Steel Horses Leather Roads

A Second Chance, Small Town Romance

Cher Terais

Aggrandis Group, LLC

Also by Cher Terais

A Wanderlust Romance

Bali Blue

Mess on the Mara

Tempest in Tulum

Stay even more connected by scanning the QR Code below to get bonus content for Cher Terais' books.

https://linktr.ee/Cher_Terais

The trip doesn't stop here! The Booked Club and The Chapter Lounge communities have launched!

Go to my website for all the deets: https://cherterais.com/home

A Second Chance Romance

Steel Horses
Leather Roads

Cher Terais

Aggrandis Group, LLC

Book Cover by Cher Terais

Illustrations by Cher Terais

1st edition 2025

www.cherterais.com

E-book ISBN: 979-8-9987125-0-0

Paperback ISBN: 979-8-9987125-1-7

Hardcover ISBN: 979-8-9987125-2-4

Author's Note

Dear Reader,

Some stories come to you in whispers. Others kick the damn door down.

Steel Horses, Leather Roads did both to me.

This novel is fiction... mostly. But the soil it grew from? That's all real. There really was a Mr. Ecklands—my 12th grade Computer Aided Design teacher, God rest his soul. He was the first teacher that didn't just see the straight A's he saw the chaos from wince I was hiding and pulled me aside to say, "You're good at this. You've got vision." That seed of belief never left me. And yes, he did play a pivotal role in the real life meet cute of Cara and Corian.

And yes, there really was [is] a Corian (whose real name I'll keep tucked in my back pocket like a well-folded love note), and yes... there really was an Aunty Renee, a Marcus (my younger brother Torio), a Waynan (the essence of Waymond, my dad and the 1st black cowboy I knew), and a Ja'Kari, who lives in real life as my eldest daughter,

S'Kari—wise, witty, with a mouth that's too damn grown even though she is.

If you've ever wondered how much of this is true, here's your cheat sheet:

Corian = Will remain unnamed (and will stay that way)

Cara = Cher (yes, that's me)

Marcus = Torio

Waynan = Waymond, my daddy

John Ecklands = Will remain unnamed, Rest in Heaven.

Ja'Kari = my eldest daughter, S'Kari

...and so on and so forth. Some names were changed. But the emotions, the choices, the regrets and reconciliations? Those came straight from the heart.

I wrote this book with Beyoncé's Cowboy Carter in my ears and the scent of hot Georgia red clay in my nose. I wrote it while watching grown Black men ride tall in saddles, boots worn from life and legacy, looking like walking, breathing poetry. I wrote it in awe of our community's strength, our softness, our rhythm and rituals—especially trail ride culture. That whole world deserves to be seen and celebrated. Because Lord... Black Southern cowboys? They are so damn fine to me. Always have been. Always will be.

To my accountability circle—authors Mila Hunt and J. Nichole—you saw this story even before I did. To my beta readers Chevina Phillips and Sallie Mojica-Ravelo—thank you for your gentle but honest feedback, your late-night messages, and your belief in these pages. And to the ones who don't even know they inspired parts of this? Just know I was paying attention.

In September 2025, I'll be celebrating the release of this book the way it was meant to be celebrated: on horseback, under wide skies, with a real-life trail ride in South Georgia, surrounded by community, culture, and rhythm. And yes... I now want a big Black or chocolate brown Friesian stallion named Beau-Bee, after my daddy's first race horse. (Because what's a legacy without a little flair?)

Thank you for riding with me. Thank you for believing in Black love, Southern roots, and stories that won't stay quiet.

We've still got miles to go on leather roads, chasing dreams that lead us home. But this time... I'm gripping the reins and the wheel.

— Cher Terais

Lily, Georgia | Warner Robins, Georgia | Atlanta, Georgia (and sometimes, Paris and the rest of the world!)

"For my daughters, who carry my fire.
And for the legacy of Black Southern love that shaped this story.
We are the riders and the road."

~ Cher Terais

Part 1 – Setting the Stage

Steel Horses, Leather Roads

(Verse 1)
Started out with dreams, hearts
full of fire
We were just kids, living wild and
wired
But life came fast, tore us apart
Left me with a broken soul and a
faded heart
They say Iron sharpens iron, but
you're leather I'm steel
On this crossroad of love
You grip your reins, I gripped my
wheel

(Chorus)
Ridin' on a Steel horse, Down a
leather road,
Tipped your hat and was on your
way
Had to keep living, but never
stopped loving,
Place too small I couldn't stay
Jaded on love, letters unread
Vanished like a ghost, story un-
said
Ridin' on a Steel horse, Down a
leather road,
Glass hearts were meant to break

CHAPTER ONE

Chapter 1 — Cara

You should know better than to *'shit where you eat'* was my exact thought the moment I heard Michel's mildly impatient voice call out to me from the living room of my flat. "*Mon cherie*, do you need any help in there? We need to leave if we are to make our reservation on time."

I was in my bedroom, rushing to slip into the fitted black dress I had at least had the forethought to pick out this morning before leaving for work, knowing Michel would be here promptly at 6:30PM to pick me up for our weekly dinner date.

I'd long ago made it a staunch rule never to rush for anything. The life I'd built for myself here in Paris allowed me to saunter through it. Rushing was for those who didn't have their shit together. But... this was the third time this month I'd kept him waiting because I couldn't—didn't actually even try—to leave work on time to get ready.

Michel and I had a situationship of sorts. We'd met a little over two years ago. He was a super-rich, well-connected investor in Paris commercial real estate, and he flaunted his money like he tried to flaunt me on his arm. We'd met on a previous hotel project. My interior design firm turned that hotel into a luxury masterpiece as well. He'd shot his shot, and I'd turned him down for months.

He was also an investor, though not the only one, on my current project, the Rue d'Orleans boutique hotel. I sighed, thinking about the phrase I'd gotten from my daddy. His words and his old beat-up guitar were the only things he'd left me.

It was an unbidden memory from when I was a little girl and used to sit on a milk crate in our garage watching Daddy tinker on the '69 Chevy Chevelle he used to covet. He'd tinker. I'd watch.

Our neighbors across the street had erupted in a loud argument that day, voices sharp enough to cut through the country music drifting from Daddy's small radio. Daddy had shaken his head and turned the country music up, then went back to tightening a bolt under the hood.

He muttered under his breath, "That's why you don't shit where you eat." I didn't understand, but now it was clear. Here I was 'eating where I shat.'

A long-ago thought from a long-forgotten place.

The saying meant, don't invite trouble into places that you hold sacred or find peace in. My workplace was sacred, and here I'd gone and invited in trouble by sleeping with an associated business interest.

Michel had finally worn me down, and I took him up on a dinner date. That had been a year ago, and he was smitten. I was not. He was nice and all, something to do. It helped that he was extremely handsome, had great conversation, and did amazing things with his tongue when I'd finally allowed our dealings to take a turn towards intimacy. So far, I'd warded off any of his advances for... *more*. My work was always the excuse that kept him at bay.

Michel was gracious enough not to show his irritation at my lateness. He would wait patiently outside the door of my 13th-floor flat. These days the door attendant readily admitted him, and I'd swiftly go in and past him with a kiss on his cheek to apologize for my lateness. Tonight was no different.

So, I understood the increasing impatience in his tone. I threw him a bone and yelled back, "Come help me." Another Cara-ism I'd gotten from back home, this one from my mother no doubt, was if a man is acting impatient, put his ass to work. In this situation, I needed help with the zipper of the black number I knew would distract him from his mild irritation with me, with its plunging neckline, the side boob and cleavage I was serving was about to shut that whining shit coming from Michel all the way up.

I'd started going gray back in my early thirties and now fully embraced my full head of silver tresses. I'd gotten it styled earlier this week in a precisely cut bob haircut. It was giving Amanda Priestley from 'The Devil Wears Prada.' I looked damn good. And the look on Michel's face when he stepped into my bedroom and saw my full ensemble confirmed what I already knew.

He wasn't a slouch either. Michel's presence filled the room as I caught his appreciative look in the floor to ceiling ornate mirror I stood in front of. He made steps across the room, pressing his body into mine as he kissed my neck and slowly eased my zipper up, his hand grazing the upper curve of my ass like silk.

"Cara," he breathed near my ear, his heavy French accent curling around my name like a caress. "You look... magnificent."

I smirked, stepping away from him, adjusted my earrings and grabbed the matching clutch ready to leave. "And you, Michel, are as charming as ever. A glass of wine before we go?"

"Always," he replied, his gaze never leaving mine.

I felt the weight of his admiration. "You don't look a day over thirty-five, Mon Petit," he said over the glass of Burgundy I'd poured him. "When are you going to allow me the honor of officially taking you off the market—"

"Uh-uh," I wagged a finger in the air. "We've talked about this, Michel. My work is my baby and my man, right now. Let's just enjoy each other, please." He fell silent for a moment. But tonight, he pressed a bit more.

"You do something to me, Cara," he said, eyes crinkling at the corners as he narrowed them sexily. *Handsome bastard.* He continued, voice low, "You're like this city. Timeless. Impossible not to fall in love with."

"Paris definitely has that effect, doesn't it?" I replied, clutch in hand, walking towards the door.

"You know it's not Paris I'm talking about loving, Cara," he murmured.

I smiled back at him but kept moving. I was not going to allow him to bait me into that conversation again.

He dropped it, and the rest of the night unfolded just fine. Laughter and flirtation. He didn't press, but I still felt the undercurrent of him wanting something deeper. My coldness put him off, sure. But it drove his ass crazy at the same time. I was playing with fire and eventually was going to have to cut his ass off or give in.

I desired Michel; there was no doubt about that. His physique, his charm, the way his voice could make me forget everything else—it all ignited desire in me. But it was *only* desire. I'd closed myself off to the *more* he was asking for a long time ago.

Our night ended in my bed, of course, with our bodies entwined. Both of us were lost in the moment. Michel knew how to take his time;

his touches were deliberate, his kisses full of promise. For a few blissful hours, I allowed myself to let down the walls I'd built.

We dozed off, with the warmth of his body next to mine. The shrill ring of my phone in the middle of the night pierced my sleep. Disoriented, I grabbed it from the nightstand, Michel stirring beside me.

"Hello?" I murmured, my voice thick with sleep.

The voice on the other end was solemn. "Cara Mackey?" The caller asked.

"Yes. Who's calling at this hour?" I asked back, my irritation clear.

"My apologies, Ma'am, for forgetting the time difference. I'm calling on behalf of the Ecklands estate. John Ecklands has passed away, and his wife Bonita asked me to call you at once."

CHAPTER TWO

Chapter 2 — Cara

I sat at my desk, still in shock from the call I'd received the night before. Mr. Ecklands was dead. My mentor, the man who had believed in me when no one else did. The man whose guidance had shaped my career. *Gone.*

I felt guilty. It had been years since I'd tried to reach out to him, even though I received birthday cards from him and his wife every year for the last 30 years. He kept up with every important event in my life. Every one of my projects featured in Architectural Digest, Décor Magazine, all of them, he knew about.

He'd call and leave messages about how proud he was of me. I took those calls for granted. I willfully ignored his requests over the years to come home and visit. On the last such call, he'd told me he was working on something major for Lily, GA, and he wanted me to be part of it. He had gone into little detail, but he was so excited it about that I'd told him, "Maybe."

My 'maybe' was one excuse after the other for not coming home. I was busy with this project or that one. I never told him I never came back there because Lily had been the place that had broken me. Every memory was too much, and I willfully ran from it and all that remained there a long time ago. And now it was too late for that 'maybe' to ever come. Except, maybe it wasn't. The lawyer on the call last night made it very clear, that John Ecklands' dying wish was that I came home, NOW.

The summons home had me slipping out of bed and away from Michel's reach and expressions of concern. Had me sitting at my desk in deep contemplation at work this morning.

I was mid-thought as I looked around my office at what I'd built here in Paris by taking his advice over the years. He had always told me to chase my dreams and never to settle for less. And now, losing him felt like a reminder of how much more I still had to do here. And how, leaving now to go home, for what, I was unsure as the lawyer was extremely vague, explaining that he could only divulge Mr. Ecklands' wishes in person, per *John's* wishes.

Sighing, I leaned back in my chair, the soft leather cradling me as I surveyed the sprawling samples of fabric spread across my desk. I wasn't left with much choice about whether I was going.

"Jean-Pierre!" I called, glancing toward the open door of my office. I needed to get my house in order, for what might be an extended leave of absence. "Did the House of Dior samples arrive?"

Nothing. Just the faint murmur of Jean-Pierre chatting with the intern. If it were anyone else, my patience would wear thin. But Jean-Pierre was too good at what he did for this to be more than a mild irritant.

"Jean-Pierre!" I said louder this time.

There was a flurry of motion before his tousled head appeared in the doorway, a guilty smile playing on his lips. "Yes, yes, Cara, they're here. I was cataloguing them with Bonet. The new collection is stunning!"

I pushed my glasses up the bridge of my nose, my voice laced with authority. "Bring them in. I need to see everything."

He hurried in, arms laden with neatly bound fabric books, his enthusiasm palpable. "I've already got favorites," he said as he placed them on my desk.

I gave him a pointed look. "Jean-Pierre, remind me—who is the lead designer on this project?"

"You are of course," he replied, grinning sheepishly.

"Exactly. Which means I get the last word." I teased, knowing that he'd be more than capable of taking care of things here in my absence. "Now, let's see these." I flipped open the first booklet, my manicured nails brushing against the lush fabrics. The collection was indeed breathtaking: brocades with intricate patterns, velvets that begged to be touched, and a particular cream fabric embroidered with black vines and golden filigree that immediately caught my eye.

"This one," I murmured almost to myself, running my fingers over its surface. The fabric was understated, yet exquisite. It was perfect for Rue d'Orleans. *Orleans* meant gold. The fabric itself was rich, and the gold tones would counterbalance the riot of color in the hotel's lobby with its amazing garden view. To Jean-Pierre, I stated, "This is it. This is the fabric we will use for the circular banquette around the fountain."

He leaned over my shoulder, nodding slowly. "I knew you'd like it."

The Rue d'Orleans Hotel was weeks away from being ready for us to start fully implementing my firm's design vision, but its soft launch completion date was set, and I wasn't leaving anything to chance.

Every detail had to be perfect, from the hand-carved moldings to the floral arrangements that would greet guests in the lobby. This wasn't just another boutique hotel. It was *the* boutique hotel, destined for spreads in every lifestyle and travel magazine worth its salt. This was the worst possible time ever that I would need to go home. But this time, I had to.

"If you're sure, I'll get it ordered right away," Jean-Pierre said.

"When am I ever not sure?" I teasingly shot back. "Order it. And make sure it's expedited," I said, standing. "Great eye." I winked at him, giving the credit he fully deserved, for suggesting we go with the Dior brand even though they were mostly used for apparel and not interiors.

I grabbed my scarf, knotting it neatly around my neck before pulling on my trench coat, to protect me from the late spring chill and wind of the city. "I am going out for a moment, but when I return, I need to speak with you and the team." I glanced down at my watch. "Have everyone in the conference room at one." I smiled glumly at him as I swung my Birkin over my shoulder. I was meeting Delia, the assigned architect on the Rue d'Orleans project, for lunch anyway. And would walk there to clear my head.

"Yes, of course, Cara. Is everything okay?" he asked, concern furrowing his brow.

"Um, yeah. I'll share details when I return. I'm heading out early for my lunch date with Delia."

"Shall I call up a car, to take you?"

"No. No car. I'll walk."

"Cara, it's windy outside!" he exclaimed. "You'll catch your death."

I smirked. "A little chill never stopped me. And I need to take a detour by the Lock Bridge. I spotted a flower blooming in the most captivating shade of pink. I want a dye mixed to match it for the bed linens."

Jean-Pierre sighed, resigned. "As always, you're impossible."

"No, darling," I said, throwing him a wink. "I'm perfection."

The streets of Paris were alive. The scent of freshly baked bread wafted from the *boulangeries*, french bakeries, and conversations hummed from cafés. Sunlight glinted off the Seine. May in Paris was beautiful even if still chilly. The wind nipped at my cheeks as I walked to the Lock Bridge. I needed the cool air to still my mind. I hadn't been back to Lily, GA since shortly after graduating high school and enlisting in the Army Reserve. I ran from it. Tried never to look back. But it seemed Lily and all I'd left behind there finally caught up with me.

I arrived at the bridge and snapped a photo of the pink flower, its rare color perfect for the Rue d'Orleans. Satisfied, I continued to the trendy bistro where Delia was waiting.

She spotted me first, waving from across the crowded space. Her presence was a soothing balm—another Black woman thriving in a city that could be equal parts inspiring and isolating. As I reached the table, she pulled me into a warm hug. Though we'd already planned to meet, I needed to tell her about my plans to go home for a little while

"Cara," she said, her tone professional, and as ready as ever to get down to business while still being warm, "As always, you look fabulous, and I've got updates for you."

"That's great, because I have something that's come up and I'm going to need you and my team on top of everything while I'm away." I said, while taking my seat across from her, chancing a glance in her direction to ensure she heard me.

Her smile only faltered a bit as an inquisitive brow raised. She didn't miss a beat and continued, "Let's get to it, then. Care to share?"

Not really but I started by explaining the call I got last night. I felt comfortable enough talking to Delia, another girl also from down south Georga in Paris. We'd met just shy of six months ago on the Rue d'Orleans project. soon after she'd arrived in Paris. We became fast friends as soon as I detected the unmistakable twang in her voice. We clicked instantly, even though she was from Atlanta and was almost twenty years younger.

Delia was good people and when she asked what was so hard about going back home, I gave her the raw truth, even though I knew the tears that were now streaming down my face would be inevitable. Thank God for the waiter who caught my distress and inconspicuously brought extra napkins and a warm smile of understanding to the table. She sat them in front of me, not missing a beat to move on and help another customer as Delia squeezed my hand across the table.

"My family as I knew it, died in Lily," I said. The demise actually started before we moved back to my daddy's hometown. For brevity, I surmised it to say, "It was where me and my younger brother Marcus were dumped as kids, and would have had to figure out life on our own, had it not been for Mr. John Ecklands, my aunt Renee, and..." My words trailed off as I fought to remove the last person I wanted to think about from my memory, "Yeah, um, they were our lifelines after my Mama and Daddy died in a car crash."

I strategically left out how said car crash happened. It was too much for me to even think about right now. Hince the reason, going home was not on my list of happy things to do, all these memories would be dredged up soon enough.

"Anyways," I continued, "I'm telling you this because I need you to be my lifeline right now." I chuckled wistfully. "I know you don't work for my firm, but please look out for my team while I'm away. Jean-Pierre will be great, but Delia, keep them straight for me will you girl?"

"You know I got your back, Cara. Don't you worry about that. Let's get down to business, shall we?"

I nodded, knowing Delia would indeed have my back while I was away. "Tell me, what's the status of the construction and build out?"

She pulled a tablet from her bag, scrolling expertly. "Good news first. Sixty percent of the spaces are ready for your team to start. The lobby, guest rooms, and most of the public spaces are clear for your design team to start applying the F.F.AE, flooring, fixtures, finishes and all."

I nodded, sipping my cappuccino. "And the not-so-good news?"

"The wet areas," she said, her tone pragmatic. "There's a plumbing delay in the commercial kitchen. So that is off limits. And since the lobby bar and restaurant areas butt up to the kitchen, they are off limits as well. The public bathrooms are also off limits for now. It's not catastrophic—three weeks delay at most—but I wanted to flag it early."

I set my cup down, considering. "A few weeks... we can manage, but it needs to stay that, or the grand opening launch will be delayed. Coordinate with the contractors to ensure no slippage. I'll have Jean-Pierre adjust the marble delivery if necessary."

Delia nodded, her expression confident. "I'm on it. Everything else is progressing smoothly, and your timeline should hold."

I leaned back, satisfied. "Good. Let's keep it that way. In a couple of months, Rue D'Orleans is going to be the crown jewel of Paris."

"Not just Paris," Delia said with a grin. "The world. Now go take care of home, girl. This *here*, is under control."

After getting back to the office and letting my team know I needed to go home for a little while, I went home to pack.

CHAPTER THREE

Chapter 3 — Cara

My plane touched down at Atlanta Hartsfield-Jackson at 4PM Eastern, the heart of rush-hour. Normally, I'd have been more than happy to kill an hour to let the traffic die down by shopping in the international terminal--the Louis Vuitton and Prada stores there were usually heaven for me. Not today, though. Today I walked through the airport numb, thoughts of John Ecklands on my mind and the two-and-a-half-hour drive to Lily. I just grabbed my bags, went through customs and headed straight to the rental car terminal.

I'd flown through Atlanta, many times over the years, but had sworn I'd never go back to Lily. I'd packed my bags and ran off to chase bigger dreams. I'd kept that promise until now. Life has a funny way of eventually changing the plan. And so, here I was... A meeting with my team and a quick call to tell Michel I was leaving for a little while, a little while undefined, to go home to take care of family business. I'd booked a flight and had basically let the past take over to pull me home.

I picked up the keys to a Porsche—same make and model as the one I drove back home in Paris. Funny how "home" and Paris fit together so easy now, while Georgia felt like a place that didn't belong to me anymore. Still, here I was.

The air hit me as soon as I stepped outside: thick, heavy, and full of memories I'd spent years trying to bury. Driving through Atlanta's familiar streets, I felt the weight of it settle on my chest. I lived here for a few years while in college at SCAD and the first few years of my interior design career. Before long, the city lights faded into miles of highway and then came the weathered signs and rusting mailboxes. Lily hadn't changed much. Dusty roads stretched endlessly, bordered by cotton fields and whispers of dreams left behind.

Except for Marcus's sprawling estate. Built right on Mackey land, it stood tall and shiny where a near-dilapidated house once leaned against a backdrop of trees. Daddy inherited those 50 acres from his father. The inheritance would prove more of a burden than a blessing. First, my daddy didn't have money to maintain or clear it. And someone had to pay the taxes on it. If it wasn't for my Dad's sister all that land and the house on it would have gone up in smoke. The house itself even back then looked like it might crumble if the wind blew too hard.

But now? That land was a prize. Marcus's prize because I wanted no part of it.

A lot of the trees were gone, cleared to make way for something big and bold, with manicured lawns and a private gate that screamed success, Marcus's house. It was the only thing around here that appeared untouched by time.

I parked in front of Marcus's estate, the house standing tall against a backdrop of trimmed lawns and cleared trees. His success was the kind of anomaly Lily didn't see often. Most people here clung to routines and regrets, but Marcus had built something extraordinary—first in the NFL, then in landscaping. That boy who'd been teased for his ragged sneakers now owned land people would kill for.

Marcus opened the door before I even knocked. "Sis," he groaned, pulling me into a bear hug, "It's good to see you." Even though we talked on the phone, now via Facetime, at least two times a week. How we grew up, that was a blessing in and of itself. We hadn't physically seen each other in person in over seven years, at Aunty Renee's funeral up in Ohio. This was my first time ever coming to his house. His arms wrapped around me like the safety net I didn't know I needed until now.

"It's good to see you too," I said, the words catching in my throat. I cleared my throat, willing them away as I pulled back just enough to get a good look at my little brother. "Still working out every day like you're still in the league, I see."

He grinned, while flexing the muscles in the back of his arm, "Damn straight," he said, "You see them horseshoes, don't you." He bragged playfully, just like he used to when we were teens. Marcus started playing football around the age of five. Originally just for fun, as we'd gotten older, it and his coaches had become his lifeline like my journal and Mr. Ecklands had been for me. He started working out like a beast even back then. He'd become a starting player over the years. So much so, it was inevitable for the scholarships and eventually the NFL to come-a-calling. It wasn't until then that I felt safe enough to flourish in my own endeavors. Marcus was safe, and that's all that mattered.

I mushed him in the chest now, just like I'd done countless times when we were kids. "Boy, you are still corny, I see." We both laughed at my light ribbing as a big sister was supposed to do.

"And you still my biggest hater, I see," he said, pulling me back into another bear hug.

"Naw, for real though, you look amazing. I miss the shit out of you!"
Pulling back from his embrace, I moved past him and walked up the steps
to the massive wrap-around porch. "And this house is fire. The pictures
you sent don't do it any justice. I know Raynice, had to have picked all
the finishes."

"On the inside, hell yeah. But what you see on the outside from the
mailbox, through the gated fence up to after feature on the outside of
the house down to the shingles was all me. Don't act like you the only
one with class." He joked.

"You did your thing-thing, lil bro. The landscaping is phenomenal."
I looked out at the expanse of the yard, eyes freezing when they hit just
past the clearing beyond the landscaped borders of his main property.
Marcus's gaze followed mine. His voice sobered a bit as he grabbed my
elbow and guided me towards the front door.

"Want to see the inside?"

I didn't immediately answer. My mind was still on the old house
beyond the clearing. Its faded shutters barely hanging on. I thought he
would've torn it down. A wave of emotion washed over me. It started the
closer I got to Lily. But seeing the near dilapidated structure rocked me.

We settled on the porch, the rocking chairs creaking as we swayed in
silence. He didn't push me to talk. He never did even when he'd catch
me crying sometimes when we were younger. That house was still there.
Seeing it for the first time brought the past rushing back.

*It was a humid summer day. A few weeks out from the start of my
senior year in high school. I sat at the edge of the church pew, clutching my
journal like it was the only thing holding me together. The air was thick
and suffocating in the sanctuary of the small church. The doors were left
open so a breeze could blow through the non-airconditioned space.*

The organ hummed faintly, and whispered condolences blurred togeth-
er. My parents' caskets sat side by side, covered in colorful flowers that did
not mask the reality of our loss. Marcus was beside me, his hand gripping
mine, his silent tears stronger than any words.

I didn't understand why they were being buried here. Daddy was from
Lily, sure, but this wasn't our home. Until a few weeks before, we lived an
hour north in Warner Robins near my Mama's family. Not here. It didn't
matter. Nothing made sense to me anymore.

I felt the weight of the congregation's stares. Pity. Curiosity. Judgment.
What would happen to the Mackey kids now? I didn't look up the en-
tire ceremony. Instead, I scribbled furiously in my journal, pouring every
dream, every fear, every piece of myself onto the page.

"Their calling for one of us to say some words over them." I still didn't
move. "You've got to say something, Cara. I'm too scared." Marcus whis-
pered when they called again for the family to speak. We were the only
family here.

But I couldn't either. I didn't have any words. They been swallowed
by the pages of my journal and the ache in my chest. My finger blindly
traced the inscription just on the inside of the journals worn cover. Mama's
handwriting looping across the page: For Cara, my dreamer. The world is
yours.

Later, at the burial, the sun blazed cruelly overhead, its brightness at
odds with the darkness I felt inside me. The preacher spoke, but all I heard
was the thud of dirt hitting wood. Marcus stood still, his jaw tight, but his
pain radiated like heat. Unspoken but palpable. I clung to my journal and
his hand like they were the only things left tethering me to this world.

The rocking chairs creaked softly as the silence between Marcus and
me stretched. It wasn't an awkward silence—just the kind that comes

when two people who experienced the same trauma could say more with looks, gestures and a shared past than words ever could.

"I never thought you'd ever come back to Lily," Marcus said, breaking the stillness. His voice was soft, but there was a knowing edge to it.

I let out a small laugh, shaking my head. "I didn't either."

He leaned forward, elbows on his knees, studying me. "It was sad to hear about old man Ecklands. He used to ask me about you all the time. Would say, "Talked to your sister the other day. Can't wait to see her again as if he was sure you'd come back." Marcus was quiet for a spell before looking over at me. "Guess he had one more trick up his sleeve that finally got you back here. How long you staying?"

I glanced toward the old house, its weathered shutters barely hanging on. "Long enough," I said slowly, "for the reading of the will and to see what this big thing is that Mrs. Ecklands and his wife needed me hear in person to do. The lawyer asked that I be at his office tomorrow to honor his last request at 3PM sharp."

Marcus nodded, his gaze distant now, like he was mulling something over. "He was good to us, you know. Always looking out for you. For both of us."

I swallowed hard, Marcus's words pressing on me. Mr. Ecklands had been more than good to us—he, his wife and Aunty Renee had been a lifeline when we needed them most. It was at Aunty Renee's funeral the last time I'd seen Marcus in person. And now, Mr. Ecklands' was gone now too.

Marcus stood, stretching. "You're welcome to stay as long as you need to. Glad you're finally home. No matter the reason why," he said, his tone firm in that little-big-brother way of his.

He stepped off the porch to grab my bags from the car but not before chuckling and tossing a smirk laced, "Still love steel-colored horses, I see..." His words were in reference to the steely, silver Panamera 911 I'd rented. I narrowed my eyes at him and his double entendre, referencing the horsepower under the hood of my rental and the conjured memory of a wiry young boy sitting proud on the back of a beautiful shiny gray, very rare stallion named Steel. That memory and the boy that rode in on it could go straight to hell.

I rolled my eyes at Marcus as he continued to laugh. The sun was starting to set, casting long shadows across the fields. For a moment, I stayed put, letting the familiar sounds of Lily wash over me—the rustle of the wind through the trees, the faint hum of crickets.

For the first time in years, I allowed myself to think about what coming back here might mean. Not just for Mr. Ecklands' estate, but for me. The dreams I'd written down in my journals over the years had taken me far away from here. I was afraid to talk about, let alone journal about and unpack these feelings that coming back to Lily had brought.

CHAPTER FOUR

Chapter 4 — Corian

It was almost 8:00 PM when I heard Ja'Kari calling my name from across the field. Her voice carried over the warm Georgia air, sharp and urgent.

"Damn it!" I cursed under my breath; the words lost on the horse in front of me. The rawness in my voice matched the scrape of the tool in my hand, which should've been hitting the horseshoe but missed completely, smacking into my fingers instead. I flinched at the sharp sting, biting back a stronger curse as I looked down at the fresh cut.

Ja'Kari never came near the stables. 'Too many gnats out here around those ol' sweaty horses,' she'd say. That was what had me more rattled than the blood dripping from my knuckle. I tore a strip off my worn cotton shirt and tied it around my finger. When I stepped out of the stable, I spotted her running toward me, her legs bare under those damn cutoff shorts she insisted on wearing. The closer she got, the shorter they seemed.

She was my baby girl, my only child, and no matter how grown she thought she was, I hated it when she paraded around like she didn't have home training. If I could legally smash those cowboy boots into dust and replace those shorts with something that didn't stop halfway up her thighs, I'd do it in a heartbeat.

Before I could get the words out, she came to a halt in front of me, her breathing ragged. "Dad," she gasped, "it's Mr. Ecklands... I mean, his wife—something's wrong."

All thoughts of her shorts, the tools in the stable, and my aching finger fell away. Without a word, I threw my hat on and followed her toward the house, holding it down against the wind as we hurried across the field.

By the time I reached the kitchen phone, I could feel my heart pounding harder than it should have been. I grabbed the receiver, pressing it to my ear with more force than needed. "Mrs. Bonita, is everything okay?"

Her voice was soft but steady, the kind of tone that came from a woman who had seen more than her fair share of life's burdens. "Baby, you know John loved you like you were his own son. If it weren't for his wishes, I would've called you two days ago when he was on his way to meet the Lord. He's gone, baby. But don't you fret none. He went on to glory with a smile on his face and a light heart."

The words hit me square in the chest, knocking the air clean out of my lungs. "Miss Bonita..." I started, but the words stuck. "Why didn't you call me? I should've been there. I would've—"

"Shh now," she said, her voice firm but kind. "John and I have known his cancer was back for a while. We made peace with it, Corian. He didn't want no fuss, just peace."

I swallowed the knot in my throat and nodded, though she couldn't see it. "I'll come by and sit with you. Help with whatever you need—funeral arrangements, anything."

"There won't be no funeral, baby. John wanted to be cremated, and we've already started the arrangements. But I do need you to come to the lawyer's office tomorrow at 3:00 PM sharp. Can you do that for me?"

"Yes, ma'am. I'll be there."

"Thank you, Corian. And don't you worry. We'll talk more tomorrow. You just get some rest now."

When the line clicked, I let the receiver fall back into place. I sank into one of the chairs at the breakfast nook, staring at the table without really seeing it. Mr. Ecklands was like a second father to me, in some ways more than my own. My daddy's body might've given out long ago, but his voice and iron will were still sharp as ever. Mr. Ecklands, though... he was the one who taught me how to think beyond the ranch, who pushed me to go to Prairie View and get my degree in mechanical engineering. Without him, I wouldn't have had the life I have now.

He was also the one who introduced me to...

The memory caught in my chest, sharp as a barbed wire fence. Before I could fall too deep into it, I felt a small hand on my back, warm and steady.

Ja'Kari.

Her touch gave me permission to feel what I'd been holding back, and the tears came before I could stop them. They were slow at first, sliding silently down my cheeks, but then they came faster, harder, breaking through the wall I hadn't realized I'd put up.

"Daddy," she said softly, her hand never leaving its place. That single word, spoken with so much love, was all it took to shatter what was left of my resolve.

Mr. Ecklands would be sorely missed. And as my daughter's hand moved in soothing circles, I let the grief take me, even as another memory pushed its way to the surface, unbidden and undeniable.

It was dawn, and the ranch lay quiet except for the occasional soft nickers of the horses in the stables and the faint rustle of wind through the paddocks. The sun crept over the horizon, bathing the expanse of land in a warm, golden light. Rows of immaculate fencing stretched as far as the eye could see, each enclosure holding some of the finest Thoroughbred horses in the country. My family's ranch was renowned for breeding and training champions—Arabians with their high endurance, Friesians with their commanding beauty, Tennessee Walkers with their smooth gait, and even the occasional rare Akhal-Teke, their metallic coats shimmering in the sunlight.

"Corian!" my father's voice cut through the stillness like a whip, pulling me from the quiet beauty of the morning. I'd been staring at the horizon too long, my mind drifting to the metal-gray Friesian stallion I named Steel. Steel was my pride, my masterpiece. I had broken him myself, earning every inch of trust and respect from that horse through sweat and patience.

But I knew better than to keep my father waiting.

I jogged toward the barn, wiping my hands on my jeans. Inside, the air was thick with the smell of hay, leather, and saddle oil. My father stood tall, his frame as solid as the beams holding up the structure. Beside him were my two younger brothers, already busy brushing down the new foals.

"You think those horses train themselves?" he snapped, his sharp eyes catching me the moment I stepped inside. "This ranch is your legacy, boy. You don't walk away from something like this."

I nodded silently, but my chest tightened. I wanted to tell him about Prairie View, about the scholarship Mr. Ecklands said I had a shot at. But the words died in my throat.

"Now go saddle up Steel and check the east paddock. Make sure the fencing's still intact. And get the tractor ready; the south field needs mowing." My father's tone left no room for argument, and I turned to obey. My

unspoken dreams heavy on my shoulders was apparent in the way Darren's eyes tightened when he saw them slump.

Later that day, as I worked under the hood of the old tractor, the frustration boiled over. I loved machines, the way they worked, the way you could bring something to life with your own hands. But I also knew my father wouldn't see it that way. To him, the ranch was life, and anything outside of it was a betrayal.

"You're thinking too much again," my brother Darren said, leaning against the side of the barn. He had a smirk on his face, but his eyes were serious. "You gotta find a way to tell the old man what you're going to do. Man-up and make peace with it, Corian. Take that academic scholarship and go to Prairie View, or not. But don't drag this out. It'll kill you."

Those words stuck with me. Even now, years later, I could hear Darren's voice in my head. He was right, of course. But it was Mr. Ecklands who eventually helped me make the choice and tell my daddy. Prairie View won out, but not without a cost. The relationship with my father and me was never the same after I left and he certainly couldn't wait to hit me with the "I told you so," when I came back home. The ranch became a symbol of everything I was trying to hold on to and let go of all at once.

CHAPTER FIVE

Chapter 5 — Cara

I loved my condo in Paris; it embodied everything about who I was—modern, elegant, and unapologetically bold. But stepping into Marcus's home, I had to admit it was stunning, though I couldn't believe he hadn't called on the best interior designer he knows. *Me.*

Raynice, his wife, had designed it, and while I couldn't give her the praise she deserved in person—she was out of town for work as a traveling nurse—I couldn't help but admire her choices.

From the moment I walked in, I noticed the details: an open-concept living area with soaring ceilings, a sleek glass staircase that seemed to float in midair, and custom floor-to-ceiling windows that framed the meticulously landscaped garden like a living work of art. The furniture was clean-lined and modern, but warm tones and soft textures kept it from feeling too sterile.

Still, I couldn't help but imagine the ways I would've made it even better. A pop of color here, better lighting choices there. But it was beautiful, I had to give her that.

The house had six bedrooms, which still felt excessive for two people with no kids. But Marcus had explained his reasoning—he wanted to host family reunions and be the go-to spot for friends and family. I wasn't sure how often they actually had friends over, but since neither of us had kids, family gatherings would be small. The thought was nice, though. And speaking of kids, they were a hell no for me. I also understood Marcus's hesitation to have kids came from a much deeper place. We'd talked about it before on one of our many heart to hearts over the years.

He'd confided in me that his years as a linebacker, from Pop Warner to the NFL, had left him cautious about starting a family. While he hadn't experienced any signs of traumatic brain injury, he knew the risks and didn't want to chance it. Watching the news and seeing former players spiral into violence or mental decline had left an impression on him. It broke my heart to think about it, especially since it meant the next generation of our family wouldn't come from him—or me, for that matter.

Of course, my reasons for not wanting kids were far less noble. I didn't want rug rats running around my house touching my nice things. I'd earned the right to have a beautiful home without sticky fingerprints and endless clutter. And honestly, that desire came from how Marcus and I grew up—cramped in a house that was constantly falling apart, with repairs that never got done and corners of the ceiling that sagged with water damage.

The only place I could find comfort was my bedroom back then. I saved every dime from babysitting jobs to make it mine. I'd buy things to transform it into a space that felt pretty, safe, and separate from the chaos just outside my bedroom door. I first fell in love with interior design back then. I'd fantasize about lavish furnishings and luxurious bed linens and fluffy towels to wrap around my body after a long hot bath in a marble tub. A far cry difference from the threadbare towels with the ratty holes in them that we actually had. Those fantasies stayed with me long after I left that life behind.

Now, I wandered through Marcus's house, marveling at the sprawling kitchen with its oversized marble island and chef-grade appliances. The library, with its dark oak shelves and tufted leather chairs, made me want to curl up with a good book. But the room I loved most was the guest room where I'd be staying. It had a wall of windows that opened to the garden, lush with hydrangeas and jasmine, and a private patio where you could sit and feel the quiet settle over you like a blanket.

By the time I sank into the bed, exhaustion had caught up with me. Between the nine, almost ten-hour flight, the emotions stirred up by being back in Lily, and the sheer size of this house, my body was done. But I couldn't fall immediately to sleep as a faint sense of unease over meeting with Bonita and the late Mr. Ecklands' lawyer lingered.

The engine of my rented Porsche roared beneath me like a loyal beast, eager for the open road ahead. Marcus's estate, nestled on the outskirts of town, gave me twenty uninterrupted minutes of country road to lose myself in the hum of the engine and the wind rushing past.

I shifted into a higher gear, and the car surged forward, my grin widening with every mile. I loved fast cars, always had. But as much as I enjoyed the Porsche, it wasn't the car I'd grown up dreaming about.

That honor belonged to a '69 Chevy Chevelle. Midnight blue, with a growl that sent shivers down your spine. My dad had promised to buy me one just like his when I was a kid, back when life still made sense. Back before everything fell apart.

Dad had been an aeronautical engineer, a certified genius with his hands and his mind. He built race cars in his spare time and bragged about his undefeated streak on the streets. I believed him—how could I not? Watching him tune engines in our garage, his grease-stained hands moving with precision, he seemed invincible.

But life wasn't kind to invincible men—or their wives and children. The crack epidemic rolled in like a tidal wave through Warner Robins, GA, where we lived, just like it did across many towns and cities around the U.S.. As smart as my dad was, he wasn't immune. And somehow or another he introduced crack to my mom. First, the good government job he had on base went. Then any and everything that had a modicum of value around our house would mysteriously vanish. That included mine and Marcus's computer, our bikes, sometimes the meat out the freezer. Eventually the whole house was gone too. Then the bad decisions, and then...nothing.

I'd learned to take care of things around the house the best I could. Would wash Marcus's and my clothes in the bathtub so we could go to school clean and knew how to fill out the free lunch forms at school so we could eat during the school day. But when shit hit rock bottom, they packed what little belongings we had left, and we moved an hour away to where my dad grew up in Lily, GA. And this is where he and Mom died. Everything shifted after that. Had it not been for My dad's sister, Aunty Renee, coming down from Ohio where she'd moved years ago, Marcus and I would have been left to fend for ourselves, or worse separated and sent to foster care.

Even still, we were barely scraping by in the rundown house we inherited on the Mackey property. The place was falling apart, but at least my brother and I had a place to call home and were together.

Aunt Renee was an unconventional caretaker, to put it kindly. Her version of parenting was more hands-off than on. Still, she was there, which was more than most would've been.

I tightened my grip on the wheel, shaking off the thoughts as I pushed the car faster. The past was too heavy for an afternoon like this. For a moment, I let the car's power consume me, the thrill washed over me.

The road narrowed as I neared Lily's town square, a place frozen in time. The same brick storefronts lined the streets, the same clock tower loomed over everything, its hands ticking steadily, a silent reminder of time's passage—and its refusal to stop.

At the light, I slowed, my chest tightening as memories surfaced unbidden again.

I was 17, stepping off the school bus here for the first time in my eclectic clothes, the ones I pieced together from whatever I could find. Hand-me-downs be damned, I'd made them my own. Bright colors, bold patterns—I didn't care if they didn't match. They were clean and they fit.

But it didn't matter how much effort I put into making them work. The whispers still followed me. "That's the Mackey girl," they'd said, their voices dripping with pity—or worse, curiosity. "You know her parents died, right? She and her brother live with that strange aunt of theirs."

I gripped the wheel tighter, the humiliation from years ago pressing down on me like it had just happened. I hated how this town had a way of reaching into the past and dragging it into the present, no matter how far I'd gone--or come.

A sharp honk behind me startled me out of my thoughts. I glanced at the light—green. I stepped on the gas, my heart racing as I sped forward, catching a glimpse in my rearview mirror of the car behind me. A sleek, gunmetal-gray Mustang. Its windows were tinted, and though I couldn't see the driver, I could feel their irritation radiating as the car slipped past me, moving with an ease that was as confident as it was aggressive.

Everything in me wanted to mash the gas and make whoever was in that Mustang eat my dust. I knew the Porsche could overtake him. Yeah, that was a dude's car. I just shook my head instead and shot the driver a bird. Beautiful car, but whoever was driving it was a jerk.

By the time I reached the lawyer's office, I'd managed to push the Mustang—and everything else—out of my mind. Parking the Porsche, I glanced around the square. People bustled in and out of the shops, and I caught a few lingering looks in my direction. Were they really staring, or was it my imagination? Back in the day, I would have been self-conscious at the stares, the old whispers sometimes still played in my head.

"Let them stare," I sighed, as I climbed the steps to the lawyer's office, squaring my shoulders and holding my head up high, refusing to let anyone—or my own insecurities—shake me.

The bell above the door jingled as I stepped inside, and the scent of lemon polish and old paper greeted me. Behind the reception desk sat a middle-aged woman with soft curls, her nameplate reading *Dot Chandler*.

"Good afternoon," she said, her tone warm and polite. "You must be Ms. Mackey."

"Yes," I replied, slipping easily into the polite tone I'd perfected growing up in Georgia.

She smiled and stood. "Mr. Hensley is expecting you. I'll let him know you've arrived."

With that, she walked toward the heavy oak door that had *'Conference Room'* on its placard. I adjusted my blazer and took a deep breath, trying to steady myself.

A moment later, the door from the outside swung open. The same bell jingled, causing me to turn in the direction of the sound.

"Cara?"

The deep voice froze me in place, my heart lurching as my head snapped up.

There he was.

Corian Demetrie.

He stood in the doorway, broad and rugged, his salt-and-pepper hair framing a face that had only grown more handsome with time. His eyes widened slightly as if he couldn't quite believe I was standing there.

For a moment, I couldn't speak. My tongue felt heavy, and my thoughts jumbled together. He looked good—too good—and that realization hit me like a sucker punch.

"Cara?" he said again, this time softer, his disbelief clear.

I straightened my spine, forcing a polite smile to my lips, even as my chest tightened. "Corian," I said, my tone calm and measured.

Dot gestured toward the room. "Mr. Hensley will see you both now."

Both? Of course. Whatever this meeting was about, it wasn't just with me and the attorney, apparently. And now, I had to face it— and *him.*

CHAPTER SIX

Chapter 6 — Corian

The table in Attorney Hensley's conference room was big enough to seat twelve—five on either side, one at each end. Solid mahogany, polished to a high shine.

The kind of table that didn't just take up space—it owned it.

I studied it a little closer.

I knew this craftsmanship.

This wasn't just any table. This was definitely a John Ecklands designed.

Simple. Built to last.

I ran my fingers along the edge as I made my way down the length of it, my boots tapping against the hardwood floor. When I reached the far side, I pulled out the chair and settled in.

Middle seat. Full view of the room.

That was me—always needing to see the whole picture. Always needing to know what I was walking into.

The surprise of seeing Cara here had me deep in my head and if it were another night, I'd likely go out to my garage and tinker on the car, I'd been restoring now for the better part of 20 years. That's where I went when I needed to think and clear my head. I wouldn't be able to tonight, though. I'd have to leave the over-analyzing for another time.

Ja'Kari had asked me to be her plus-one at a bank event at The Orchard House tonight. Some kind of corporate dinner for Bank of Dooly's management team, the kind of thing she usually brought her fiancé to. But Derrick was out of town, and my baby girl wanted her old man on her arm.

I'd never say no to that.

Hell, these moments were rare enough as it was.

Then she walked in.

Cara.

She hesitated, just for a second, before stepping inside. But I caught it.

Like I always did.

Some things don't change.

She scanned the room, eyes flicking over everything but me, trying to decide where to sit. Most folks would've thought she was just taking her time. But I knew better.

She was nervous.

I knew it the way I knew the land out on my family's ranch. The way I could tell a storm was coming before the first drop of rain hit the dirt.

And I knew her.

Seventeen-year-old Cara had the same tell.

Whenever she was uneasy, she'd twist her left thumb inward, toward her palm. When she was angry, she'd twist it the other way.

Right now?

That thumb was locked tight.

I smirked to myself. Still the same.

Or maybe I just never let myself forget her.

Attorney Hensley cleared his throat, breaking the silence. "Ms. Mackey, if you would take a seat. Doesn't matter where. Then we can get started."

Cara finally moved. Chin up, shoulders back. And she took the seat to Hensley's right.

Of course.

I bit back a smirk.

Still competitive as ever, too.

And just like back then, in Ecklands' drafting class—when we were kids, trying to prove ourselves—Cara was still gonna take the power seat.

I had no idea what this meeting was about—not really. I wondered if she did.

I mean, our longtime mentor had just passed away. Maybe he'd left an old tractor to me. Maybe a few tools from his shop. But what of Cara?

But from the tight set of Cara's brows as she turned her head expectantly at the lawyer, I knew she was just as in the dark as I was.

For all we knew, Mr. Ecklands could've left behind a stack of debts or some unfinished business.

Nah. Not Mr. Ecklands. He was always solid-as-a-rock to both of us, more me, over the recent years as Cara had left Lily in her dust years ago.

Hensley flipped through the thick stack of papers in front of him, sorting and straightening them. Cara looked at him intently while I took the moment to study her.

Really study her.

It had been years. Almost thirty, to be exact.

And damn. She wasn't seventeen anymore.

The long, skinny legs, the thick French braids—gone.

In their place sat a woman. Poised. Controlled. Regal, even.

Her skin was still that same deep, rich mahogany. Smooth as ever. But now, silver streaked through her near shoulder cropped hair—the kind of silver that didn't age a person.

It crowned them.

She looked expensive.

I could see it in the cut of her blazer, in the simple but elegant jewelry she wore. She wasn't flashy, but everything about her screamed quality.

She was different.

And yet... she wasn't.

Hensley's voice finally cut through the silence.

"John Ecklands and his wife, Bonita, came to me many years ago," he began. "As you both know, they never had children of their own, but their love for this community was well known. What you may not have known is that John had been battling prostate cancer for quite some time. When he was diagnosed, they revised their estate plans to ensure their legacy would be placed in trusted hands."

Hensley looked between us.

"You two have been named the sole heirs of the Ecklands estate."

The room went still.

I barely moved, but beside me, I caught the sharp inhale of breath from Cara. Her fingers flexed against the polished wood, but her expression didn't crack.

Hensley kept going.

"Bonita," Mr. Hensley said, looking at his watch, "Was supposed to stop by but may have gotten side-tracked as she has decided to move to New Orleans to be near her family. The estate they are leaving to you both is extensive—195 acres, including their home."

That house.

I knew it well.

Spent too many summers there, working odd jobs for Mr. Ecklands. Hell, I'd helped replace the damn roof about five years back. Hadn't known then I'd be patching up a house I'd one day own.

And the pond.

It was tucked away behind Mr. Ecklands' house, hidden from view unless you knew exactly where to look.

That little stretch of water and embankment was a world of its own.

I remembered the bank of it blanketed in wildflowers, stretched like an untouched canvas—bursts of purple, yellow, and deep blue swaying in the breeze. The trees leaned in close to the water, their branches casting dappled shadows over the surface, shielding it from the rest of the world.

It was always so quiet there. Still.

And Cara loved that place.

I'd found her there more than once, curled up on the grass, knees drawn to her chest, scribbling in that worn leather journal of hers. Some days, she'd hum to herself, completely lost in whatever she was writing.

But whenever she caught me watching—snap.

She'd close the journal in one quick motion, fingers tightening around the cover like it held every secret she never planned to share.

That damn journal.

It was the one thing I never got past. The one thing that made me wonder what part of her life I didn't have access to.

One time, though... I got a peek.

I crept up behind her, quiet as I could, and snatched the journal right out of her hands.

"Corian!" she'd shrieked, scrambling to her feet.

But by the time she lunged at me, I'd already flipped it open and caught the first few lines of something that might've been a poem. Or a song.

Something about steel and leather.

Before I could read more, she'd snatched it back and taken off toward home, her braids flying behind her. I didn't see her again for days after that.

She avoided me like I had the plague. Wouldn't talk to me at school, wouldn't look my way. I ended up having to slip a note to Marcus, her little brother, and ask him to pass it along.

They didn't have a phone at home, so that was the only way.

It was a stupid apology. Something like "Sorry for being a jerk. You can hit me if you want."

I didn't know if she'd read it, but two days later, she was back at the pond.

Didn't say much, but she let me sit next to her while she wrote, and after a while, she handed me a fistful of wildflowers.

She never mentioned the note.

Or the poem.

It was the first place we kissed.

And the first place we argued.

A place filled with too many memories. Ones I hadn't let myself think about in years.

I wondered if she remembered it like I did.

Or if time had erased it for her.

"On paper, the estate—including land, assets, and liquid funds—holds a value of $8.7 million," Hensley continued. "However, there are conditions."

Of course there were.

Hensley continued, "I don't know the full set of conditions that you will both need to agree to. But there is a time commitment and both of you will need to agree to these," he pulled two envelopes from the stack of papers and slid one to me and another to Cara, "conditions. John penned two letters; one for each of you to read. Further details are enclosed. Once you have read them, please think it over then reach back out to me for next steps. Let's say, within the week?"

This time Cara exhaled slowly.

"I loved Mr. Ecklands, I did" she said, her voice tight, measured. "But I don't know if I'll be here in a week. Are you sure you can't share more details, Mr. Hensley? My home is in Paris, and this sounds all a bit mysterious." She splayed her hands looking down at the envelope with her name scrawled on the front as if it would bite her.

Paris.

I'd heard rumors of her moving there around the same time her brother moved back to Lily.

Someone mentioned it at a party.

But I couldn't remember who.

Didn't matter.

What did matter was the growing knot in my throat when she said the words. 'I live in Paris.'

Thirty years ago, we had talked about living there *together*.

She'd made a life there.

Without me.

I clenched my jaw, forcing down the tangle of emotions rising in my chest. None of that mattered now. What mattered was she'd been moved on and her life in Paris was ultimately none of my business

I reached for the pen. Without hesitation, I signed my name on the document stating I'd received the letter and stood to leave.

I would do anything Mr. Ecklands asked of me.

Cara, on the other hand?

She was already looking for her exit route. Still the same Cara.

Chapter 7 – Cara

I left the lawyer's office with a measured calm, each step carrying the weight of the pressing demand that Mr. Ecklands had placed on both me and Corian. Before we parted ways, the lawyer had made it unequivocally clear: the letters needed to be read—one addressed to me, the other to Corian. And whatever was enclosed in them needed both our agreement. Like Corian, I picked up my letter, signed the receipt for it and left the lawyers office with a promise that I'd reach out later in the week.

I drove to Marcus's house, where I now had free reign. A brief message on my phone confirmed that he was at his office in town. Good. I wasn't prepared to face the Ecklands' ask, let alone talk about it; and Marcus was going to want to know every detail.

What I needed right now was a distraction. I didn't want to think about last will's and testaments, inheritances, or... Corian. Marcus's home, that I had not fully explored would have to do for now.

I walked through the rooms again, admiring what Raynice had done with the place. I adored my sleek, modern condo in Paris—it was an expensive reflection of my identity—but I had to admit, Marcus and Raynice's home felt like—a home.

I eventually made my way to the garden. The moment I sank onto the stone bench, the familiar scents of hydrangeas and jasmine immediately hit me. I remembered the flowers growing wild around the old Mackey house. That was at least one thing that made living there barrable. The smell of them drug my mind back there. I hadn't intended to relive that day—the day I first met Corian Demetrie—but there was no escaping it. It seemed the past had a way of elbowing its way back into the present, no matter how tightly I tried to keep it at bay. The site of him and the smells in the garden conspired to remind me, coaxing those memories to surface despite the walls I'd spent years building around them.

Ainty Renee's raucous laughter and loud country yells almost pissed me off. "Gon' on out yonder and catch that chicken, now Cara!" She'd hollered. "Look at you acting all sadiddy like ya' too good to catch what you eat."

And that did it. I wasn't about to let that little white ball of feathers get the best of me. It had only been a month since our parents' funeral, yet Ainty Renee wasn't having any of us moping around or feeling sorry for ourselves.

"When I found out my brother was on that stuff," she said to both Marcus and I not long after the funeral, "I told him it was gonna be the end of him—but no, nobody listened to ol' Ainty Renee. Him and your Mama stopped talking to me after that. But now y'all are back home in the country, where they never should have carried you away from. Now I'm gonna have to teach you how to take care of yourselves. We ain't got much, and God knows ain't nobody lived in old Joe's—your granddaddy's—house

in years. So, the first order of business for today is catchin' that chicken, wringin' its neck so we can pluck it, and I can fry it up for supper."

Her belly shook with laughter as she turned away from the look of pure disgust on my face at the thought of eating that dusty chicken. Then again at the scene of me chasing that ornery bird—making a fool of myself, no doubt—before hollerin' over her shoulder for Marcus. "Go on in there and grab my notebook so I can write down these numbers Jennie Mae just called in."

Sure enough, Ainty Renee, whose name until now I thought was Annie Renee, until I learned that Ainty was just how country folks around here said Aunty and she was everyone's aunty--Ainty... and I mean everyone's. She was also the town's number runner—and aside from me catching that chicken, those one- and two-dollar plays that people called in were how we ate.

I kept running behind that chicken until I entered the woods and could no longer hear any of ol' Renee's hollerin'. The chicken had bolted to the left, vanished out of sight, and there I was, scouring under and around the low brush, trying to track that mischievous little joker. Then, out of nowhere, I heard, "Whoa, whoa, whoa!" Had I not leaped back in time, falling to the ground, the fiercest, most determined horse I'd ever seen would have run me clean over.

I scooted back into the brush, my backside scraping against the rough ground, and looked up in awe at the big, beautiful horse. What surprised me even more was the wiry young boy who had jumped off its back and was reaching out his hand to help me up.

First off, it might have been the very first time I'd ever seen a horse up close. Second, I'd never really considered that Black folks rode horses. And third, I recognized the boy from school. I didn't know his name, but

I knew he was popular, played football, and every girl seemed to be after him—and I could see why.

He rode that horse bareback and, shirtless, his tall, wiry frame appeared chiseled like patinated copper. His hand stayed outstretched as I stood there, momentarily stunned by the jumble of thoughts racing through my head.

Then it struck me—I probably looked like a complete mess: cut-off shorts, an old beat-up sweatshirt, barefoot, running through the woods chasing a chicken like a fool. On any other day, I wouldn't have been caught outside without proper shoes, but it was just after daybreak, and Ainty Renee had woken me up, stompin' around the house, yellin' for me to go catch that chicken—without even giving me a chance to put on shoes.

And on top of that, my braids were two days old, and I hadn't had a moment to wash my face. Now, here I was, face to face with one of the most handsome boys at school.

When he saw me hesitate, he took his hand and wiped it down the front of his worn jeans, then laughed. "Girl, let me help you up," he said. "Everybody around here is doin' some yard work or chores or whatever their folks got 'em doin', so quit bein' shamed and shy—let me help you up."

I accepted his help, placing my hand in his outstretched one, and he lifted me as if I were nothing more than a feather. "Ain't you the new girl?" he prodded.

"Yes, I suppose you could say that," I replied softly. My brother and I have been here for about a month now, but we only started school here last week. They're still sorting out my classes—apparently some of the gifted courses I'd been in aren't available now, so they're working to ensure I don't lose the credits I've already earned.

He chuckled softly, then said, "Well, I'm sorry 'bout frightenin' you smart girl. My dad's got me trainin' this new Morgan mare, and for some reason she wouldn't listen when I tried to keep her outta' the woods—it's like she just brought me here on her own."

He took a breath long enough to refocus his attention on the horse, speaking directly to it. "It's all right, girl; you're gonna learn. I'll be gentle with you, and next year, you might even fetch a high bid at auction. Seems like you just wanted a new friend." Then he turned back to me and stuck his hand out again. "I'm Corian, by the way. I live just on the other side of this grove—our properties are butted up against each other." He whistled, then added, almost to himself, as if he couldn't believe his own eyes—it might be the first time in all these years I'd seen anyone on old man Mackey's property. "Are you a Mackey?"

"Yeah, I'm Cara Mackey," I replied, my gaze lowering to the ground and left at that. 'Yeah, I'm Cara Mackey, eldest daughter of Paul and Laria Mackey, addicts that tragically died in the car accident off Hwy 27 didn't quite seem like the right thing to say to some strange boy I went to school with. That would just be a buzzkill. I didn't have to say anything further; his next line said it all.

"Oh, yeah, that's right. I heard my dad talkin' about your parents. I'm sorry for your loss."

His words were so gentle that I couldn't help but quickly lift my eyes to his, searching for sincerity in them. Most boys his—our age—especially ones as handsome and popular as he was—didn't have an ounce of empathy. But Corian was different, at least that's what I saw in his eyes.

Perhaps I was staring too intently; he shifted his gaze, a nervous blush creeping over his features. Then he asked, "What are you doin' out here in these woods?"

No sooner had that question left his mouth, than that dumb chicken strutted right between us and halted our conversation. With a swift twist of his wrist, Corian picked it up by its head, executed some maneuver, *and popped its neck. He handed it to me, grinning, "Y'all gonna eat good tonight," he smiled as I grimaced. Then we locked eyes and both burst into laughter.*

I couldn't help but exclaimed, "This chicken is precisely why I'm out here—chasing it around because Auntie Renee told me to do it, though I'd never been certain how until you did that! So, thank you for wringing that chicken's neck for me."

"I gotta get on back before my dad starts hootin' and hollerin' 'bout where I am with this prized horse. But you can tell your folks you wrung that chicken's neck yourself if you want," he replied.

Corian was getting ready to walk away, leading the horse by its reins, but before it budged, it trotted up to me first and nuzzled my neck. I didn't know what to do—I'd never been this close to a horse before, never had one touch me like that. I froze.

"She really likes you. You know you can come by the ranch anytime, and I might even teach you how to ride her, if you want."

"Really?" I managed, but still a bit stunned. Quickly, I added, "She's absolutely beautiful—I'd love to learn how to ride her."

"Yeah? Well, that's dope. You seem to have a way with her; I might even let you name her—"

"Leather," She blurted without much hesitation.

"Huh?" I asked.

"You should name her Leather. It was the first thing I thought of when I looked up at her from the ground—the way the sun glinted off her glossy brown coat and mane made her look like polished, beautiful leather."

He dipped his head in a quick, strong nod, lips curling into a thin smile. "Leather it is, Cara Mackey." Tugging the reins, then grabbing a fist full of Leathers mane, he swung himself up on her back in a way I'd only seen cowboys do in movies. Before he led Leather back to his side of the grove, he tossed over his shoulder, "Nice meeting you again, Cara. See you at school Monday."

For that brief instant, I watched him disappear into the trees, a small smile tugging at my lips as I felt a fragile crack in the well-fortified walls I'd built around myself—a vulnerability I usually denied.

When I returned to the nearly dilapidated confines of our family home—with its creakin' floors, peeling wallpaper, and that old broken swing in the yard—I assumed the thrill of my encounter with Corian would fade. But it lingered. As I carried the chicken into the kitchen and saw Ainty Renee's and Marcus's mouths drop open in disbelief, a burst of pure, sunshine-like warmth exploded within me. I yelled, "Yeah, we eatin' good tonight!" I laid the bird on the counter and savored that small victory Corian had unwittingly given me.

I recalled that defining morning after Ainty Renee had taken us in after my brother and I were thrust into a new, uncharted world—a world unified by the dense woods between the Mackey, Demetrie, and Ecklands properties.

I sighed at yet another memory dredged up, this time caused by seeing Corian For the first time in nearly thirty years. All these memories made me feel vulnerable... Vulnerability, I believed, came at too steep a cost—a risk of losing control. Similar to how I lost control over Corian back then. That day in the woods and the weeks and months after hinted at the possibility of something more: a fleeting chance at love. Corian had been that guy. Until he wasn't.

Let me get this over with so I can get back to my life in Paris. I pulled Mr. Ecklands' letter from my bag and began reading it right there in the garden under the encroaching dusk.

Chapter 8 — Cara's Letter

*D*ear Cara,

   I hope you're reading this in a quiet moment, somewhere still enough for you to hear the truth in my words. I imagine you sitting with that same thoughtful look you used to have in my classroom, the one that told me you were listening even when you were too stubborn to admit it.

   I want you to know something—I never once doubted you. Not when you sat in that drafting chair, piecing together a future bigger than this town. Not when you told me you were leaving, even though I could see how much it hurt you. And not when I could hear the sadness and disconnect in your voice from being away from your roots for so long. Heavy is the head that wears the crown.

   You were always meant for more. And you proved me right.

   But here's something I've learned, something time has taught me in ways both kind and cruel—success is only as sweet as the people you share it with. I have had Bonita by my side for most of my years, and though we never had children of our own, we were never without love. That's why you and Corian mattered so much to us. We saw something rare, something beautiful, and I won't pretend that watching it fall apart didn't ache.

You never had to tell me what happened between you two. I didn't need to know the details. —I knew you two well enough to know that whatever it was, you both were broken by it. I saw it in the way your eyes lost some of their fire just before you left for good. I saw it in the way Corian anchored himself to responsibility when he was once all light beam around you. And I see it now, in the way life has carried you forward, but never quite let you forget.

I am not a man given to regrets, but I do have one: I wish I had found a way to help you hold on to love. Because love, real love, the kind that roots itself deep, does not often come twice in a lifetime. And you, my dear girl, have always deserved a love that does not waver.

So, I ask you this—do you still believe in what you once dreamed? Not just in the designs, the plans, the buildings that carry your name, but in the life you imagined? The life that was never meant to be lived alone?

Building a community center for the people of Lily is my dream, my legacy. By now, you should be made aware of this project from my attorney. The project if you will be a killing off of the old, that old raggedy cotton gin. And an ushering in of the new. My legacy is also yours. A modern facility in the heart of Lily, Ga where young minds like yours and Corian's once were, can took shape, where futures can be drawn in pencil before being built in concrete and glass. I leave it in your hands, not just to complete, but to understand the bigger picture of what home can be.

I have put together a list of things that I need you and Corian to do. Yes, I could have put the list in this envelope, but that just would have been too easy now, wouldn't it? Here's a bit of homework for you. Go back to my lawyer and get further instructions on where you can get the list. You will find the list to be challenging, my dear, but the rewards will be grand! As *these are not just tasks. They are the steps back toward something I know you've never truly let go of. Some items on the list will test your patience, others your heart, but all will require two things—trust and a desire to carry out a dead man's wishes. Yes. By the time you read this letter, I will have left this world. And I go in peace knowing that you and Corian will see this through.*

No, no, no, no, noooooo. I rolled my eyes away from the letter to stare up at the heavens. How the hell could I say no to a dead man. I refocused on the letter.

I know I cannot ask you to see what I see. But if you give yourself the chance, maybe, just maybe, you will find that some things are worth rebuilding.

Wow. I see what you did there, Ecklands.

For me, for the town of Lily. But most of all, for you.

With love and endless faith,

John Ecklands

Chapter 9 – Corian

The clang of metal against wood rang out as my boot connected with SJ's empty feed pail, sending it skittering across the barn floor. The crossbred Friesian and Morgan colt didn't flinch—just flicked an ear and watched me, like he was used to my frustration. Hell, he probably was. The stable was my space where I came to mull things over. Things like the ranch's down trending financials. Now I had much more frustration to add to the pile of horseshit building up.

The scent of fresh hay and saddle oil filled my lungs, but it did nothing to settle me as it usually did. My hands curled into fists at my sides. The barn was quiet except for the rhythmic huffs of the horses and the occasional creak of old wood settling. SJs dark eyes tracked me.

I had a bond with the horse whose initials were short for Steel Jr., sired by the very first horse I'd broken for myself. Bred with the very horse named by you guessed it... The runner, the track star, Cara Mackey. Leather and Steel, we'd once called the duo; a stallion and a mare that were equally as smitten with each other as I was with Cara when we were teenagers.

The flick of SJs ear made brought me back to the manure of my present predicament.

The ranch's financials, the lawyer's office visit today, and Cara Mackey. I didn't even want to think of the latter two items on the list so I stuck with the ranch's financials...

They were a damn mess, and even though we had a few overseas sales pending, nothing really had popped off with the European market just yet. Farms and ranches across America were dwindling. Competition for thoroughbred breeding overseas in places like Dubai was growing stronger. We would need to establish those overseas connections and innovate more if we were going to keep the ranch running.

And now, on top of that, Mr. Ecklands had dropped this community center project in my lap.

I exhaled hard, dragging a hand down my face.

"You look like hell."

I turned to see Darren standing in the barn's entrance, arms crossed, leaning against a post like he had all the time in the world. My younger brother always had a way of showing up when I was two steps from losing my damn mind.

"Feel like it too," I admitted, rubbing my temples. "*Gotta'* figure out something, D."

"I've been continuing to work the overseas angle. Germany's thoroughbred market is booming right now. Currently most of their imported breeds come from Ireland, France and the UK. But they need unique pedigrees and bloodlines that they can't find in Europe. The jockey clubs in Turkey are on the rise as well. It's a niche market there but they are paying top dollar for great stock to cross breed with their

Anadolu and Turkish Arabians." His words trailed off. "Something tells me you weren't talking about the ranch," his brow raised at me.

I hesitated, then sighed. "Went to the lawyers office for the reading of Ecklands' will this afternoon."

Darren's eyes sharpened. "Yeah. The old man had more faith in you than you did in yourself. Not surprised. He leave you anything?"

I let out a dry chuckle. "Yeah, well, a lot of something. Wants me to turn the old cotton gin into a community center. Dying wish and all. Per the lawyer, he wants to leave his legacy by turning that monstrosity into a place for the kids and to preserve our history."

Darren let out a low whistle. "Damn."

"Yeah. Fuck knows why that damn cotton gin ain't been torn down. It's a good thing, but I don't have the time or the means to make it happen." I exhaled heavily. "And on top of all that... Cara's back."

Darren's brows lifted even higher while his chin dipped to his chest, "Cara? From back in *high school*, Cara?"

I nodded. He stepped forward, resting his hands on the stall's edge. "Oh shit. The plot thickens. Is that why you look like someone knocked the wind *outta'* you?"

I let out a humorless chuckle. "Something like that."

Darren was quiet for a beat. Then changed the subject, clearly not wanting to touch the Cara conversation with a ten-foot pole. "You ever thought about calling Jax?"

I frowned. "Jax?"

Darren nodded, casual but watching me closely. "Yeah. Our other brother?" He quipped, lips twisting as he shook his head, admonishing me. "I know he's a hell of a lot younger than us, but don't you think it's about time you quit treating him like he's still that snot nosed aggravating ass kid he used to be?"

To that I did chuckle. "That little shit was always getting in the way."

Jaxon Demetrie was our little brother, cocky as hell, and had made himself a damn fortune in virtual and augmented reality tech out in California. He could sell a dream to anybody—but the one thing he'd never bought into was this ranch.

"Ranch is bleeding money, right? He's *makin'* big tech dollars, and you know that boy loves building shit. You need innovation—Jax knows innovation and how to make money moves."

I scoffed. "Jax ain't interested in this place, D. Never was."

Darren shrugged. "He ain't interested in *shovelin'* stalls and *breakin'* horses. Hell naw. But makin' money? That's his game." He paused, then side-eyed me. "Besides, what's the alternative? Just keep *runnin'* this place the same way until it folds?"

My jaw tightened. I hated how damn right he was.

Darren leaned against the stall door, crossing his arms. "Let me keep working the overseas angle. In the meantime, call Jax and let lil *bruh* help with the innovation piece, while you figure out what you're going to do about this legacy building community center shit. Let us help. And then you'll have time to focus there. Now the means... Wait, the old man didn't leave any money behind for you to carry out his wishes?"

Darren's question paused me. I had signed and didn't stick around the lawyer's office to read the fine print or the letter that Mr. Ecklands left. I was too caught up in my feelings around Cara making a life in Paris without my black ass. And said as much to Darren, minus the in my feelings part.

I sighed, rubbing the back of my neck. "Yeah. Hell, I don't know all the details yet." I glanced back at the bench where I'd dropped the letter from Mr. Ecklands. "Just know a contingency of what I agreed to was that it had to be done with the other person named in the will."

Darren's brows drew together in confusion.

I finally said it. "Cara's named in the will too. She's supposed to be handling the design. But I doubt she will stick around for that."

Darren let out a low whistle. "So, if she bails, it's all on you?"

I nodded, jaw clenched. "Not that I wouldn't do anything for John Ecklands and his wife Bonita. But, yep. If Cara bails, I will help my dead mentor's legacy come to fruition."

A long beat of silence passed between us.

Darren's gaze flicked past me—to the crumpled envelope sitting on my workbench, still sealed. His expression darkened. "You planning on reading that letter anytime soon?"

I exhaled sharply. "I will."

"When?"

"Damn, Darren—"

"When, Corian?" Darren stepped closer, voice low but firm. "You signed a deal with a dead man, and you don't even know the fine print? That ain't you, big bro."

My temper flared. "What does it matter? Ain't like I would've said no to whatever it is."

Darren shook his head. "Nah. You just don't wanna read it 'cause you know Mr. Ecklands always saw through your bullshit."

I sucked in a breath, but Darren wasn't done.

"You're out here *holdin'* up the weight of the world, and for what? This ranch? A community center dream you just found out about?" He glared at me, hands on his hips. He let out a pent-up sigh then straightened, a realization dawning. "Or is it guilt over how you let the love of your life slip through your fingers all of them years ago and now the pigs done came home to roost?" My eyes shot up to his then. He studied me. "Yeah, big bro. It's high time you *face* what you've signed up for... *All of it, including her.*"

My pulse thumped in my ears as I stared at the letter. Darren's words sat heavy.

Then he let out a breath, shaking his head. "I already know how this goes. You're gonna sit here, stew on it, pretend it don't bother you. But you gonna read that letter, Corian. *'Because* you don't walk away from what needs doin'."

He clapped me on the shoulder, then turned to leave.

At the door, he paused. "And think about Jax. Ain't about what he wants—it's about what you need."

Then he was gone, leaving me alone with SJ, the ranch, and a whole bunch of thoughts swirling in my head about that unopened letter waiting for me on the workbench and the woman who got the matching envelope.

I grabbed the letter and sat down on the bench to read it.

CHAPTER TEN

Chapter 10 — Corian's Letter

D*ear Corian,*

If you're reading this, then I suppose I've finally managed to get you to stop for a moment. Lord knows you've spent your whole life carrying more than your fair share, always putting everyone else first. I have watched you hold up this ranch, this family, this town—sometimes with both hands, sometimes with just sheer will. And I respect that. I always have.

But now, I need you to listen to me, son.

I know what happened between you and Cara. Between you and Monica. Between you and the life you thought you were headed toward. Funny thing about life, it will take you on a ride that can heal or break you. I think your path has done both healing and breaking for you and you just did the best you could with what you were dealt.

For the record, Monica is an amazing woman and mother, and she put up with a lot from you. Yall both were given some lemons. But that Ja'Kari is some sweet lemonade conceived of you two. Yes, son. You did right by Monica. You built a life, raised a daughter, and when it was time to part ways, you did so with grace. You gave ten years to duty, to family, to doing what needed to be done.

But before that, there was Cara. I loved you both as much as I imagine I would have loved my own children had Bonita and I been blessed with them...

I watched you leave for Prairie View with the world in your hands, and I watched you come back, carrying a different weight than the one you left with. And I don't begrudge you for it.

You did what a man is supposed to do. You stood up, took responsibility, and honored your commitment. And for that, I couldn't be prouder of you.

But, Corian, tell me this—when did honor become the thing that kept you from happiness? When did you decide that and under whose counsel? That will be a question that you will one day need to answer and reckon with.

Here you are, all these years later, still carrying a burden that isn't yours to carry anymore. You did what was right back then, but now, son, you've got to make amends for your mistake.

Damn. The old man really did see through all my bullshit over the years. I'd never verbalized that marrying Monica out of duty rather than love was the biggest mistake of my life but right here in this letter, the old man had clocked it with full clarity. I kept reading.

And I don't mean the mistake of getting Monica pregnant—that brought you Ja'Kari. I mean the mistake of believing that a mistake would close the path to true love forever.

Cara. Period with a 'T' as the youngins say it.

I know you still love her. Even if you won't say it, even if you think the love you hold for her doesn't matter anymore. Even after all these years, I saw it in the distant look in your eyes whenever you came to the house and saw her picture when you thought nobody was watching. I see it in the way you've lived—steady, strong, but never letting yourself reach for what you wanted out of life.

You and Cara were young, but what you had together? That wasn't just young love. That was the kind of thing people spend lifetimes looking for. And I know you lost it. I know it broke both of you in ways neither of you ever admitted.

So now, I'm asking you to fix it.

The community center is my dream, but it ain't just about me. It's about Lily. It's about the next generation. And it's about making sure two of the brightest students I ever had—two people who built dreams out of nothing—finally build something together.

You and Cara have work to do. Not just with your hands, but with your hearts. And I'm going to ask that you do it together.

Once you've thought all this over, call up my lawyer and he will get you the list. The list isn't just a bunch of tasks I need you to do. They are steps. Steps that will take you both threw your past, and maybe—just maybe—toward something you thought was lost for good.

Do this for me. Do this for Lily. But more than that, do this for you.

With pride and faith in the man you are,

John

Chapter 11 — Corian

The only upscale restaurant in Lily was a small, dimly lit place that tried too hard to be sophisticated. It was the only restaurant in town with white tablecloths and a paper menu. But the food was your run-of-the-mill soul food.

I would have rather just went to mom and pop's for dinner rather than be sitting at a banquet sized table full of these stiff ass banker types that my daughter worked with. But anything for Ja'Kari. I was it. Her plus-one at her work event to celebrate some VP getting promoted because her fiancé was out of town.

With all the boring bank talk going on around us, I caught her studying me over her half eaten plate of black-eyed peas and rice with smothered chicken. She sat down her glass of wine, tilting her head and whispering, "Alright, out with it. You're shoulders have been tense during the whole meal and you've had this distant look all over your face. Everything okay, Dad?"

I exhaled hard, ran a hand down my face, then let out a dry chuckle. "It's complicated."

Before Ja'Kari could reply, the restaurant door swung open, and my body betrayed me before my mind caught up.

Cara.

I could feel Ja'Kari's eyes on me before they darted to not what, but who had just captured my full attention at the entrance. I could see curiosity lighting up her face out of the corner of my eye as she tracked my reaction. I tried to school my expression, but my jaw tightened of its own accord, and my fingers tensed around my glass. Too late. She caught it all.

A wicked grin stretched across my daughter's face. "Well, well, well," she murmured, her voice thick with amusement. "Who's that?"

My chest tightened, so I didn't respond to Kari's probing.

"Mm-hmm." She arched a brow. "Let me find out the *complications* have something to do with that stunning woman who just walked in?"

Even though I had yet to respond to her, Ja'Kari's gaze whipped back to me, and she kept ongoing. "Oh, I see now. You do know her." Ja'Kari stated rather than asked.

My attention was too focused on Cara to give in to Ja'Kari's keen questioning.

How the hell could this woman be so similar to the Cara I knew back then, but still so much—more... More composed, more polished, more... Cara. *Perfection.* Her silvery-gray bob framed her face like she'd walked out of a high-powered fashion magazine. Her skin shone in the dim lighting of the restaurant like burnished mahogany. That skin had a history that tangled with mine in ways I'd never forget.

"Who is she?" Ja'Kari finally asked.

I didn't answer. Hell, I couldn't. Because Cara's gaze had just landed square on mine and me *and* Ja'Kari both openly stared in her direction. When Cara's lips parted slightly, in what looked to be the makings of a smile for a second—just a fraction of a second—everything else disappeared. Then, just as quickly, recognition marred her face, and she turned away.

That's all I needed to see, though. A moment of hesitation in her gaze. I don't know what the flicker of light I saw in her eyes meant, but I knew then that the unfinished car in my barn wasn't the only thing I might have a sliver of a chance to fix.

And just like that, the years faded away...

Twigs crunched beneath my boots as I swung up on Leather's back. She was a beauty—sleek, brown, her coat shimmering under the slanted morning light like polished leather. I could see why Cara chose that name for her. Leather was a Morgan mare. The kind of horse that turned heads. The kind of horse that needed patience, precision, and a steady hand.

And she had nearly run over the girl standing wide-eyed in front of me just a week ago. Yet, that same girl seemed to have a way with calming this queen down.

I reached out, offering my hand, watching as Cara stared at Leather like she might bite. A mess of tangled coils framed her face. No braids this time, her cottony black mane hair was beautiful. She wore the same sweatshirt she'd worn the day we'd met in the woods. But this time with a pair of oversized jeans and flip-flops. City girl through and through. Because who else would be in a horse pasture with flip flops on.

Cara hesitated a moment more before she finally took my hand, and the moment our fingers touched, I felt it. A current. Not the kind you expect from a handshake. Something sharper, unexpected.

She barely weighed a thing as I pulled her up and behind me on the saddle.

She tensed for a moment, her hands gripping my waist tighter than necessary. I felt the hesitation in her touch, the way she fought to relax. "Ain't gonna let you fall, city girl," I said over my shoulder, my voice softer than I intended. "Just hold on."

Leather shifted beneath us, sensing the unfamiliar weight. I adjusted the reins, steadying her. "Have you ever been on a horse before?"

"Been on one? I've never even been near a horse before the other day."

I smirked. "Well, you're in for a ride."

I nudged Leather forward, keeping her pace slow as we left the clearing and moved toward the open field. The rhythm of her steps was steady, the warmth of Cara pressed against my back something I knew I shouldn't be noticing—but damn if I wasn't.

"Relax," I murmured again. "Let yourself move with her."

It took a moment, but eventually, I felt her body ease, the tension melting bit by bit. I turned slightly, just enough to see her profile, the way her lips parted slightly in awe as she took in the land stretching before us.

"Wow," she breathed. "It's... beautiful."

Something settled in my chest at the wonder in her voice. I'd seen this land my whole life, but through her eyes, it was something new. Something different.

"Yeah," I said. "It is."

As we approached the ranch, I spotted my father near the main corral, arms crossed, eyes narrowing the second he saw me riding up with Cara behind me.

"What the hell you doin', boy? Wastin' time paradin' some girl around when there's work to be done?" Daddy's voice was a familiar crack of thunder, sharp and unforgiving.

I felt Cara stiffen behind me. Before I could say yes sir to my daddy, the screen door creaked open, and there was Mama.

"Waynan Demetrie, you hush all that fussin' right now," she called, stepping down from the porch with the kind of authority that made even my father pause. "Ain't nothin' wrong with Corian teachin' the girl how to ride. Nobody stopped you from teaching me when we were right around that same age."

Waynan exhaled sharply, muttered something under his breath, then stalked off toward the stables.

Mama walked right up to us, her knowing gaze sweeping over me first, then settling on Cara. A slow, approving smile crept across her face. Then—like only she could—she winked at me before turning her attention fully to Cara.

"You're Mack's daughter, Cara, aren't you?" Mama asked already knowing the answer. "Waynan and I went to school with your daddy."

Cara responded, "Oh, I never thought I'd meet any of my dad's school mates."

"Oh yes, half the folks living around here still went to school or knew your daddy. He was a genius in school but was a beast on the road. Had the fastest car on the circuit. He used to drag race," Mama said matter-of-factly. "Used to have the hardest '69 Chev--"

"Chevy Chevelle," Cara finished the sentence. "He told us stories about his car."

"Yeah... it's a shame that he sold it all those years ago.." Mama paused, like she was going to say more but thought better of it. Then she smiled kindly at Cara touching her beautiful hair. "Girl you look just like your mama. So beautiful. I see why Corian here can't keep his eyes off of you."

"Mama!" I said, not able to contain my embarrassment.

"Oh hush, I'm just teasing with you, son. Finish up with Cara, before your daddy pitches a fit. Cara it was very nice meeting you, dear."

"You gonna sit there and pretend she's not what's got you over here all in your feelings tonight?" Ja'Kari's question pulled me back to the present. "You ain't gonna go speak to her?" Her lips curved in a sly grin.

I grunted, swirling the bourbon in my glass. "Ain't got nothing to say."

Ja'Kari scoffed. "Right. And I'm the Queen of England." She leaned forward, chin resting on her palm. "So, what's the deal? First love? Or old heartbreak?"

My jaw flexed. I wanted to respond all the above. "Mind your business, Kari."

Ja'Kari hummed, clearly pleased. "Interesting."

I shook my head. "It's really not."

She chuckled, stealing a glance toward Cara's table. "Well, from the way she looked at you, I'd say it is. She is."

I sighed, setting my glass down. "Drop it, Kari."

"Alright then," she said, arching an eyebrow. "But from the way the two of you just looked at each other, *baybeee...* don't be surprised when mystery-woman haunts your dreams tonight."

She sat back, sipped her wine, and grinned like she'd just hit the jackpot.

Ja'Kari's coworkers had already paid the tab, and we rose from the table just as Cara was doing the same across the restaurant. It was as if the universe had been waiting for the perfect moment to put me in this damn position.

I turned, and there she was—mere feet away. No escaping it now.

Her gaze met mine, her expression unreadable, though something flickered in those dark eyes of hers. Recognition. Maybe even hesitation.

Ja'Kari, ever the instigator, arched a brow and smirked. "Well, don't be rude, Daddy. Aren't you going to introduce us?"

I cleared my throat, shifting on my feet. "Uh... Cara... this is my daughter, Ja'Kari."

Cara's lips parted slightly before she recovered with a smooth nod. "Nice to meet you."

Ja'Kari shot me a sidelong glance, her smirk growing. "Likewise."

The tension stretched thick between us, heavy with words unspoken, unfinished business pressing in from all sides.

And for the first time in years, I had no idea what the hell to do next.

CHAPTER TWELVE

Chapter 12 – Cara

I tapped my card against the screen, a satisfied little thrill running through me as another package was secured. A new pair of Amina Muaddi slingbacks? Click. A structured Jacquemus blazer? Click. A Gucci Bamboo 1947 bag? Why the hell not? Lily, Georgia, might not have a single luxury boutique within a hundred and thirty miles, but that's why express shipping exists. And thank God for that, because a bitch needed retail therapy right about now.

The wind rolled lazily across Marcus's porch as I sat in the rocking chair spending a small fortune to sooth my spirit. The ruffling pages of the home design magazine I'd discarded on the wicker table beside me and the clacking of my nails on the tablet screen weren't loud enough to drown out my roiling thoughts.

My thoughts were stuck on replay of the scene yesterday in the dimly lit restaurant. I couldn't stop thinking about a set of deep captivating eyes on the beautiful face of the young woman in the restaurant with that damned Corian Demetrie. Her eyes weren't exactly his but were his enough for me to know that I was staring right into the face of his daughter. On top of everything else that'd happened from the memories being dredged up just from being in Lily, the impossible demand of legacy building by Ecklands, and running smack dab into *him*. I wasn't ready for this.

Ja'Kari.

After reading the letter, I just wanted a good glass of wine and a change of scenery from my brother's garden. I should have known that going to the one decent restaurant in town... the only one that had real wine glasses and linen napkins that there would be a chance of running into him. And did. Corian had the nerve to be there too, sitting across from the daughter I had never met, never thought I'd have reason to meet. She was grown, polished, beautiful.

She had Corian's smirk and his same level-headed stillness that had once steadied me when I thought my world was too chaotic to hold on to.

The chance meeting hadn't been hostile or even awkward. It was just... heavy. Too much history in the space between us. And I had barely been able to keep my food down.

I exhaled sharply, hitting place order one last time just to shut my brain off.

"Something must've rattled you good," Marcus drawled from the doorway, a grin pulling at his lips as he stepped out onto the porch.

I shot him a glare over my glasses. "What are you talking about?"

Marcus folded his arms, his designer sweats hanging loose on his frame, because money or not, this man still embodied Sunday-morning-in-the-South leisure. "Because, I know you big Sis and you don't shop like this unless you're pissed or shaken. And since you can't stand losing control of your emotions, I'm guessing it's the second one."

I pursed my lips and tucked my phone under my thigh like that would erase the multiple order confirmation emails in my inbox.

He sat beside me, reaching for the glass of sweet tea I had abandoned on the porch railing, taking a sip.

"Ew, put my glass down. I don't know where your mouth been." I glared at him, not so much for drinking out of my glass, but for knowing me too well.

"Aw shut up and stop worrying about where my mouth been," he said, emptying the glass. "Obviously I'm not worried about what man yours has been on." I swatted at him like I used to do when we were teenagers. We both chuckled. When that died down, I looked out across the field, but Marcus's eyes stayed on me, expectant. He was my younger brother by two years, but growing up, we were so close that many thought we were twins because of how protective we were of each other. We were almost clairvoyant in how we could pinpoint each other's moods and feelings without ever saying a word. There was no need in me holding back from him.

"I ran into Corian again last night," I paused, looking out at nothing in particular, "and Ja'Kari," I said, letting the words fall between us.

He blinked at me a few times. stuttered back to life to said, "Oh damn. Awkward?" He questioned, and I cocked my head and raised both brows at him. "Don't answer that," he said as soon as I twisted my face at him. "Awkward is probably an understatement."

I shifted in my seat. "She looks like him."

Marcus hummed. "She would. Bet that fucked you up, didn't it?"

I clenched my jaw. "It didn't fuck me up, Marcus. It just—" I exhaled sharply. "It's just. *Fuck.*" I squeezed my eyes tight. "It's one thing to know he had a kid. It's another thing to look her in the face and see..."

See what we never got to be.

I swallowed hard. I wasn't mad at Ja'Kari. She wasn't a villain in my story. Hell, all this happened thirty years ago. If anything, she was proof of how time had moved on, of how life had shaped itself without me.

And that's what stung the most.

Marcus, annoyingly perceptive as ever, clearly read the battle happening behind my eyes. He let the silence sit for a beat before nudging me again.

"And what about Mr. Ecklands' letter?"

I bit my lip. I hadn't told him everything yet. Only that there was a letter and a request that I stick around long enough to help realize the man's dying wish.

Mr. Ecklands, the man who had seen me before I even knew how to see myself. The man who had put a drafting pencil in my hand and said, create something better than what you come from. The man who had left behind a challenge.

Not just a challenge. A damn near impossible one.

He wanted us—me and Corian, of all people—to turn that abandoned cotton gin into his legacy. A landmark for the people of Lily.

And it hit me, suddenly, why I had spent my entire adult life carving out beauty in places that had never belonged to me. Why I needed to create something softer than where I had come from.

Maybe it had never just been about high-end hotels or Parisian brownstones. Maybe, deep down, I had always been trying to prove I could make something beautiful out of my ruins.

I let out a slow breath.

"I'm doing it," I said finally.

Marcus stilled beside me. "Come again?"

I turned to face him, my grip tightening around my knee. "I'm taking Mr. Ecklands' challenge, the cotton gin, the whole damn thing."

He studied me for a long moment, and I braced for whatever half-smart comment he was about to lob my way.

But instead, he grinned, wide and knowing.

"You sure about that, sis?"

I squared my shoulders and narrowed my eyes at the landscape. "Yeah. I'm sure."

Because, yeah, this was about Mr. Ecklands and his legacy. But a small, reckless part of me? It wanted Corian to feel my goddamn presence as keenly as I felt his absence all those years after he'd up and gotten that girl, *Monica,* pregnant. The only reason I knew her name is because, Mr. Ecklands had let it slip once during one of the earlier calls he'd made after I left Lily behind. And I certainly would never forget her face.

For John and Bonita Ecklands, I'd transform that cotton gin, once a symbol of hardship and labor into something beautiful right in the heart of the place I vowed, I'd never return. And Corian? Well, he was just going to have to fall in line. This was going to be my show. And if it burned him up to watch me take the lead? Even better.

Marcus was still grinning like he had just won something. I hated that grin. It was the same one he used when he beat me at anything—Monopoly, spades, hell, even something as stupid as who could eat the hottest wings without tapping out.

I shot him a warning look. "Don't start."

"Oh, I'm starting," he said, stretching his long legs out like he was settling in for the show. "I see the competition burning in your eyes. That poor man is about to catch *hell,* isn't he?"

"Watch," I narrowed my eyes in Marcus's direction and pursed my lips together, the wheels on how to be the biggest pain in Corian Demetrie's ass were already turning.

"Buckle up Lily, GA, Cara Mackey is back." Marcus just shook his head, muttered under his breath. "This is *really* rich. Miss 'I Left and Ain't Never Coming Back' is about to roll up her designer sleeves and get her hands dirty." He let out a low whistle. "One more time. *You sure?* Ain't no Saks out here in Lily, GA, sis."

I lifted my chin. "So? Amazon exists."

He snorted. "Amazon don't sell patience. And that's what you gon' need when you realize this ain't just about a blueprint or getting under your ex's skin. This ain't Paris, Cara. You ain't working with million-dollar budgets and glass walls. You gon' have to deal with the bigotry, the permits, the history. The *people*."

I already knew that.

This wasn't a hotel with an endless budget. There were no high-profile investors, no sleek executive meetings in a Parisian penthouse. This was a rundown, rusting gin mill with a roof probably seconds from caving in.

And I had just signed myself up to fix it.

Marcus leaned in, his voice dropping like he was offering me a way out. "You really think you got the patience for this?"

I stared out at the land in front of us, the dirt road that stretched alongside the old Mackey house beyond the clearing, long and bumpy. I had spent so many years running from this place. From the heat, the slow-moving clock, the reminders of everything I tried to bury.

But wasn't that what Mr. Ecklands saw in me?

The ability to bring something to life out of nothing?

I sucked in a breath. "Yeah. I do."

Marcus studied me, and for once, he wasn't smirking. "Then *you* better buckle up," he said finally, shaking his head. "Cause this is gonna be a fight. Against the town, with Corian, against yourself."

I held his gaze. "Good."

I wanted the fight.

But let's be clear—this was a *detour*, not a destination.

I was going to come in, get the job done, make sure Mr. Ecklands' vision didn't die with him. And then?

Then I was taking my black ass right back to Paris. But first, the list.

Part 2 – Building and Growth

(Verse 2)

Necessity called, I had to roam

You took your path, I took my own

Family drama, it weighed me down

Two dreams too big for this one-horse town

They say Iron sharpens iron, you're leather I'm steel

On the crossroads of love

You grip your reins, I gripped my wheel

(Chorus)
Ridin' on a Steel horse, down a
leather road,
We forged our own ways
Had to keep living, never stopped
loving,
But I couldn't make you stay
Jaded on love, letters unread
Vanished like a ghost, story un-
said
Ridin' on a Steel horse, Down a
leather road,
Glass hearts were meant to break

Chapter 13 — Corian

The Mustang's tires hummed against the cracked asphalt, my fingers drummed against the steering wheel as I ran my tongue over my teeth. Irritation sat low in my chest like an unwelcome friend. Mr. Ecklands had always been a man of wisdom, a man who saw further than most—but for the first time, I was questioning his methods.

A list. He said reach out to his attorney for the list and I did.

Instead of the list, though, I got further instructions: "Go to the Ecklands' home to get the list before Bonita leaves for New Orleans." This was beginning to feel like a game of whack-a-mole.

I exhaled sharply, glancing at the envelope on the passenger seat like it might suddenly give up the rest of the details.

Damn man always did have a way of making people do things the hard way.

I shifted gears, the Mustang responding smoothly as silk beneath my grip. The road leading to the Ecklands' place was familiar. If I closed my eyes, I could probably navigate the turns by muscle memory alone. My hands had gripped this same wheel on this same stretch of road more times than I could count but today felt different.

Pulling up to the house, I barely had time to put the car in park before I saw her.

Cara.

She stood on the porch, knocking on the door. I imagined her perfectly manicured nails tapping against the wood. She turned at the sound of my car pulling up.

Our eyes briefly met, before she turned back around giving me her back. I didn't need to see her face to know her mood—it was woven into the stiff set of her shoulders, the way she shifted her weight like standing still was an inconvenience.

Of course she'd be here already. *How the hell did the old man pull this shit off? How was he playing both of us like puppets from the inside of an urn?*

Rolling my head around my neck to remove some tension, I killed the engine and stepped out of my car. The afternoon heat pressed down on my skin. I took my time walking up, not bothering to announce myself. But the second I hit the bottom step, she turned, eyes locking on mine. Then she sucked her teeth and slid her eyes past me to my car. Rolling her eyes, she said under her breath, "Steel gray mustang. That was you... *Figures.*"

I didn't look away. But instead of asking what she meant, I changed the subject.

"You got the same damn message I did, huh?" I said, nodding toward the door.

She arched a brow, then rolled her eyes while her arms crossed over the sleek black fabric of her top. "What was your first clue?"

Okay.

"Could've been the way you were knocking like you had somewhere better to be."

"I do."

I chuckled under my breath. "Right."

Before she could fire back, the door creaked open. Bonita stood there, dressed like she was already halfway out the door—purse in hand, suitcase by her side. She gave us both a once-over, and seeing the sour look on Cara's face she laughed. "Y'all ain't changed a bit. Come on inside."

We stepped inside, and it was like stepping into a time capsule. The scent of old books, polished wood, and something faintly sweet lingered in the space, a reminder of years past. The weight of memory settled heavily in my chest, but I shook it off, focusing as Bonita reached into the drawer of Mr. Ecklands' old desk.

She pulled out another envelope, just one, setting it on the desk between us. Her eyes softened as she looked between me and Cara, studying us.

"This here is what you're looking for," she said gently. "John put a lot of thought into this. He believed in the both of you. Always did. Said you two were his brightest students, but more than that, he saw something special between you."

Cara shifted beside me, her arms crossing over her chest, but she didn't say a word. I swallowed hard, keeping my gaze on the envelope, already dreading what puzzle Mr. Ecklands had cooked up for us this time.

Knowing him, this list would be a damn scavenger hunt with riddles, obscure references, and a whole lot of unsolicited wisdom.

Bonita sighed, a wistful smile tugging at her lips. "He'd want you both to see this through—together."

A car horn sounded outside, signaling her ride was here. She glanced toward the door, then back at us, hesitating just a moment longer.

"I know y'all have been through a lot," she said, her voice quieter now. "But if there's one thing life's taught me, it's that some things, some people... they're worth fighting for."

She patted my arm, then reached out and gave Cara's hand a light squeeze. With a smile, she pulled a set of keys from her pocket and pressed them into Cara's palm. "This place belongs to the both of you now. John wanted it that way. Take care of it... and each other."

With that, she grabbed her suitcase and keys, and with one final glance at the two of us, she stepped outside. Through the window, we watched her climb into the waiting car, giving a small wave before she was gone.

The silence left behind was thick.

I exhaled slowly, staring down at the envelope. "Oh God. What scavenger hunt will the old man have us on now?"

I glanced at Cara, but she was already reaching for the envelope.

"Go ahead, then," I muttered.

She tore it open with a flick of her wrist, pulling out a folded sheet of paper. As her eyes scanned the words, something in her expression shifted—just a flicker, but I caught it.

She handed it to me without a word.

I took it, smoothing it out with my thumb.

The scrap of paper had a hand written note in the same scrawling script of Mr. Ecklands' original letter.

Cara & Corian,

Yes, so you both have decided to take on my challenge, I see. Otherwise, Bonita would have given you an entirely different message.

I imagine you're both wondering how in the world you're supposed to do everything I've asked and am about to ask of you—on top of your other priorities of life. Well, rest assured, I've thought about that, too. My intention was never to make your lives harder. Quite the opposite. The lesson here is simple: two are always better than one. The right partner makes even the heaviest loads lighter. And a shared vision? That can move mountains.

The fact that you're both standing in this house, reading this letter at the same time, means you are already beginning to understand the legacy I want to leave behind.

Now, a few ground rules.

Because this estate now belongs to you both, any and all decisions about its future requires two signatures. That means all business conducted in the estate's name must be handled in person—right here in Dooley County. No running off to Paris or disappearing into ranch work to avoid each other.

And since I know you're both stubborn as mules, let me ease at least one of your concerns. I didn't just leave you with a dream; I left you with the means to make it happen. By now, my lawyer should have informed you that the estate's liquidated value is approximately $8.7 million dollars. But I didn't build all this just for it to be cashed in and forgotten.

Instead, I've set up a dedicated account at the Bank of Dooley, under both of your names. This account is to be used exclusively for funding the completion of the community center and any other projects tied to this estate. There's more than enough to cover everything, but—and this is important—any withdrawal requires both of your signatures. No exceptions.

Money should never be the thing that holds you back. Make it grand, my children. Make it something that will last.

Now, about the list.

The world has changed, but Dooley County unfortunately is still as backwoods as ever. Which means we're not as modern as young Cara here probably thinks. Things take time. People need convincing. And some battles will be harder than others. But I trust the two of you to see this through.

John Ecklands

P.S. Oh and don't worry about Bonita. She was the brains behind all our investments and will finally be able to hit every casino down in Mobile, New Orleans, and Vegas to play the slots 'til her and her sister's hearts are content.

I let out a breath, glancing at Cara, who was staring at the letter with an unreadable expression.

"Well," I muttered, rubbing a hand over my beard. "What fresh hell did the old man leave us this time?"

Cara ignored me and reached for the second slip of paper inside the envelope..

THE LIST:

1. Secure the permits for the cotton gin restoration.

2. Clear the overgrown trails around the property and schools.

3. Design and build the community center without totally tearing down each other or the old cotton gin—together.

4. Plan a town fair and trail ride for the grand reveal and ribbon cutting event.

The muscles in my jaw flexed. This wasn't just some checklist to keep us busy—this was a damn gauntlet. Every single thing on this list didn't even look simple on paper, and in a town like Lily, GA? Every step would be a battle, a negotiation, or a headache waiting to happen.

And speaking of headaches—Cara was going to be the biggest one of all. If I couldn't even get her to look at me without that ice-cold glare, how the hell could I get her to work with me? No matter how bad I wanted to pretend we could just focus on the work, I knew better. This wasn't just about the gin, the town, or even Mr. Ecklands' legacy.

This was about us. And whether either of us was ready to admit it or not, we were gonna have to face that, too.

Fucking Mr. Ecklands. Even from the urn, he was still schooling us.

I cautioned a glance at Cara to see if perhaps she was thinking similar thoughts.

She lifted her chin and said, "Looks like we have our work cut out for us."

I met her gaze, a slow smirk tugging at my lips despite myself. "Hope you brought your work boots, Paris."

She scoffed. "Hope you brought some skills other than riding a goddamn horse."

I huffed a laugh, shaking my head as I folded the paper and tucked it into my back pocket.

And this was only the beginning.

Chapter 14—Cara

I pulled my laptop closer, staring at the open calendar, my perfectly balanced life now split in two. My fingers drummed restlessly against the desk as the weight of it all pressed against my temples. Paris. Lily. The Rue D'Orleans. The Cotton Gin. Corian.

I exhaled sharply. The first call had to be Jean-Pierre.

I pressed dial, and before the first ring finished, his voice filled the receiver, bright and clipped. "Cara, *chére Madame*! Please tell me you're calling to say you'll be back in Paris by next week. I am drowning here. The Dior textiles arrived, and let me tell you, the rouge is all wrong. I mean, I know it's not technically something I'd need your help with, but my soul is suffering without you here. You are missed."

I pinched the bridge of my nose. "Jean-Pierre, breathe. First, I need you to focus on the neutral palettes for the lobby seating. That's priority one. Second, Delia will be point on everything while I'm here. You both have to hold the line. And... you are exaggerating anyway. How are you my loyal, worker bee?"

A dramatic sigh. "Oh fine," he gave in, instantly calming the extra, "And when, may I ask, will here stop being there?"

"I don't know yet," I admitted. "But trust me, if I could clone myself, I would. Just hold down the fort. I have to take another call."

"Fine, fine," he huffed. "But only because Delia is terrifying and I value my life. All is well here but keep your phone by your side in case we need you."

I hung up and inhaled deeply. The next call was harder. I scrolled to Michel's name, hesitating.

Then I pressed call.

"Cara," he answered, his voice warm, expectant. "What time should I pick you up from the airport?"

I closed my eyes. "Michel, I won't be back anytime soon."

A beat of silence. Then, "Hmm. *Ma chére,* what does that mean, no time soon?"

"There's a project here, family related—I guess—that I need to handle." Now would have been the perfect time to say 'this isn't working for me anyway. Sorry I've wasted your time'. But I hesitated long enough to allow his irritation to creep into the conversation.

"I see," was his clipped response.

"I'm not quite sure how long it will take," I sighed. Choosing my next words carefully. "Michel, I have some unfinished business here that I don't quite want to get into. It's not just this...*project*—it's more of a personal, *umm* thing." *Shit.* I was really about to rip the Band-Aid off. In the midst of all the turmoil I was in just being back here, Michel's growing feelings for me could not be a distraction. *Yeah, not when Corian Demetrie done pulled up on your ass,* said a small voice in the back of my head. "I need to be honest with you. I can't give you what you want. So maybe now is a good time for us to *you know*, *umm* go back to a more professional situation." I waited for his response.

His exhale was measured. I could tell his European sensibilities disguised any raw emotion he may have felt. He sighed. "You've always had one foot out the door, chérie. I was just hoping, one day, you'd as you say, *'you know'* come around."

"I never meant to mislead you, Michel," I whispered. "You deserve someone who can be all in and being here dealing with my bullshit. I just need to sort some stuff out."

Another pause, then a quiet chuckle. "You are usually infuriatingly honest, Cara Mackey. Right now, it seems that you are holding something back. But I won't press. Take care of you. *Bon courage, mon amour.*"

The line went dead, and something in my chest tightened. Not regret. Just... closure.

I dialed Delia at once.

"Cara," she answered, direct and to the point. "What do you need?"

"You, actually."

"I figured. Your texts seemed strained. What's up?"

I filled her in quickly—the cotton gin project, the demands, my sudden second life in Lily. She listened without interruption, absorbing every detail like she always did.

"Well, we've got it covered here," she assured me. "Just don't stray too far away from your phone in case the Rue d'Orleans and team needs you."

"I won't," I promised. "I just need time to figure this all out, here."

There was a brief pause before Delia's voice softened, just slightly. "You sure everything with you is good? You didn't say anything outright, but something about the way you're vaguely describing things makes me wonder."

I hesitated. Delia had become an amazing friend, but I wasn't ready to share that everything here, including agreeing to work with Corian had me a bit frazzled.

"It's about this project, Delia. That's it."

"Hmm. Okay. Well, I'll let you get back to it then," she said.

"Thanks Delia. Talk again soon."

We hung up.

***

Almost a week had gone by before we could get the Cotton Gin discussion on the docket for review by the citizens of Lily. The town hall was standing room only. A low murmur filled the space. Tension hummed beneath the surface like an electric current. Lily might not have been an openly hostile community, but bigotry was still a thing here in a place where cotton was once king and the descendants of those kingdoms were still land owning tax paying citizens.

Corian stood beside me, arms crossed, his presence a steady force I was both grateful for and irritated by. He looked calm, but I knew him. I could tell he was reading the room, jaw tense in preparation for the pushback that was surely coming.

"First order of business," Mayor Gibson began, adjusting his glasses. "The permit application for the restoration of the old cotton gin into a community center."

A low rumble swept through the crowd.

"Now hold on," came a voice from the back. "That building is part of Lily's history. It's been standing for over a hundred years. And now, what? You want to turn it into some modern thing?"

A few murmurs of agreement rippled through the crowd.

"History?" I countered, keeping my voice steady. "The cotton gin stands for a past that doesn't serve all of Lily's citizens. This is about creating a future. A place where kids can gather, where businesses can host events, where the town can grow. That's honoring history in a way that matters."

Corian spoke next, his voice low but firm. "This project is already funded. We're not asking for money. We're asking for a chance to make something better than an abandoned husk of a building."

Mayor Gibson nodded slowly. "The permit application is under review, but it's not just up to me. The community has to be heard."

Outside, on break, the mayor stepped out and lit a cigarette. He glanced at us and exhaled, the smoke curling in the cool night air. "You two are in for a fight, but it's one worth having. Ecklands already told me about this project before he passed. I can't tell the town to roll over but know this—you're going to get those permits. This process is just the dance we have to do."

I nodded, the tightness in my chest loosening just a fraction. "Good to know we have at least one ally."

Corian glanced back at the door. "We're going to need more."

Back inside, when the debate resumed, a woman in the second row stood. Tall, lean, and confident, she pushed her hat back on her head. "I think it's time we stop talking about history and start making some. That old building? It's a hazard. An eyesore. The young folks don't care about what it used to be; they care about what it can become."

I blinked, recognizing her instantly. "Kima?" I was surprised to see the only girlfriend I had in Lily back in high school. Except for having curvier hips and a body built like a thick and tall goddess, she virtually looked the same. Beautiful, buxom and as confident as ever in a pair of cutoff shorts, cowgirl boots and a hoodie that read 'Where Them Fans At.'

A smile split her face. "Cara Mackey. Look at you back in Lily. And ready to give these good ol' towns folk hell to boot." She hollered, pulling me into a hug then pushed me back to give me a full once over. "Give them hell," she said nodding to the left side of the room, "and all of us something to be proud of." To this she nodded to the right.

A murmur of agreement swept through the right side of the room, including several of the Black farmers, homesteaders and ranchers standing in support. The tide was shifting, and I felt it.

Corian leaned in slightly, voice low. "We'll at least get fifty percent of the vote based on the makeup of this room. We're closer than I thought."

I scoffed. "Yeah? Too close if you ask me," I said, moving away from his closeness.

He didn't flinch. But I saw the comeback brewing in his eyes—the way he registered my meaning, understood every layer of it before delivering his own blow. "Yeah, and we know how you like to run from closeness, don't we."

My spine went stiff, heat rising up my neck. "Maybe this time, you won't give me a reason to run."

His lips barely twitched, a glint of something unreadable flickering behind his calm. "Guess we'll see, won't we?"

I turned back toward the council, jaw tight. This wasn't over. We might win the fight for the project, but the one brewing between me and Corian was just heating up.

Chapter 15 — Corian

" and in conclusion," one of the council members said, adjust-
• • • ing his glasses, "given the historical and cultural significance
of the property, and the potential positive economic impact, the board
will now vote on granting the necessary permits for the project."

A murmur ran through the room. My hands clenched on my knees as
I watched the members exchange looks before nodding, one by one.

"All in favor?" the chairperson asked.

A chorus of ayes filled the space.

"All opposed?" Silence.

He nodded and scribbled something down. "Motion approved. Mr.
Demetrie, Ms. Mackey—you have your permits."

A quiet exhale left my chest, but the tension in my shoulders didn't
fully disappear. Then I caught sight of Cara.

Damn woman had the most beautiful smile on her face. That was the
biggest win of the night.

I turned back toward the chairperson. "What's next?"

"You and Ms. Mackey will need to come by the county office to officially sign the paperwork," he said. "After that, you'll have full clearance to break ground."

"Perfect." Cara stood smoothly, brushing off her dress. "Corian and I will take care of that first thing in the morning."

I opened my mouth to argue—about what, I didn't know—but she was already walking off. My eyes followed her for a second longer than they should have. I shook my head.

Tomorrow was gonna be a long-ass day.

The next morning, the county office was quiet, the kind of quiet that made my boots sound too loud against the tile. Cara was already there, dressed sharp in a cream-colored blouse and tailored jeans, signing her name with smooth precision.

"You're late," she murmured without looking up.

I grunted. "Had things to do."

She made a soft, unimpressed sound but didn't argue. Instead, she slid the clipboard across the counter toward me. I took the pen, hovering over the paper for a second before pressing my name next to hers.

It was done. No turning back now.

The following afternoon, Cara and I sat in my office at the ranch, trying—and failing—to put together a vision for the community center.

She had her laptop open, scrolling through reference images, while I stared at the blank floor plan like it was a damn foreign language.

"Look," she said, finally breaking the silence. "We need to stop wasting time and figure out a concept."

I scoffed. "You think I'm *wastin'* time?"

She gave me a flat look, then gestured toward the floor plan in front of me. "You've been staring at that same blank page for ten minutes, Corian. You look lost."

I frowned. "I'm thinkin'."

"You're brooding." She tilted her head, studying me. "Which, I'll admit, you do very well. But it's not helping us get anywhere."

I leaned back, dragging a hand down my face. "You ever thought about the *kinda* folks who'd actually use this place? Ain't just for show—it's gotta work for the people here."

Cara's eyes flickered, something unreadable crossing her face. "I know that."

I muttered under my breath, "Yeah, sure. Meanwhile, you're probably over there looking at some frilly, whimsical nonsense that ain't got a damn thing to do with making this space functional."

She shot me a sharp look. "Excuse me?"

I shrugged, not backing down. "Tell me I'm wrong."

She narrowed her eyes and turned the laptop toward me, her lips pressed tight with purpose. "This is what I was looking at."

I leaned in, ready to pick it apart—expecting some cold, big-city concept that looked good in magazines but had no soul.

But what I saw? Was different.

Wide, flexible rooms with natural light. Kitchen layouts that made sense. Spaces made for work *and* rest. It wasn't just pretty—it was smart. Grounded. Black Southern thoughtful.

The kind of design that didn't just look good—it *belonged*.

And damn if it didn't stop me for a second—not because it was fancy, but because it felt like home. Like she saw this place, *really* saw it—and wanted to honor it.

I had to admit, Cara and I working together like this—side by side, sharp and stubborn—it reminded me of the first time we ever had to build something together.

Senior Year

We damn near killed each other.

"I'm not putting a fountain in the middle of the walkway," I snapped, arms crossed.

"And I'm not letting you turn this into a boring, empty field," she shot back, eyes flashing.

Mr. Ecklands cleared his throat and peered at us over his glasses. His look was stern but the controlled smirk at the corners of his lips clearly showed his amusement. "Mackey and Demetrie, stop disrupting my class and figure it out," was all he said, shaking his head before returned to his grading.

Cara had turned to me, her hands on her hips but voice hushed. "We need something inviting, Corian. People should feel like they want to be here."

I had pointed at the rough sketch she'd done. "And you think this is practical? A bunch of benches and a water feature? This is a high school, not a damn park."

"Exactly," she huffed and crossed her arms as if her point was proven.

We had gone back and forth, neither of us willing to give an inch—until, somehow, we did. We had found the middle ground, a compromise that worked. And it was one of the best projects of the year.

I exhaled through my nose, grudgingly impressed. "Guess not."

She smirked, then reached for her notebook, flipping to a fresh page. As she tucked a strand of hair behind her ear, I felt something shift in my chest. She scribbled in her notebook, and I studied her... I still wanted Cara Mackey. The thought was swift and hard. I had to wrench myself back to the task at hand. The community center.

Maybe we could still do this. Maybe, like before, we could find a way to meet in the middle. Just like back then, our oil and water mix. And her concept ideas weren't half bad. Little did she know though, I wasn't just staring at a blank page, I was deep in thought on how we could turn this into more than just a space. Could Cara and I use what we already knew and loved to give the town not just a beautiful space, but some real function for all its citizens; the children, the farmers, ranchers and other business owners to use? I wanted the community center to be a space for everyone. It was time to call Jax.

Later that evening, after Cara left, I pulled out my phone and scrolled through the contacts.

Darren's words echoed in my head. 'Think about Jax. Ain't about what he wants—it's about what you need'.

I hesitated a second longer, then hit the call button.

Jaxon picked up on the second ring, his voice smooth and measured, the way I imagined he handled every business deal he closed. "Corian. This is unexpected."

I smirked. "Got a proposition for you."

"Oh?"

"The ranch. And... something else."

Jax was quiet for a beat, then let out a low breath, the kind that told me he already knew this was coming. "You need my help."

I huffed a short laugh. "Don't make it sound like I'm *beggin'*."

His chuckle was polished, effortless. "Wouldn't dream of it." A pause. "Let's hear it."

After I explained everything to him, Jax and I switched over to video. While he had started off with his usual smooth, detached tone, I just knew the wheels in his head were turning.

"So, you're telling me you've got the green light on this community center, but you don't actually have a concrete vision for it yet?" he asked, arching a brow.

I rubbed the back of my neck. "I've got ideas. Cara's got ideas. We just... haven't exactly met in the middle yet."

Jax smirked. "Shocking."

I ignored that. "And then there's the ranch. We're bleeding money. Darren thinks you might have some ideas on how to modernize things. Keep us relevant."

Jax leaned back in his chair, steepling his fingers. "Darren reached out and we chopped it up a bit. He's right. The ranch needs innovation, Corian. Not just a new coat of paint. We're talking about a whole shift in approach."

I sighed. "I ain't turning the damn ranch into a tech startup, Jax."

Jax rolled his eyes. "I'm not suggesting that but hear me out. What if you integrated augmented reality into your training and breeding programs? Buyers could get a fully immersive experience of the horses—bloodlines, training footage, health metrics—without ever setting foot in Georgia."

I sat forward, curiosity peaked. "Well, that will cost money. The community center is funded, but that doesn't extend to the ranch," I exclaimed.

"Well no, it won't but let's not let that stop us from brainstorming. I think it'll be easy to get the funding for a great venture. What you thinking?"

I was thinking about ending this call but decided to play along. "I like where you're going with the AR bit."

Jax jumped in with an excitement I'd never heard him express about the ranch. "And it doesn't have to stop at just the ranch. We could apply this to agricultural programs too—real-world training for farming, livestock management, and sustainable land use. There's your tie in to the community center. Continued funding for both it and the ranch.

Jaxon was full out grinning now. Guess who has money for that?" He asked.

I shrugged, a blank expression on my face.

"Fort Valley State University. They're throwing funds into agricultural and technological innovation. If we tie them in, they could fund training programs at the ranch and use the community center as a satellite location for their students."

I exhaled, processing it all. It did sound good, but I still had to contend with the fact that I could indeed handle the mechanics of it all, but the tech behind it? I didn't have a clue how to broach that conversation with the university. "So what? You gonna build this out and quarterback the conversations and grant proposal from your fancy high-rise in L.A.?"

Jax steepled his fingers, thoughtful. "As long as you and 'old girl' can design the space, let me worry about the tech, how to integrate it and the funding for the ranch."

I raised a brow. "So, you ain't coming down?"

He smirked. "Didn't say that. But I might need to see it firsthand before I start throwing my money and resources at it. I'm in big bro. I think you really got something here. Consider me an investor."

I shook my head, feeling something I hadn't in years—relief. For once, I wasn't carrying everything on my back alone.

Jax exhaled sharply, then added, "What you think about this Turkey trip Darren's talking about?"

I blinked. Surprised at how read in Jax seemed to be on everything Darren and I had discussed.

"He mentioned it when we talked earlier. Cappadocia. Horses are big business there. Some of the best bloodlines come through that region. If you're serious about investing in the ranch, expanding our reach internationally is feasible. Darren can take point—scout out the breeders, negotiate deals, and establish connections for importing our horses in to breed with theirs."

"Say less, big bro. If you're in, I'm in. No half-stepping. "

With that, we ended the call. The distance between me and my little brother seemed to evaporate. We weren't as far apart as I'd thought. And if the Demetrie brothers could come together for the ranch, maybe I could find a way to meet Cara in the middle too.

CHAPTER SIXTEEN

Chapter 16 — Cara

The crunch of dry leaves under my boots is the only sound breaking the thick quiet between us. We'd started the day with a crew of volunteers, cutting back years of overgrowth along the old trails that ran through the town's heart. Mr. Ecklands had given explicit instructions—clear a 30-acre radius around the property. At first, it seemed excessive. Did the town really need that much space for walking and bike trails? But the more we worked, the more a pattern emerged. This wasn't just about clearing pathways; it was about uncovering something.

The deeper we cut into the brush, the more we noticed how the trails weren't just random. They led somewhere. They wound deliberately toward something we hadn't quite figured out yet. An old marker post, half-buried under decades of tangled vines, hinted at something more—a connection we weren't seeing yet. The thought lingered in my mind like an itch I couldn't quite scratch.

Now, it's just me and Corian, the rest of the crew gone, leaving the two of us alone in the hush of twilight.

The sun was low, casting long shadows between the oaks and pines, their branches draping across the trail like skeletal fingers. A sharp breeze cut through the humidity, and I rolled my stiff shoulders, feeling the satisfying ache of a day's hard work. This was Mr. Ecklands' second request on the list—to clear the trails that once connected the county's high school, middle and elementary schools back in the day when horses were the main transportation to get around. Clearing these trails would give the current students of each of the school's clear and easy access to the new community center that would stand on these grounds. They would be able to walk, skate or ride their bikes without the fear of being hit by a car on these long country roads.

Also, while researching some of the details about the history of the cotton gin, I discovered that these trails didn't just connect to the schools. They also held a forgotten history of young Black sharecroppers, cowboys and cowgirls moving from one place to another.. The past was woven into the dirt beneath our feet, and for the first time since I got back, I felt the weight of the roots pulling at me.

Corian swung his axe one last time, severing a thick vine before letting out a low grunt. He stepped back, reaching for the hem of his sweat-drenched T-shirt, and tugged it over his head in one smooth motion.

Sweet. Mercy.

The man's body looks like it was carved out of sin—broad shoulders tapering to a firm, chiseled waist, every muscle sculpted by years of hard work. His skin glowed under the last traces of sunlight, slick with sweat, and the way his back flexed as he moved made my mouth go dry.

He ran the shirt over his face, then draped it over his shoulder like some kind of goddamn romance novel cover model. I was caught totally off guard, when he suddenly shifted his gaze at me and asked, "You ever think about why he wanted this much space cleared?"

I swallowed, forcing my gaze back to his face. "I uh, I have, actually." My voice is a little too breathy. I clear my throat. "At first, I thought it was just about making the land useful again, but..." I trail off, looking down the path ahead, the way it bends through the woods like it's leading somewhere we haven't fully realized yet. "Most of these trails connect the three schools in the county back to the site where the old cotton gin stands and where the community center will be. But this trail here cuts away from the schools. I'm not sure where this one leads."

Corian nods, his gaze following mine. "City girl, something tells me this ain't just about some old trails, Cara. He knew something. Something we don't see yet."

The thought sends a shiver down my spine. Mr. Ecklands had always been a step ahead of everyone, guiding people in ways they didn't understand until it was too late to turn back.

"I found an old marker post earlier," I admit, nudging a boot at the ground. "It was half-buried under the brush. Couldn't read much of it."

Corian exhales, resting his axe on his shoulder. "And we just so happen to be cutting through here, opening it all up." He looks at me then, his dark eyes knowing. "He is leading us somewhere."

I nod, my fingers brushing absently over my arm. "And we're walking right into it."

A heavy silence settles over us, thick with the unspoken. Mr. Ecklands' influence doesn't end in death. He's still pulling the strings, still nudging us toward something bigger than either of us expected.

"Didn't think you had it in you, city girl," Corian finally said, looking around at how deep into the brush we had come, a teasing lilt in his voice.

The man hadn't changed—at least, not in the ways that counted. He still had that presence, the kind that filled a space effortlessly. It used to comfort me. Now, this giant of a man with biceps that could bench press my whole body, had me rattled in ways I wasn't ready to admit.

I tossed my work gloves onto a tree stump and sigh. "I didn't grow up here like you, Demetrie. I was dropped here, planted in soil I didn't ask for. But I made it work then and will do the work now So cut it out with this 'city girl' shit." I huffed, arms crossed glaring at him.

His lips twitch, but he doesn't argue. Instead, he watches me, his gaze moving over my face, lingering a little too long. The air thickens between us, a slow, charged stillness wrapping around us, thick as the summer air, pressing in like the hush before a storm.

"Oh I remember how tough you were back then. I respect it. Respect that fact that you're out here now getting your hands dirty." Corian said.

His words land heavy, like a stone in the middle of a still pond, sending ripples through places inside me I thought were long settled. *Is he baiting me?* Either way, my chest tightened, my pulse betrayed me, and I hated that he could still do this—still get under my skin like we never left *us* be. I turned away, pretending to brush dirt off my jeans. I shouldn't be feeling this—this pull. This quiet awareness that settled between us like an old, worn-in space neither of us knew how to fill.

"We should head back. It's getting dark," was all I could muster in response.

CHAPTER SEVENTEEN

Chapter 17—Cara

I needed a break from all things Demetrie. From the way Corian looked at me, it felt like he still had a claim on something long since shattered. From the way my body betrayed me every time he got too close, like muscle memory refusing to forget. From the pull of a past, I thought I had buried under steel and glass, tucked away in a life I'd built oceans away.

I was unraveling, piece by piece, and I needed air before I lost what little sense I had left. I needed laughter, something light to cut through the tangled mess in my head. I needed Kima.

I'd run into Kima at the town hall meeting a few days back, our eyes locking across the room in silent recognition before she'd sauntered over with that same bold energy I remembered from high school. She hadn't changed a bit—still sharp, still calling me out on my nonsense, still one of the few people in this town I trusted to tell me the truth. We'd exchanged numbers, promised to catch up, and now, I was cashing in on that promise.

Kima, Corian, and I had all graduated together, but while Corian and I had been tangled up in love, heartbreak, and everything in between, Kima had been the steady one. The friend who saw through the mess and called it for what it was. And right now, I needed my friend.

Pulling into the long gravel driveway leading to Kima's eco-farm, I exhaled, rolling my shoulders as the sight of her sprawling property came into view. The last time I saw this place, it had been a modest homestead farm, nothing more than a few acres of tilled land and a small clapboard house where Kima's family had worked the soil with their bare hands. Back then, it had been functional, practical—nothing like what sprawled before me now. Tiny homes and yurts dotted the landscape, tucked between vegetable gardens and wildflower patches. A few volunteers—young, carefree, probably chasing some back-to-nature experience—milled about, tending to rows of crops. This was Kima's world now, and I had to admit, it was thriving.

I barely had time to cut the engine before she was striding toward me, a grin stretching wide across her smooth, sun-kissed face.

"Look who finally remembered her roots," she teased, hands on her hips. "Paris must be real dry if you're back here digging up old dirt. And girl, when I saw you and that damn Corian together at the town hall? *Bay-bayyy*, I was fit to be tied! Fill me in, bitch!"

"Nothing much to tell."

She smirked, folding her arms. "Mm-hmm, and I'm supposed to believe you just popped up after umpteen years of being gone? Like I didn't just see you at that town hall sneaking glances at Corian like he was the last biscuit on the table?"

I rolled my eyes. "Girl, can we pretend for five minutes that my life does not revolve around that man? I'd much rather catch up with you—talk about how you turned a little family homestead into this empire." I gestured around us, my voice softer. "I mean it, Kima. This place? It's incredible."

Kima arched an eyebrow but let it go—for now. "Alright, alright. I'll behave. But girl, we got some catching up to do. I want to hear everything—Paris, work, and yes, even a little about what's got you back in Lily. But first, let's go inside, and day-drink like we ain't got responsibilities."

"Damn right! Cheers to that." I hugged her neck.

Kima linked her arm through mine and started walking me toward her porch. "I got you, girl. But you know I'm not letting you leave until you spill every last detail."

We settled into her open-air kitchen, a mix of rustic charm and modern efficiency, the scent of fresh herbs and roasted vegetables lingering in the air. She handed me a glass of homemade sangria before plopping down across from me, eyes sharp and expectant.

"Alright, talk to me. How bad is it?"

I sighed, swirling the drink in my hand. "It's... frustrating. Infuriating. Maddening." I took a sip. "And unfairly attractive."

Kima cackled. "So much for talking about something else first," Kima's eyes twinkled as she lifted a brow before continued, "So basically, nothing's changed."

"Not true." I set my glass down. "We're different now. He's different. And I hate that I keep catching myself looking at him like—" I groaned, rubbing my forehead. "Like I forgot how much he wrecked me."

Kima hummed, sipping her sangria. "Sounds like you remember just fine. But the way I see it, Mr. Ecklands didn't just throw y'all together for nostalgia's sake. Man had a plan."

I shook my head. "Yeah, well, his plan has me tangled up in something I'm not sure I want."

Kima shot me a knowing look. "But you're still here, Mackey."

I didn't have a response to that. And I wasn't about to go down that road—not yet. I tilted my glass, finishing the rest of my sangria before sitting it down with a decisive clink.

"Tell me more about what you've got going on out here," I said attempting to change the subject. "I mean, tiny homes, sustainable farming? This ain't the little family homestead I remember. You turned this place into a whole eco-movement."

Kima studied me for a moment, like she knew exactly what I was doing but again she let it go and didn't press me more about Corian. *For now.* She leaned back in her chair, swirling her drink. "Yeah, girl, it's been a journey. Started small—just me and a few volunteers. But you know how it goes—word gets out, people start showing up looking for something different. Now we've got full-time residents, workshops, and folks coming in from all over. Urban farming, eco-tourism, hands-on education—it's bigger than I ever imagined."

I nodded, genuinely impressed. "That's incredible, Kima. And the more I think about it, the more I see how this could tie into what we're doing with the community center. There's so much potential here."

Kima grinned. "Mm-hmm, now you're talking. We could set up something real—connect young people with real skills, real work. Show them a different way to make a living and be part of something bigger than themselves."

I tapped my fingers against the table, my mind already turning with possibilities. Before I could tell her just how much I appreciated her, my phone buzzed. A message from Corian. "Back at the trails in the morning. We need to talk."

I exhaled sharply, setting my phone face down on the table opting to not respond to the message before said, "We need to sit down and really map this out. This could be exactly the kind of foundation the community center needs."

Kima nodded, but her gaze flicked back to my phone, still sitting face-down on the table. "We will. But first..."

She smirked. "You gonna tell me why you just looked like you got hit with a bag of bricks when Corian texted you?"

"You caught that, huh?" I said, never able to get much by Kima.

"Oh yeah. Especially the that 'I'm in trouble by my ex-boyfriend' that was on your face before you flipped that bitch over." She said chuckling, referring to my cell phone.

I groaned, rubbing my temples. "Girl, the way this man gets under my skin. It's criminal. I swear, it's like he breathes, and I forget every good decision I ever made."

Kima let out a sharp laugh. "Oh, this is even better than I thought. Keep talking."

I shook my head, reaching for my glass again. "Nope. I'm cutting myself off before you start planning a wedding—meanwhile, I'm trying not to kill this man. You know how bad he hurt me, Kima. You were there. You saw what it did to me."

Kima's smirk softened, and she reached across the table, giving my hand a squeeze. "I did, and I don't blame you for keeping your guard up. But Cara... y'all still got something. It's written all over you. The way you talk about him, the way you react just hearing his name. You can lie to yourself all you want, but I see it clear as day."

I swallowed hard, staring at the deep red in my glass. "Feelings don't change what happened. Or how much it hurt."

"No, they don't," Kima agreed. "But pretending they don't exist doesn't make 'em go away, either."

The next morning, with Kima's words still rolling around in my head, I made my way back to the project site. The crew was already gathering, the air thick with the scent of damp earth and freshly cut brush. Corian stood near a pile of tools, his sharp gaze locking onto me the second I stepped out of my car.

Here we go again.

CHAPTER EIGHTEEN

Chapter 18 — Corian

The chainsaw ripped through the morning quiet, sending the scent of pine and fresh earth into the air. I wiped the sweat from my brow with the back of my arm, already regretting the thick heat settling in for the day. The crew was working steadily, clearing out the last of the overgrown brush. We were making progress, but my focus kept slipping, my gaze flicking toward the parking lot every few minutes.

I was waiting on her.

Cara.

She pulled up just as I turned toward the tools, stepping out of her car with that same mix of confidence and hesitation she always carried around me. Something about her felt different today—like she had more on her mind than she was ready to admit. I wasn't sure what changed, but I felt it. A shift in her energy, a weight in her eyes. Maybe it wasn't my place to ask. Maybe I'd lost that right a long time ago. But hell if that was gonna stop me from trying.

When I did, she kept her focus locked on the straps of her gloves, pulling them on with sharp, deliberate tugs. Her jaw was tight, her shoulders squared like she was bracing for something—me, maybe. But it was the flicker of hesitation, the way she exhaled just a little too slow before turning away, that gave her away. She twisted her thumb against her palm—small, subtle, but I caught it. I knew that tell. She only did that when she was nervous or anxious about something. Was it me? Or something else entirely?

"Morning."

"Morning," she echoed, tugging on her gloves like she was bracing for a fight.

I smirked. "Something wrong?"

"Nope."

She turned toward the trail, marching forward like she had something to prove. I watched her for a beat before falling into step beside her. She wasn't gonna make this easy, but that was fine. But this wasn't some game. Not anymore. I'd already lost once—because I'd been too young, too stupid, too scared to let her go and trust she'd come back. And instead of waiting, I made the biggest mistake of my life. So no, this wasn't about the thrill of the chase. This was about whether I still had a chance to make it right with her at all.

"We need to talk," I said, keeping my voice even, waiting for the inevitable resistance.

Cara let out a sharp, humorless laugh. "Oh, let me guess. This is where you tell me we should talk about our feelings? That we need to go over the past one more time like that's gonna change it? Because, Corian, I—"

I blinked, then let out a low chuckle, crossing my arms. "Damn, Cara. That where your mind went? You been thinking about me that hard?" I watched the way her eyes narrowed, the way her lips pressed into a thin line, and I bit back a smirk. "Relax, city girl. I was talking about the community center. Jaxon and I came up with an idea—one that could bring in real money and make this whole thing self-sustaining. Figured you'd want to hear it."

That got her attention. She paused, her mouth pressing into a thin line like she was trying to figure out how to save face. I could almost see the tug-of-war happening in her head—throw attitude, make a snarky comment, or admit that it was a damn good idea. She settled for a slow nod, crossing her arms as if she wasn't fully conceding. "Go on," she said, her voice measured, but I didn't miss the way her fingers tapped against her elbow—a dead giveaway she was thinking hard. She glanced at me, her skepticism giving way to curiosity. "I'm listening."

I kept walking, stepping over a fallen branch before continued. "Jaxon's been working with some serious investors in the tech world. People who want to back initiatives that blend innovation with community impact. He thinks we could integrate a program that teaches young people about virtual design, AR, construction modeling—real, hands-on skills that could turn into careers."

Cara slowed her steps, considering. "That... actually makes sense."

"I know." I glanced at her. "We'll need space, the right people to lead it, but the funding's there if we move fast."

She nodded, chewing on her bottom lip like she always did when she was thinking something through. "It could work."

Cara exhaled, rolling her shoulders like she was still working out whatever tension sat between us. Then, as if deciding to shift gears entirely, she spoke. "Kima's got something big. I was at her farm yesterday, and it's not just land—she's got a whole ecosystem going. She's running sustainable farming initiatives, hosting workshops, and bringing in young people to learn hands-on skills."

I raised my eyebrows, impressed. "Damn. That's more than I expected. She's really built something out there."

She nodded, her fingers tapping absently against her hip. "It's bigger than just farming. She's got programs teaching people how to live off the land, workshops that bring in specialists, and a rotating crew of people who come in to volunteer and leave with actual skills. If we link it to the community center, we could be giving folks real careers, real independence."

I let out a low whistle, shaking my head. "That's not just solid. That's game-changing."

Cara brightened just a little, and for the first time this morning, I saw something other than frustration in her eyes. "I know, right? And she's already got the structure in place. We wouldn't have to start from scratch—just integrate it. It could be the backbone of the whole thing."

I let out a low whistle. "That's solid."

"Yeah." She looked at me then, really looked at me. "We might actually pull this off."

We.

The word settled in my chest, unexpected and heavy in a way I hadn't prepared for. She said it without thinking, without guarding herself against it, and that alone had me gripping tighter onto the handle of my axe.

I glanced at her, taking in the way she was looking at me—not with skepticism or hesitation, but with something closer to belief. To trust.

It shouldn't have meant so much. But damn if it didn't feel like the first real step forward, we'd taken in years.

The moment stretched between us. I cleared my throat, breaking the silence. "We should—"

A break in the trees stopped me mid-sentence.

A clearing.

I knew it before I even looked. The way the sunlight filtered through the branches, the way the air shifted, the way the pond stretched out before us was like something out of a dream.

The past slammed into me so fast I had to stop walking.

I hadn't been here in years. Not since Cara. Not since *us*.

Cara took a step forward, and I saw it hit her, too. The way her breath caught, the way her hands clenched at her sides.

The pond had been ours.

The place where she'd handed me a fistful of wildflowers instead of an apology. The place where we fought for the first time. Where I stole her first kiss.

And where we gave ourselves to each other for the first time.

I forced a breath through my nose, running a hand over my jaw. "Didn't realize we'd cleared this far."

Cara's voice was quiet. "Neither did I."

I glanced at her, my pulse kicking up at the way she was looking at the water. Like she was seeing ghosts. Like she wasn't sure whether to run or stay.

Cara took a sharp breath, then turned abruptly, like she needed to escape before the memories swallowed her whole. But in her rush, her boot caught on a root hidden beneath the underbrush.

I moved without thinking. One second, she was pitching forward, and the next, she was in my arms, my hands gripping her waist, her body pressed flush against mine.

The air between us shifted, turned electric. Her breath hitched, and my pulse thundered in response. Every inch of her was familiar, but damn, feeling her against me again after all these years? It was a punch straight to the gut.

Her hands landed on my chest, palms flat, as if she meant to push away—but she didn't. Neither of us did.

I swallowed hard, my voice rough. "You good?"

She nodded, but she didn't move.

I should've let her go.

But I didn't want to.

The past wasn't done with us yet.

Chapter 19 — Cara

The pond had always been my place, my quiet, my refuge—the emotional ground zero of everything Corian and I once were and lost.

And now, wrapped in his arms for the first time since we were teenagers, the memories, the emotions, the heat crashed into me so hard I couldn't breathe.

My body remembered him, but my heart still refused to forgive. I pushed away, panicked and breathless, needing space. Corian let me go, but in his eyes, I could see the essence of who we were back then.

This place had always been magic.

A secret world, hidden from the rest of Lily, where time slowed and everything felt bigger—brighter. The water stretched wide and still, mirroring the sky like a piece of another world had been left behind just for us. The bank was wild, blanketed in soft bursts of purple and yellow, the flowers swaying lazily in the thick summer air. The trees leaned in close, casting shadows that moved like whispered secrets across the surface.

It was where I ran when life broke too loud. When the grief of losing my parents swallowed me whole. When I needed somewhere—anywhere—to write myself back into being.

I'd sit cross-legged in the grass, journal balanced on my knee, letting my thoughts spill across the page like ink was the only thing keeping me together.

And somehow, Corian always found me.

He'd stand at the tree line some days, just watching—quiet, steady. Waiting until I invited him in. Other times, he'd sit beside me, close enough that I could feel his heat, but never close enough to push. And then there were the days he couldn't help himself—days he'd snatch my journal with that crooked grin, teasing me until I tackled him just to get it back.

That's how we had our first fight here. That's how we had our first kiss here. That's how I knew—really knew—I loved him.

It's where I gave him everything. I was fifteen the first time I saw Jason's Lyric—sprawled across Marcus's bedroom floor, a pillow clutched to my chest. The TV glowed in the dark, casting a soft halo around the room. The air was thick with the scent of hot grass and Georgia clay drifting through the open window.

Jada and Allen made love by a pond that shimmered under soft, golden light. It wasn't just sexy—it was sacred. Two people carving out a world that didn't belong to anyone else. That scene struck something in me. Not because it was fantasy—But because I knew that place.

The pond on Mr. Ecklands' land looked just like the one in that movie. And when Corian and I tangled in each other for the first time by our pond, that scene was all I could think about.

That day started out the way they always did when I went to the pond—with silence.

The sun hung low, pouring gold through the trees, and the pond caught every drop of its rays like it was hoarding light. Honeysuckle and heat clung to the air. It was hot. A Southern stillness that made everything feel suspended.

I was barefoot in the grass, legs curled under me, journal open but forgotten. My pen sat slack in my fingers. This time I didn't hear him approach—I felt him. That familiar pull just before his shadow spilled across the page.

Corian didn't say a word. Just sank down beside me, thigh brushing mine, his body warm and close and steady like it always was. We sat like that for a long time. Not touching. Not needing to. The quiet between us was a thing we knew how to hold.

Then his hand grazed mine.

Not a grab. Not a pull. Just... a touch. Testing the air between us like a question he was too scared to ask out loud.

I turned to look at him.

His eyes were darker than the water—stormy and sure—and for once, his teasing grin was gone. What I saw instead was hunger, and fear, and something that looked a lot like what I thought love might look like. It looked like exactly what I felt for him.

I didn't speak. Didn't breathe. Just leaned in.

Our lips met like we'd been rehearsing it in dreams. Soft at first. Careful. But it built fast. Hot. Sharp. Like we'd been waiting too long and couldn't afford to wait another second.

His hands found my waist. My back. My face. Always moving like he wasn't sure what to hold first.

I kissed him harder—because, I was sure. And I needed him to know.

We tumbled onto the grass like it had been waiting for us. Like the flowers and dirt and sky all conspired to make space.

He hovered above me, chest rising fast, his breath catching as he brushed the hair from my cheek.

"You sure?" he whispered.

I nodded. "Yeah."

That's all it took.

No music. No speech. Just skin and breath and sunlight and nerves.

He undressed me like I might vanish. One slow tug at a time. Not clumsy—careful. Like each piece of me was a secret he wanted to memorize.

And when he finally moved inside me?

It wasn't perfect. It wasn't smooth. It was everything.

His forehead pressed to mine, both of us shaking, gasping like we were drowning in each other. The grass scratched my back. A bee buzzed somewhere nearby. A bird called out across the pond like it had something to witness.

And when we came undone, we didn't cry out. We held on.

His fingers were laced with mine. His lips brushed my shoulder. And my whole soul stretched open in a way I didn't know could be done.

I thought it meant forever.

I felt it.

I gave him everything that day—my body, my heart, my faith in the idea that love was something that could last.

But a few months later, he gave himself to someone else.

And had a whole baby to show for it.

The present slammed into me so fast it made my stomach twist.

The weight of his arms around me, the heat of his body pressing against mine—it was too much. Too real. Too familiar. My body remembered him in ways my heart refused to.

Panic curled in my chest, rising fast.

I pushed against him again—harder—breaking the moment before it broke me.

Corian's hands lingered on my waist for a half-second too long before he let me go, his gaze dark, unreadable.

"You good?" His voice was rough, strained.

I took a shaky step back, nodding, but my pulse was a runaway train. "Fine."

Liar.

His eyes searched my face, his jaw tightening like he wanted to say something. Like he knew. Maybe he did. Maybe he still read me too easily, still saw through the walls I had spent years fortifying.

I cleared my throat, crossing my arms as if that could shield me from the way my skin still burned where he'd touched me. "I gotta go."

A muscle jumped in his jaw. For a second, I thought he might push. Might make me say the thing I refused to acknowledge.

But he just nodded. "Yeah. Let's go."

I turned first, walking away before he could see the tremble in my hands.

But I knew, without a doubt, that he felt it too.

Goddamn John Ecklands.

Chapter 20 — Cara

The red clay crunched beneath my boots as I walked the path across Marcus's land. The late-afternoon sun cast long shadows behind me. The old house came into view slowly, like it was daring me to keep going. It sat hunched at the far edge of the property, barely standing, sagging under the weight of time.

From Marcus's porch, it looked like nothing—just another broken-down shack swallowed by brush. But up close, I could visualize what it used to be when we lived here for such a short time so long ago. Snatches of memory played out in front me as I got nearer and just as quickly faded like a picture developing in reverse.

Daddy brought us to this place that he had once called home when there was nowhere else for us to go. He'd brought us here when the job was gone. When the house in Warner Robins was foreclosed on. The dignity. All of it. *Gone.* We landed here like orphans before we even were.

I remember that day we'd first pulled up and dad had to brush the cobwebs from the door before mom ushered us into the front room.

"Awe it ain't that bad," she said in a shaky whisper when she'd seen me wipe a tear from my eye. Our house hadn't been all that great before. But *this? This* house was rock bottom. Mom was so sad that day. My dad was high out of his mind, but this was a rare day when she was sober. I could see the brief moment of clarity in her eyes that day. She didn't want her kids living here. Not long after that, my parents were gone. Just like that. And then there was just me, Marcus and Anty' Renee.

I'd long since forgiven my parents. As a grown up, I could only empathize with a woman who'd followed the man that had vowed to lead her and her family, even if he led them to their detriment. I hadn't been back here since the day I left for the Army Reserves. And even now, I wanted to turn around, run past Marcus's porch to my car, then head straight to an airplane that would carry me far away from here. But my feet kept going, like they knew what I needed before my heart did.

One of the steps gave a little but held. The porch groaned under my weight as I stepped onto it. The screen door was barely hanging on, its rusted hinges yawning open as I tugged it. Inside, dust motes danced in the late evening sun that seeped in through the bare windows. Time had ceased to exist here.

The living room was empty—no furniture, no pictures. But I could still feel it all. The echoes of silence for a little while after our parents were gone. Then Anty' Renee's raucous laughter and loud talking as she schooled Marcus and I on country living.

None of us could outrun the grief though. All of us experienced it in our own corners of this old house. Anty' Renee cried in the night when she thought we were asleep. Marcus paced in the early morning on the back porch before heading off to an early morning practice up at the high school. Me, I poured my grief into that old red leather journal. Every page soaked in the weight of what I couldn't say out loud. My tears bled through ink, turning sorrow into song, pain into poetry. Love, rage, hope—every wild and aching part of my heart lived there, bound between the pages.

I moved through the house quietly, steps slow, breath shallow. The hallway was darker, the paint on the walls peeling in long, curling strips. I stopped in front of the door at the end of the hall. The room where I slept but never felt like mine.

I entered and went straight to the closet. I opened the door tentatively then crouched low, fingers reaching for the baseboard. It still had that small, splintered edge I used to worry with my thumb. I slipped my fingers behind it and tugged. The panel popped loose.

Behind it sat a small metal box, dented and rusted at the corners. My name was still scrawled on top with a pink glitter pen: *CARA M.*

I hesitated.

Then I opened it.

Inside, everything was exactly how I'd left it.

A picture of me and Marcus with mom and dad before the drugs. A busted pair of hoop earrings. A cassette tape labeled *"Car Mix – Daddy's Songs."* A dried-out pen. And underneath it all, like it had been waiting for me, was my red leather journal.

I let out a breath I didn't know I was holding.

The cover was worn from years of handling. My initials were scratched into the corner. I flipped it open and there it was—first page I landed on, front and center:

Steel Horses, Leather Roads—For C.D.

I pressed my hand to my mouth.

God.

I wrote this for Corian. Back when I was eighteen and thought love meant forever. Back when I thought I could give him some pretty words in a song, and they would say everything I didn't know how to.

I'd carried the journal around like it was sacred. Always scribbling in it during lunch, after school, whenever I had a quiet moment to myself. He teased me about it.

"Let me find out you tryin' to be Lil' Kim," he'd said thinking I was writing rap lyrics.

He had no clue of my love for country music. He'd caught a glimpse once, maybe thought it was a poem. Never knew it was a country love song—for him.

Because I never gave it to him.

I was planning to. I finished it the night before graduation. I was going to show it to him then, but I'd gotten scared and chickened out. The whole summer went by, and I left that song right there, waiting for the right time. Then there was that night he'd picked me up on his motorcycle and we rode down to Slosheye Trail.

He thought he could scare me by telling me stories of the haunted trail and the *haints*, the most southern way of referring to ghosts or spirits, which would torment you at night out by the old cemetery. I one upped him and told him to take me and dared him that I'd lay on one of the graves. Of course he wouldn't let me when I tried. He was more afraid than I was. I planned to give it to him that night too but chickened out again.

Before long, August came around. I'd gotten into Savannah College of Art and Design but wasn't sure how I would pay for it.

Of course I had a full academic scholarship, but it was a private school and that wasn't enough to pay for everything plus room and board. I enlisted in the Army Reserve. He begged me not to go. Desert Storm had since ended, but tensions in Bosnia were picking up. I enlisted anyway. It was my way out. Money for college. The only way I knew how to go after my dreams was like he was going after his. He gave me the silent treatment for weeks when I told him. I was shipped off to basic training the day before Corian flew to Texas. He'd gotten accepted to Prairie View.

Six months later, finished with my training, the Army flew me home from Ft. Lee, Virginia to Atlanta. Rather than taking a bus to Lily, I booked a flight to Houston and rented a car. I drove the 40 miles to Prairie View straight from the airport. I had my red journal and this time I wasn't afraid. Mr. Ecklands told me how to find his dorm. I walked into his room preparing to surprise him just as the petite, honey-skinned girl standing behind him as he looked out the window said the one word that changed all of our lives forever.

Pregnant.

His baby.

I never said a word. Just tucked the journal away and quietly closed the door and disappeared.

I sat on the floor in that dusty old closet, cradling the journal in my lap like it might break. My fingers traced the lyrics, my chest tight with everything I had never said.

The song wasn't just about Corian. It was about Daddy too. About running. About trying to hold on to something that always slips through your hands no matter how tight you grip but eventually finding your way home.

Steel horses, leather roads. Glass hearts were meant to break.

I closed my eyes and held the journal to my chest until I was able to will my tears away.

I walked back across the field with the journal still tucked tight against my chest. The old house faded behind me.

From the path, Marcus's home looked like another world—the sleek lines and smooth stone looked like safety.

Marcus was on the front patio, phone to his ear, sipping from a heavy tumbler that probably wasn't just sweet tea. He looked relaxed until he caught sight of me.

"Lemme call you back," he said, already rising from the lounge chair. "Yeah, Sis just walked up. I'll call you later. Love you."

His tone shifted as he met me halfway up the steps.

"Where the hell you been?" His eyes dropped to the journal in my arms, and then further down at the red dirt covering my shoes. The teasing in his voice fell away before his eyes shifted back up to mine. "You went out there... didn't you?"

I didn't answer. Just held up a hand as I prepared to walk past him.

"Cara."

I heard the concern in his voice, saw it written across his face as I passed him and entered the house, cool air and quiet swallowing me whole.

"You alright?" he asked.

I couldn't speak.

I didn't trust what might come out if I tried.

I moved through the open space of the house, past the wide kitchen with its slate counters and subtle under lighting, past the floating staircase and the wall of Black art that always made me proud of who Marcus had become. Proud of us.

I turned into the guest room without another word, closed the door behind me, and leaned against it for a breath.

I walked to the edge of the bed and sat down, placing the journal in my lap like it needed its own moment to settle. It was time for me to confront the past. But to do it, I needed to remember it all. I removed my shoes and curled up and began reading.

Didn't even stop when there was a knock at the door—two soft taps.

"Cara?" Marcus called.

I stayed quiet.

"You need anything?" he asked.

Still nothing.

He didn't linger. I heard his footsteps fade across the smooth hardwood floor.

I closed my eyes, holding the journal like a prayer and let the memories in.

I hadn't planned on finding that song again. Hadn't planned on remembering what it meant. But I'd written it for Corian. For us.

And now it felt like a map I didn't know how to read anymore.

The lyrics echoed in my head like gospel:

You gripped your reins. I gripped my wheel.Glass hearts were meant to break.

I whispered the words to the ceiling. I wrote those words when I knew we'd have to take separate paths for a little while. Him to go to school, me into the Army. We never got to live out the rest of the lyrics.

CHAPTER TWENTY-ONE

Chapter 21 — Corian

That first half-mile, he tested everything—my grip, my rhythm, my patience. Steel Jr. had his father's fire but none of his discipline. Where Steel Sr. was all thunder and command, his colt came with something to prove—head high, hooves striking like he owned the trail.

Years ago, I might've met that challenge with force. But now? Now I know better. I didn't try to break him. I guided him—steady, sure, letting my hand and handling speak the language his blood-line already knew. He carried more than fire in his legs—he carried his lineage. By the time we hit the tree line, he'd settled just enough for me to trust him and him to trust me. We moved together like something rebuilt, not brand new.

Darren caught up just as we crested the back hill, his gelding loping with easy rhythm, his eyes scanned the horizon. He had that same steady energy he always carried—one part caution, one part quiet confidence. We rode in silence for a while until I broke it.

"You're early," I said, easing SJ into a trot beside him.

"Had an early call with some buyers overseas."

I glanced at him. "Turkey?"

"Yep."

We rode a few beats longer before Darren pulled a folded packet from his saddlebag and handed it over. "You remember that contact I mentioned—the equestrian center outside Istanbul? They're serious about striking a deal. Want high-quality Thoroughbreds for show, breeding, maybe even some cross-training with endurance. They're looking to expand, and they want something different."

I skimmed the top sheet. "Black-owned. American-trained. Southern-blooded," I whistled.

He nodded. "Said it just like that," he chuckled, "while our government is trying to do away with diversity, these Turkish investors are looking for it."

I raised a brow. "They know how cantankerous our old Black daddy is?"

Darren snorted. "I didn't lead with that."

I handed the packet back, heart beating steady. Not fast. Not unsure. Just steady.

We were finally moving as a team— in the right direction for the ranch.

Jax had shared his plans for new tech integration—livestream foaling cams, blockchain pedigrees, AI analytics for stride tracking. Crazy techy stuff. But I wasn't laughing anymore. I was starting to believe we could evolve without selling our souls.

And now Darren was working to secure the overseas market.

It was coming together.

All we needed to do now was the hard part.

"Time to tell Daddy," I said.

Darren gave me a look. "You sure you don't wanna wait for Jax to come home first?"

I shook my head. "Don't know when or if Jax is coming home and this needs to happen now while we got motion."

"Now or never then," Darren groaned.

We turned toward the barn, dust kicking up behind us. The sun was high now, and the ranch was stretching to life—stable hands moving buckets, dogs barking near the feed shed, the faint hum of the tractor in the west field.

"Let's ride out a little farther," I said. "Past the ridge."

Darren didn't ask why. He just followed.

I needed the space and time to prepare to face daddy.

The house my parents lived in sat in the middle of the old stretch of ranch land—what used to be the heart of everything before we grew up, spread out and built our own homes on the land. The barn was long gone, torn down after I came back home and took control of the ranch.

Mama had finally gotten her way—a proper kitchen with real light, a walk-in pantry, and a wraparound porch that caught every breeze. But the study? That was still all Daddy. We left the horses at the post near the gravel roundabout and walked up the path. The screen door slapped shut behind us and Mama called from somewhere in the back of the house.

"Y'all tracking dirt on my clean floors?"

"Always," Darren called back with a grin.

I led the way down the hall, past the smell of lemon oil and black coffee, to the back room where Daddy spent his days—maps of the land, ledgers older than I was, framed newspaper clippings from the county fair, and an old rifle mounted above the fireplace.

He was at his desk, reading with a pair of bifocals perched on the edge of his nose. The prosthetic leg rested stiff beside the chair, his good leg stretched out long, boot tapping lightly against the rug.

He didn't look up.

"Took y'all long enough," he said, turning the page, "thought you said you were on the way an hour ago."

Darren eased into one of the leather chairs across from him. I stayed standing.

"You wanna' hear what we came to say, or you gonna keep complaining?" Darren said, eyes narrowing at our pops. Damn if he wasn't a spitting image of the old man.

Dad closed the book slowly and took off his glasses. "That depends. You bringing me some bullshit or something worth my time? Better not be another one of your '*thirty-second brain*' ideas you're known for."

I cut in before Darren could clap back. "We've been working with some international partners to bring in new revenue for the ranch." This had Daddy's attention. He narrowed his eyes at me over his glasses as I continued. "Some investors in Turkey want what we've got—Thoroughbreds, Arabians, maybe a few of our specialty breeds."

"Black-owned ranches have weight there. And they're offering real money," Darren added.

Waynan leaned back, lips pressed into a thin line considering what we'd said. "And what do they want in return?"

"Bloodline contracts. Exclusive deals. A stamp of authenticity," I responded.

That got a grunt. Not quite approval. But not dismissal either.

"We'll still be in control of the line," I added, stepping forward. "We're not sending colts off to strangers. We raise them here, we train them here, and we choose which ones go. Only the best. They want excellence? *We* define it."

Dad studied me like he was looking through me.

"And who decides what's best?" he asked slowly. "You?"

"No," I said. "*We* do. All of us. Including Jax."

His brow twitched.

Darren leaned in, elbows resting on his knees. "We're not trying to erase what you built, Pops. We're trying to evolve it. Before it withers out here waiting on better weather."

He didn't respond. Just looked down at his hand resting on the edge of the desk.

"Y'all already looped in Jax?" he asked after a long pause.

I nodded. "He's been working with investors and a couple universities out in California and local to bring in some grant money. They're beta-testing some of his tech now."

Waynan gave me a flat look. "That boy thinks you can train a horse with a goddamn computer and some A-one?"

"AI, pops. And, well, yeah," I said. "He's trying to amplify what we do. Make it more efficient and effective. Bring us into modern day ranching using all the tech and tools out there. We'll be ahead of our competition."

The old man leaned back again in his chair, tapped a knuckle against the desk twice. A habit from his rodeo days when he used to prep for a run—grounding himself before the gate flung open.

Then he muttered, "Get him on the line."

I pulled my phone from my back pocket and hit Jax's number.

He answered on the second ring, camera on, wild locs half-tamed up into a man-bun atop his head, some big screen flashing behind him with what looked like a 3D horse skeleton spinning mid-air.

"You live?" he asked, squinting before realizing we were in Daddy's study, sitting up straight when it hit him.

"You up?" I countered.

"Barely. It's seven here but I'm working on some stuff," he waived at the screen behind him, rubbing his eyes, then sat up even straighter when he saw the old man on the other side of the room. "Pop."

Dad grunted. "Show me what you got and spare me the West Coast science fiction, won't you?"

Jax grinned. "How about I show you in person. I'm flying home in the next few weeks. I'll have demos, mockups, market data, and a bottle of your favorite bourbon. And Mama already requested that I make oxtails on one of the Sundays I'm home."

Daddy cracked a dry smile. "You *cookin'*? We all gon' die."

Darren chuckled. I just shook my head.

"Just be here," I said.

"I will." Jax's face sobered a bit before he saluted.

I ended the call and slipped the phone back in my pocket.

The room went quiet again, each of us looking around at the other.

Finally, Waynan nodded once.

"You wanna change things?" he said. "Fine. But don't bring me no half-built shit. Show me results. Make me believe in it."

I exhaled, slow. "We will."

Then he picked up his glasses and went right back to reading.

Dismissed.

Darren and I left his study to go find mama in her garden before heading back to our separate homes.

The wind was picking up. Storm clouds forming out east, heavy and gray. I needed to head over to the cotton gin to make sure the blueprints we'd left in the makeshift office over there were safe from the rain that was sure to pour in through that leaking roof.

Chapter 22 – Cara

I 'd come here to clear my head. Instead, I found Corian walking through the doorway like a storm I wasn't ready to weather.

The humidity clung to everything—my skin, my clothes, my thoughts. The cotton gin smelled like mold. Stale, forgotten, with the faint sweetness of decay. I'd spent the last hour taking photos of warped beams and scribbling notes in the margins of my sketchbook, half-cursing Mr. Ecklands for putting me in this position.

The rain hadn't started yet, but the sky had turned the color of bad news.

Corian stepped inside and shook off the mist like he owned the place. His eyes landed on the blueprints I'd flattened out across a rickety card table and then slid to me. He didn't say anything right away. Just looked. That same quiet, assessing stare that used to undo me when we were teenagers.

Not today.

"What are you doing here?" I asked, sharper than I meant.

"Saving these before the storm ruins them," he said, nodding toward the plans. "You're welcome."

"I think I'm capable of handling these blueprints, Demetrie.."

He raised an eyebrow. "Yeah? That's why they're *sittin'* under a cracked window?"

I opened my mouth, then closed it again. Not even interested in entertaining Corian's ass.

He smirked like he knew he'd scored a point, and that was all it took to light the fuse.

"This building is a damn hazard," I snapped. "You realize that, right? The roof leaks. The floor's rotted in at least two places. There's no insulation, no wiring, no foundation to build on. It needs to come down. Start fresh."

Corian crossed the room in three slow steps, then stopped on the opposite side of the table like we were opponents in some old Western standoff.

"You wanna tear down everything just 'cause it looks rough on the outside? Not wrapped up with a pretty bow just how *you* like it?

I stared at him, jaw clenched. "Don't do that."

"Do what?"

"Make this about me."

"If the boot fits—"

I shoved the small table holding the blueprints aside. "This isn't about some emotional attachment to a pile of bricks. It's about function. Safety. Progress."

Corian leaned in, voice low but firm. "And what about legacy? What about respecting what came before us?"

I scoffed. "You mean like a rotting cotton gin? A building that once processed the same crop our ancestors damn near died harvesting? That's what you wanna preserve?"

His eyes darkened. "You think Mr. Ecklands didn't know that? You think he picked this place by accident? This building *means* something. It tells a story."

"Then let's tell a better one," I said, my voice rising. "One that doesn't reek of trauma and rust. One that doesn't fall apart every time it rains!"

Thunder rolled in the distance, low and threatening.

We stood there, breathing heavy. The space between us was charged. It always had been. Even when we were kids—too close, too much, too soon. We were fire... and pressure... and a whole lot of unspoken feelings.

"I'm not here to relive the past," I said finally, quieter now. "I'm here to build something that lasts."

Corian's gaze dropped to my hands. I hadn't realized I was gripping them into fists so tight.

"And I'm here," he said, "to make sure we don't erase the soul of this place just because it makes you uncomfortable."

I stepped back like he'd slapped me.

And just then, lightning ripped through the sky—sharp and merciless—followed by a thunderclap so loud it rattled the walls and sent dust raining down from the rafters. A second later, the clouds cracked open, and the rain came, hard and unrelenting, beating against the old tin roof like it was trying to wash us both away.

We stared at each other like enemies caught in the same foxhole.

"You always gotta make it personal," I said, my voice shaking. "Always got your chest puffed out like your way is the only way."

He didn't flinch. "Better that than running from every damn thing that don't fit your picture-perfect plans. You ran from here. From me. From everything."

"You got another girl pregnant while telling me you loved me."

"That was thirty years ago, Cara."

"And you think that makes it hurt less?" I snapped. "You're so busy building a legacy," I bit out, my voice shaking with fury, "I just pray your daughter doesn't end up thinking love has to come second to pride."

His eyes narrowed, jaw tight. "Careful, Cara."

"Why?" I spat. "'Cause I spoke the truth? You're so full of your own damn self-righteousness, you can't even see the wreckage you leave behind—"

"I'm not your daddy, Cara. He wrecked you. Not me."

His words cut straight through me.

For a second, I stopped breathing.

He'd said it so cold, like it was nothing. Like all the years I spent trying to outrun the kind of love that abandoned, broke, or left without warning meant nothing.

Different men. Different mistakes.

But standing here, caught between memory and heat, the ache they'd both left behind pulsed in the same place. *My heart.*

My daddy—charming, reckless, full of promises he never kept. And Corian—who once looked at me like I was his whole damn future, then handed that future to someone else without a second thought.

The men weren't the same. But the way they broke me? Identical ugly twins.

And the fire it sparked in me felt damn near nuclear.

I moved before I could tame my feelings. My arm swung high, hand flying, aiming to slap the taste out of his mouth—

But he caught me.

His fingers closed around my wrist like steel, stopping me midair.

"Don't," he growled.

I trembled in his grip, shocked at the force, the closeness. Rain pounded against the roof above us. Thunder rolled again, loud and low like a warning.

But I couldn't move.

Couldn't breathe.

My body was still humming from the things he'd said, from the things I couldn't say back. All the years I'd buried this fire inside me—it cracked open.

And then he pulled me into him.

Rough.

His mouth crashed into mine and my whole body lit up like it remembered him.

Like it never forgot.

I pushed against his chest, tried to shove him away, but my hands were traitors. They grabbed instead—clung to the fabric of his shirt like I'd drown if I let go.

I hated him.I wanted him.I *hated* that I still wanted him.

I sobbed into his lips—one sharp, broken sound that tore loose from somewhere deep and still hurting. He didn't stop. His hands moved over my back, grounding me, holding me to him. Like if he kissed me hard enough, it might undo the past.

And maybe it did.

For one heartbeat, for one breath, for one aching, shattered moment—I let go. I kissed him back like I was starving. Like I was falling. Like he was home, and I'd just found my way back to it.

I don't know how long we were there clawing at each other grudge-kissing, in the damp space. It seemed to be mere seconds, but the rain had softened to a hush against the windows and the thunder faded by the time we finally pulled apart. Both of us was panting. My forehead pressed against his, my hands still fisted in his shirt. My lips throbbed. My face was wet—maybe from rain pouring in through the leaking roof, maybe from tears.

So much for my claim of taking care of the blueprints.

I laughed. Just once. Low. Bitter. "They're soaked." They weren't totally ruined but were certainly splattered. "Thank God they were copies from the courthouse that can be reproduced."

He didn't respond. Just looked down at me like he didn't trust himself to speak.

Outside, the clouds cracked open again—at least not in anger this time. A beam of sunlight pierced through the drizzle and streamed into the room, soft and golden. Like forgiveness. Like irony. Like a lie I still wanted to believe in.

The door creaked open, and a voice called in from the doorway, casual and unbothered. "...Should I come back later?"

We both turned, breathless, stepping back from each other like two teens caught too close

The man in the doorway tipped his weathered hat, eyes bouncing from me to Corian and back again.

"I'm Vernon Townsend," he said, stepping into the light. "Local architect."

Vernon stepped farther into the cotton gin, boots squishing against the part mud, part concrete floor.

"I, *uh*... apologize if I interrupted something," he added, adjusting the blueprint roll under his arm. His voice was gravelly but gentle.

Corian cleared his throat and brushed a hand down the front of his shirt like he was trying to smooth away the fact that he'd just had me pinned to that same spot.

I wiped my mouth with the back of my hand, ignoring the way my fingers still trembled. My voice was low, hoarse. "You're fine. We were just... wrapping up."

Vernon nodded once, polite. But his eyes said he'd seen more than enough.

"Well, I'm here 'cause Mr. Ecklands had *somethin'* drawn up before he passed. Brought me in a few months ago. I just recently got wind from one of the council members that y'all were finally making moves on the project," Vernon said, adjusting his soaked jacket with a grunt. "Figured I'd stop by on my way home—beat the storm if I could and see if I would find y'all here." He chuckled and shook his head, rain still dripping from the brim of his hat. "Didn't quite beat that storm." He then looked at us with a hint of a grin.

"John told me, 'If those two ever stop dancing around each other long enough to get started on the first items on the list, It'll mean they've both at least conceded that they'd do the best they can to figure out how to accomplish the rest of the list.' He also said y'all would need these before you start fussin' over crown molding and concrete."

He glanced between us, rain still dripping off the brim of his hat, his grin spreading slow. "Said if y'all were finally serious about the project, I should bring 'em by. Looks like I showed up right on time."

My mouth dropped open. "He said that?"

"Oh, verbatim," Vernon replied, amused. "Told me, 'Vernon, one day those two are gon' lock horns so hard, you best be ready with the tiebreaker.'"

Corian chuckled under his breath. I didn't.

Vernon shook the rolled papers in the air then moved to the edge of the table. He glanced down at the plans already there, soaked, then used the sleeve of his forearm to swipe the table dry sending the damp copies to the ground. He gently unrolled the thick set of blueprints *he'd* brought in their place. The thick paper curled at the ends so he held it open with his hand on one end and his leather bag on the other and stepped back so we could see.

My breath caught.

The design was beautiful.

A modern, eco-efficient community center with floor-to-ceiling windows and adaptive reuse of the existing structure. The main frame of the cotton gin had been preserved—refitted with sustainable materials, reclaimed wood, solar panels, and a mezzanine that overlooked the heart of the space. A performance stage, a digital learning lab, an indoor/outdoor art gallery... and tucked into the corner, an empty space labeled, 'To be decided on by Cara and Corian'.

It was everything. Beauty and purpose.

It was *us*. All that was missing was the innovation and legacy.

"John gave me full permission to adapt your input into the design," Vernon said, tapping a page with notes scrawled in Mr. Ecklands' handwriting.

Corian and I looked at each other quizzically then turned back to Vernon. "Input?" I asked.

"Right. Input from *us*? *What input*?"

I stared down at the blueprint. "You were already working on this before either Corian, or I knew Mr. Ecklands passed away?"

"Yep. As I stated, John brought me in months ago," Vernon said. "Had most of the concept already fleshed out—said the two of y'all would need a little... mediation when the time came."

Corian chuckled again, "John-*damn*-Ecklands."

Vernon gestured to the notes. "He pulled pieces from everything—old conversations, sketches, essays y'all wrote for his class back in high school. He wanted the foundation to be y'all's vision, not just his."

I stared down at the blueprint. "He... he already knew we wouldn't agree."

Vernon gave a short laugh. "Knew y'all would fight, yes. But he also knew you'd come together. Eventually."

I glanced at Corian, but he wasn't looking at me. He was staring at the drawings.

Vernon rolled the rest of the packet open. "I brought some markup paper. If you want to make edits, notes, changes—we can finalize the build plans by the end of next week. Construction crew's already been commissioned and assembled. Just waiting on y'all to finalize the plans."

My head spun. "He left nothing to chance."

"No, ma'am. John was many things. Unprepared wasn't one of 'em."

I looked back at the drawing and ran a finger along the outline of the roof.

Corian finally spoke. Softly. "We don't need to tear everything down."

I heard the double meaning in his words loud and clear. I surprised myself by answering, "We don't need to hold on to all of it either."

A pause.

And then in unison we turned to Vernon, "We can work with this."

It wasn't a truce. Not yet.

But it was something.

Vernon clapped his hands once. "Good. That's what I like to hear. I'll give y'all some time to look these over...together."

He reached for his satchel, rolling up the extra copies and scribbled notes, and gave us a look that held more wisdom than words.

With a tip of his damp hat, he stepped out the same door he'd entered, leaving Corian and I alone again.

The storm had passed.

But something else was just beginning.

CHAPTER TWENTY-THREE

Chapter 23 — Corian

O ur edits to the design Vernon had brought us were simple on paper—but layered in purpose.

A greenhouse space labeled *Kima's Farm Hub*, tucked just off the east-facing rear wing. Open glass panels. Raised beds for planting. A rain catchment system added to the roofline. Every square inch said *grow something here.*

A VR lab tagged *Jax's Ranch-Tech Program*, positioned adjacent to the media suite. With fiber wiring, dual projection space, and smart walls that could shift from simulation to classroom. It wasn't just for show. It was the future meeting the past—right in the heart of Lily.

I handed Vernon the rolled set of changes at his office just off the square.

He unrolled the sheet on a drafting table, squinting at the notes I'd added in clean, measured print.

"Hmm," he nodded. "Looks like everything is in order." He slowly looked up at me from the papers, brows raised in question.

"Yeah. Cara signed off too," I said with good-natured sarcasm.

He pursed his lips in approval and nodded his head. "Didn't think you two would get on the same side of a blueprint so quickly."

I smirked. "Neither did we."

He looked down again, then pointed to the greenhouse. "She wants this connected to the back entrance?"

"Yeah. East-facing. Better sun. And it's closer to where the kids will be getting hands-on with the farm-to-table stuff."

He jotted a note in the margin. "And this—VR lab?"

"Jax is flying in next week with a whole setup, but I told him we gotta lay the wiring now or we'll be tearing up floors later."

Vernon gave a low whistle. He paused, nodding slowly, visibly impressed.

"I'll admit it. I didn't think y'all could pull this together. But this..." His voice softened, reverent now. "*This is good*. Real good."

I didn't respond. Smiling inwardly, I tapped my knuckles once against the edge of the table and nodded.

I thought of Cara. We were past circling each other like ghosts. This was foundation work now. In more ways than one.

By the time we broke ground a week later, the sun was high and the sky clear enough to make you believe in good omens.

Folks from the council showed up in their best boots and pressed shirts. Some of the ladies from town brought lemonade and folding chairs. There was music, laughter, the sound of shovels and backhoes slicing into Georgia clay, and a couple of wide-eyed teens asking if they could help.

I kept to the edge, watching it all unfold.

Watching her.

Cara moved through the space like she was born for it—directing volunteers, flipping through the site map, adjusting tools and tents like she could see the final vision already built.

A red journal was tucked beneath her arm.

I'd spent years building horses to follow my lead and could read the land like scripture.

But I had never seen someone breathe purpose into chaos like she did.

And that shit wrecked me a little.

"Thought I'd find you brooding over here," Ja'Kari's voice cut through the wind, wry and warm. "You looking real thirsty. Stop staring."

I didn't turn right away. Just sipped the weak lemonade and let the moment settle, choosing to ignore her '*thirsty*' comment.

"I'm not brooding," I said.

"Mmm."

She stepped beside me, arms crossed, her curls pulled into a low bun, sunglasses perched on top of her head. She looked like her mother.

"She's gorgeous. Looking like a straight up boss," Ja'Kari said quietly.

"She does."

"So...?"

I finally turned to her. "So what?"

She raised an eyebrow. "So... you obviously want her, Dad. What are you doing about it?"

I let out a long breath. "Trying not to mess up the peace."

She tilted her head. "Too late for that."

A low laugh escaped me. "You got no chill, Kari."

"Daddy, I love you, but you've been walking around this place like you're waiting on somebody to give you permission to do something you already know you want to do."

I didn't say anything. Didn't have to.

"I used to think you and Mom were just too different," she continued. "Now I realize y'all just never really *chose* each other. You stayed 'cause it was the right thing. The practical thing. The respectful thing. But it was never this."

I glanced at her. "And what's this?"

She nodded toward Cara. "That."

I felt it in my gut—the truth of what she said.

"I hurt her," I said finally. "Back then. Worse than you should ever know."

"Then make it right."

"Not that simple."

"It never is. But hard don't mean it shouldn't be done."

She touched my arm then, squeezed once before stepping away. "Invite her to dinner. Not for closure. Not for some big romantic gesture. Just to tell her what you probably should've said a long time ago. I'm sorry."

I watched her walk back into the crowd, her fiancé waving from the other side with a half-eaten funnel cake and a goofy grin.

Half the day had gone by and the work at the site had wrapped for the day. Everyone else was long gone, but I sat in my pickup in the empty parking lot.

I looked down at my phone for the umpteenth time. Finally typed. Deleted. Typed again.

And then I hit send.

Dinner at my place.

Chapter 24—Cara

I knocked once, then twice.

The screen door creaked open before I could knock again, and there she was—barefoot, wearing a tank top that read *I AM NOT THE ONE*, her honey-blonde curls piled high and defiant like a crown.

Kima blinked. "Well damn."

I held up both bottles of Strawberry Hill Boone's Farm and gave her the sheepish grin I used to flash when we snuck out past curfew in high school. "Emergency."

Her eyes widened, then softened. "You brought the devil's juice?"

"I brought the devil's juice," I confirmed.

She stepped aside immediately. "Come in, bitch."

I followed her through the screen door and into her open-air kitchen. A breeze blew through the slatted windows, carrying the smell of thyme, rosemary, and tomatoes still warm from the vine. Home. That's what this place always felt like, even now with the modern farmhouse adjustments Kima had made to it.

Kima didn't ask right away. She let me breathe. Let me settle.

She grabbed two glasses from a purposefully mismatched cabinet, screwed the cap off the first bottle, and poured us both generous amounts. I leaned on the butcher block island, wine sweating in my hand, heart pounding like I was seventeen again and dying to tell a secret.

"I kissed him."

Kima stopped mid-sip, raised an eyebrow. "Girl, you stormed in here like your car was on fire and your edges were in danger. You better give me more than that."

I took a long sip. "I didn't just kiss him. I *lost it* on him. And then I kissed him. Or maybe he kissed me. Or maybe we kissed each other. It was... everything. And then I ran. Again."

She gave me a long, unimpressed look. "And now you're here. With high school wine. Acting like everybody and their mama didn't see this coming."

"I'm serious, Kima. I can't think straight. It's like my brain is all tangled up with my body and my heart's somewhere in the middle screaming *abandon ship*."

She leaned her hip against the counter and folded her arms. "Because the kiss was that good?"

I swallowed hard. "It was like... being dragged backward through every year I spent trying to forget him. And realizing I never did."

Kima exhaled an "oof," then took another sip of wine. "Okay. So. Are you mad at *him* for kissing you, or are you mad at *you* for feeling it?"

I didn't answer. Couldn't.

Kima rolled her eyes. "That man is fine, Cara. *Country*-fine. *Ranch*-fine. *Built-like-he-move-hay-bales-and-break-hearts-on-purpose* fine. And if *you* were wet and *he* was with it? *Babyyyy*."

I burst out laughing despite myself. "Kima!"

"I'm serious! You two are grown as hell. You got equity and body oil and damn near a decade of tension between you. If y'all wanna take a ride down memory lane—with protection and emotional honesty—who's stopping you? But don't do it if you're just running from your feelings again."

I stared down at my glass, her words soaking in.

She stepped closer, softer now. "Look. You don't owe that man a second chance. But you *do* owe yourself closure. So if he wants to talk? Let him. Go to dinner. Listen. And then decide if you're still mad or just scared."

I set my glass down. "Great advice," I said looking at my phone. "He texted me."

Kima arched a brow. "Of course he did."

"Dinner. His place. He said, 'One last thing I need to say face to face.'"

Kima didn't flinch. Just gave me the nod of someone who already knew where this was headed. "Then go."

"I don't know if I'm ready to forgive him."

"Good," she said, draining her glass. "Cause this ain't about forgiveness yet. This is about you letting your heart come up for air. Just... hear him out. Look him in the eye and let him say what he should've said a long time ago."

I breathed in deep. Exhaled shakily. "You always know what to say."

She smirked. "That's because I'm magic, baby. I just hide it in these hips."

I laughed again, softer this time.

Then she stepped back, studying me.

"Wear something short and flowing."

I blinked. "Excuse me?"

"You heard me. Short. Flowing. Let them legs do what they came here to do. That man's been thirsty for thirty years—might as well give him a tall glass of something to sip on if you're going to go."

I rolled my eyes. "You're ridiculous."

"I'm right," she countered. "Show up in bad bitch fashion and let him wonder if you might *ruin his life or save it, depending on your mood.* Give that man something to remember whether he earns you or not."

I sipped again, slower this time. "What if I'm not ready to hear what he has to say?"

"Then tell him that. But don't ghost. Don't run. You deserve to hear him out. And he deserves to see what he lost—up close."

I sat with that. Let it settle into my bones.

Kima poured the last of the wine and raised her glass. "To *grown ass* decisions."

I tapped mine to hers. "To wearing something short and dangerous."

She grinned. "And to making that man question every life choice that didn't include you."

Chapter 25 – Corian

I cleaned the house like a man expecting judgment. Twice.

Not that Cara was the judgmental type. But this? Tonight had to be special. I'd invited her to dinner, yes. But old memories would be brought to the surface. Tonight was about accountability. About me saying the things I should've said years ago—and being man enough to mean them.

I'd done everything I could to get it right. The roast had slow-cooked all day, seasoned down to the bone with rosemary, thyme, and garlic. Collards with smoked turkey wings bubbled low on the stove. Sweet potatoes were roasted to a caramelized glaze. A cast iron skillet of cornbread sat under a towel, to keep it warm.

Two bottles of wine—one red, one white—breathed on the sideboard. Those were for Cara. I'd poured two fingers of aged whiskey for myself and my damned nerves. I'd showered, trimmed my beard, even ironed a damn shirt. And now, with ten minutes to spare, I was pacing like a boy waiting on his prom date.

My nerves didn't usually act up. I wasn't that man. I handled business. Made decisions. Rode horses bred to throw a lesser rider and never blinked. But this?

This was Cara.

And there'd never been a map for how to navigate her.

I'd even put on the playlist Ja'Kari made for me. Said it would give me "refined, Southern *zaddy* energy." I didn't have a clue what that meant, but it didn't matter because any hint of me being cool disappeared when I heard Cara's tires crunch on the gravel. My nerves zapped and *zaddied* like a skittish colt sensing a storm.

I opened the door before she could knock.

Damn.

Cara stood there like the stars at dusk had wrapped themselves around her shoulders to show off her radiance. The short, flowy dress clung to all her right places, allowing her legs to catch the fading light as if they were dipped in gold. Her hair was up, exposing her neck and collarbone—areas I used to kiss like they held my salvation. The gloss on her lips gleamed like a dare.

She stood there, calm and collected. Like neither of us had been wrecked the other day by that kiss on the cotton gin floor.

"Hey," I said, throat tight.

"Hey," she replied, gaze holding mine for one long, unreadable beat.

"You're early."

"You want me to leave and come back?" She slickly, double pointing her thumbs over her shoulder at the over-the-top Porsche she whipped around in.

I let a slow grin curve my lips. "Naw, come on in."

She stepped inside, her heels tapping across the wood like a countdown. That same soft perfume wrapped itself around my lungs—jasmine, citrus, and something I never could name but would always re-mind me of her.

"Smells like Sunday dinner in here," she said, sliding the strap of the leather purse from her shoulder, looking for somewhere to sit it. I took it from her hands and placed it on the counter nearest the entrance of the kitchen.

"You hungry?"

She tilted her head. "Depends. Is this dinner, or a setup?"

"It's both, if I'm being honest."

She raised an eyebrow.

I poured her a glass of the red, handing it over. "But at least the food will be delicious."

I motioned toward the table, chuckling. "Sit. Let me feed you before I say something too stupid."

She walked past me, close enough to make my chest tighten. That perfume—made me weak in the knees.

I served her first, plate full and steaming, then sat across from her.

We sat. Ate. Talked around things at first. Let the food do some of the heavy lifting. She complimented my greens. I told her the flavor was courtesy of the smoked turkey Mama recommended. She raised an eyebrow when she tasted the sweet potatoes.

"You put orange zest in these?"

I nodded. "Figured I needed to add something bold if I was gonna impress you."

Her smile was small, but I could tell the orange zest worked. I held on to the feeling.

When the last of her sweet potatoes were gone, she picked up her knife then leaned back and smiled broadly. "The groundbreaking yesterday," she said, cutting into her roast, "Gave this whole project the motion we needed. The build out is going to be finished in no time."

"It is. In two months, we'll be having the commemorative trail ride and grand opening celebration." I said. "Apparently Darren was able to get your brother to help with planning it?" I raised a brow at her over the snifter of whiskey, I held to my lips.

"Yep. Isn't that crazy? And last night, Kima agreed to help with the trail ride planning too."

"Looks like the band is coming back together. We even got some new school help. Ja'Kari's got a few local businesses to agree to sponsor some of the festivities."

Cara raised her own brow. "How'd you convince your daughter to join the cause?"

"I didn't. She told me she was in before I even asked."

Something flickered across Cara's face, then faded. She changed the subject. "You remember back in Mr. Ecklands' class, when we used to draw up blueprints for our dream homes?"

It didn't escape me that she said 'homes' as if they were separate. Not how I remembered it. I chuckled and nodded. "You designed that big house with the wraparound porch. I added the underground whiskey cellar." I nodded to the bottle of whiskey on the counter. "I actually built the cellar."

She laughed, that low, rich sound that hit somewhere behind my ribs. "The big house too, I see." Her eyes arched around the huge kitchen. "No wrap around porch for me. But I guess I have gotten to see the world," she said quietly, then refocused her attention on the roast. "Guess we both got what we wanted."

"Mostly," I said just as quietly, trying not to think of the rest of the dream. Instead, I poured her more wine.

After dinner, I asked her to follow me out to the back patio. I poured the remains of the bottle of red wine into my glass and grabbed the other bottle of white and led the way. I lit the outdoor fireplace and turned on the sound system as she soaked in the glow of the fire.

Instead of sitting on the teak wood couch, she sat across from it in one of the single cushioned patio arm chairs. I was still standing when the song changed. Beyoncé's *16 Carriages* played low on the speakers.

"Mmm..." Cara sat forward and clasped her hands to her chest. She groaned in pleasure at the sound of the music. Her eyes narrowed as she appeared to savor the solemn guitar chords at the opening of the song.

"You like this one?" I asked.

Her voice was soft. "Are you kidding? I've played it about a hundred times since it dropped. Her voice... that ache. That whole 'carrying the weight of legacy and leaving girlhood behind' thing? Yeah. I feel all of that."

I watched her as the lyrics wrapped around her. She sat in the firelight, eyes on the horizon like she was seeing something I couldn't.

"You surprise me," I chuckled.

"Why? I've always loved country music. You just never noticed."

"I noticed everything. Just surprised you still do."

"So," she said, "you asked me here for a reason. What did you want to say face to face?"

I took a breath. Let the moment hold.

"Dance with me first." I surprised myself even as the words came out of my mouth, but I wasn't ready for the peace the song had placed on Cara's face to be so quickly removed.

She raised an eyebrow but surprisingly didn't argue. She let me pull her up, slid her arms around my neck as I rested mine at her waist. Our bodies fell into an easy rhythm, like muscle memory.

Her cheek grazed mine. My lips brushed her temple.

They wanted to brush her lips, but instead I parted them and began my apology. I took a breath, pulled back slightly to look at her fully in the face.

"I treated you like you didn't have the right to make your own decisions back then."

Her lips parted, just barely.

"When you told me you were enlisting in the Army, I didn't hear you. Couldn't hear you. I didn't even try to understand. I took you wanting to leave as rejection. As if your leaving meant I was being left behind. And instead of standing beside you, I shut down. Gave you the silent treatment like a coward. Because I didn't know how to hold onto you without controlling the terms."

I paused. Let it land. She remained silent.

"I was young. But that doesn't excuse it. I've spent years trying to convince myself that what happened between us was fate... that you made your choice to go into the Army and I made mine to go to Texas to Prairie View. But the truth is, I was scared. Scared to let a strong woman be strong without it meaning she didn't need me."

Cara blinked, slowly.

"I'm not that boy anymore," I said. "I realized that I didn't need to control you to love you. I just... wish I'd had the courage back then to tell you that I loved you. Always did." Cara's lips twitched, itching to shut me up, I bet, but I continued. "I'm not asking for anything. Just wanted to give you my apology. Out loud. On purpose. No pride. Just the truth."

The air shifted. She stared at me for a long time. Then stepped away and walked to the edge of the stone patio. Her back to me, she folded her arms across her chest, wrapping them around her body. After a while she stated, rather than asked, "Aren't you leaving something out?"

It was my turn to stare back at her with an equally blank expression.

Rounding on me, Cara said, "You keep talking about the silence like that's what wrecked us."

I waited.

"I was there," she said, voice tight. "At Prairie View. The day the little cute pretty girl said the words that changed *all* of our lives forever."

I froze. "What are you talking about, Cara?"

"*Yeah.* I flew to Houston. Took a rental car straight from the airport to your dorm. I was gonna surprise you that day. Tell *you* I loved you. That I wanted to fight for us. Hoping I could explain to you finally that I didn't go active duty but had enlisted in the Army Reserves. My six months of training was done and the plan we'd made to finish college, get married, build our big ol' dream house and travel the world could continue."

She paused. Swallowed.

"And I walked into your dorm room just in time to hear her say it. 'I'm pregnant.'"

I stared at her.

"Cara, what are you saying?" I shook my head in total confusion. "You came to my school?" I asked, barely breathing.

Her voice trembled, full of old wounds and new fire. "Yes. I was fighting for us. But you had already handed your life to someone else."

I stepped closer. "Cara—"

"I didn't even get mad," she cut me off. A sardonic smile on her lips. "Not then anyway. I just closed the door and disappeared, and you let me. You just..." Her shoulders dropped. "You had already let me go. Stopped talking to me before I left to go to Ft. Jackson for basic training. You didn't even say good bye. Like I didn't matter."

"I was young and stupid, Cara, but I swear I didn't just drop you, us. I had no clue you were there that day. I came home soon after and begged Mr. Ecklands to help me reach out to you. He said you asked him not to share your contact details and that you just needed time. I tried for months Cara up until just before Ja'Kari was born," I said, voice rough. "I swear to God, you mattered more than my whole life mattered, Cara and I didn't know you were there that day."

She blinked fast. "Would it have changed anything if you did know?"

"Yes." I didn't hesitate. "Everything."

The silence crackled then split wide open like the space between us had been waiting to shatter.

"I froze when Monica told me she was pregnant," I continued. "I was nineteen, Cara. Scared to death of being a dad, and just flat out young and dumb. When you left... I'd already told myself you didn't want me anymore. I thought I had time to fix it. But my whole life plan, *our plan*, fell apart in two seconds. I didn't want a baby at such a young age. And since I'm telling the truth, I didn't want to be with Monica. Almost nine months went by after she told me she was pregnant before I was able to even except the truth that I needed to man-up. I spent that time begging Ecklands, your brother, even your Aunt Renee before she moved back to Ohio to help me get in touch with you. But I had to do the right thing. I married Monica for the sake of my child. I thought that was what I was supposed to do as a man."

"That's bullshit," she snapped. "You knew my situation. You *knew* I didn't have any money. No family that could send me to college. I did the only thing I knew to do so I could play my position on *our* team. I got Uncle Sam to pay for my college, and you *dissed me for making a choice for myself!* You could've listened. Could've wrote me a letter when I was in basic you could've did all that before a baby was conceived and you didn't do any of that."

"I was ashamed," I said, my hands loose at my sides. "Didn't know how to fix the boy I was. I shut you out, yeah—and I told you why. But what I didn't say was how I convinced myself you'd moved on. That you were already out there living your life, while I was here trying to stand tall and do the 'right thing.' Be a father. Marry her. Pretend I could be what she needed."

I let the truth crack through my chest.

"But I was lying—to myself and to her. Because if I'd ever said out loud that I still loved you, I would've broken down. And I didn't know how to come back from that."

I thought back. To nights full of silence. Arguments that never touched the root.

"Monica used to ask me what I was holding back. Why it always felt like I was just... gone. I tried to be present, tried to smile, but I was walking around hollow. My family felt it too—treated her like she was just passing through, and I never stood up for her the way I should have. I couldn't. I was too busy pretending I was over you."

I paused. Let the shame sit between us.

"It all unraveled the night I called your name in my sleep."

I stepped closer.

"That broke something in her. And in me too. Because she didn't deserve to be haunted by the pieces of a woman I never stopped loving. And if I'd let myself break—back then, when it all fell apart—I don't know how I would've made it through. Not without you."

Cara stared at me, eyes shining. But not a single tear fell.

"You don't get to act like what you did was noble," she said. "It was cowardice."

"I know," I said, not shying from her accusation. I was a coward.

"I told all of them I never wanted to speak to you again. I needed you to come after me and figure out how to do it on your own," her voice cracked as tears began to stream down her cheeks.

Again, I moved closer to her. "I know. I failed you. Failed us."

This time her shoulders slumped. "I waited for you Corian."

"I'm so sorry, Cara." This time, the sting of tears clouded my own vision.

There it was. The thing between us, trembling in the air like thunder waiting to strike.

Then she stepped in closing the distance. Fast. Fierce. She grabbed the collar of my shirt and pulled me down into her.

And kissed me.

Not tentative. Not curious. But *hungry*—three decades worth of ache and fire and fury pouring into me as her hands gripped the back of my neck like she meant to rewrite history with her lips.

I groaned and grabbed her waist, lifting her slightly, pressing her against me like my body already knew the way she fit.

She tried to pull back once—reflex maybe—but I caught her jaw gently, kissed her deeper, slower now. Until her hands relaxed. Until the sob caught in her throat and melted into the kiss. Until we were breathing the same breath and lost in each other all over again.

The storm I'd been riding for years broke.

I clung to her as the fire crackled beside us, as the music shifted into something more somber, as the moon moved higher in the sky and the past finally loosened its grip. "I'm not letting go this time. Not unless you tell me to."

She didn't say a word, so I pulled her tighter.

The fire snapped again. The night thickened around us.

I growled low, grabbed her by the waist, and spun us until her back hit the patio post. My hand cradled the back of her head, her lips tasted like wine and wrath and everything in between.

"God," she whispered when our mouths broke apart.

"Do you still want me?" I whispered.

Her answer came in the way she kissed me again—desperate, slow, surrendering.

I pulled her in tighter.

Then her fingers brushed my wrist, slow, certain.

"Take me inside," she whispered.

I didn't ask if she was sure.

I just laced my fingers with hers and led her in.

Down the hallway.

Into my bedroom.

Chapter 26 – Cara

The moment his bedroom door closed behind us, I forgot how to breathe.

The room smelled like cedar and linen, like the man who had just kissed me until I came apart. Low firelight from the patio spilled through the glass doors, washing everything in a soft, golden glow. Shadows danced across the walls. My pulse thundered in my ears.

Corian stood in front of me, his chest rising and falling like he'd just finished a hard ride—and maybe he had. He reached for the buttons of his shirt, slow, deliberate. Watching me the whole time.

I stood frozen, half-drunk on wine, full-drunk on memory. This man. This *man* wasn't the boy I kissed behind the bleachers or made out with on the edge of the pond between our shared properties. This was a grown-ass man with hands big enough to break me open and the restraint to make me beg for it.

He let the shirt fall to the floor.

My throat went dry.

I took in the chest I used to sneak looks at when he changed after practice—now broader, carved with years of labor and age. That light trail of hair that dipped beneath his belt buckle? *Still there*. Still dangerous. His arms flexed as he moved, the ink on his left bicep stretching over muscle—new, beautiful, grown-man art on skin I used to know by heart.

Corian stepped toward me.

"Say the word," he said, voice like gravel and heat. "I'll stop if you need me to."

I didn't say a damn thing. I just stepped out of my heels.

His eyes tracked the motion raking back up my body to my eyes.

Then I reached behind my neck, tugged the tie loose on my dress. It floated to the floor in a hush. Bare underneath. No armor. No lace. Just me.

His breath caught.

"Jesus," he muttered.

He didn't lurch.

He approached—slow and reverent.

His hands slid up my thighs, gripped my hips, and when he leaned in to kiss me again, it wasn't soft.

It was a reclaiming.

His mouth tasted like whiskey and something feral, like everything he'd wanted to say lived in the way his tongue slid over mine. I moaned into him, my knees almost giving out when he gripped my ass and pressed me tight to his body—thick, hard, and ready.

Thirty years.

I felt every second of it in the way he handled me.

He didn't rush. Didn't stumble. This wasn't the fumbling of inexperienced horny kids. This was full-grown, full-bodied, unapologetic seduction. Every move was measured, deliberate. He kissed down my throat, down the slope of my collarbone, dropped to his knees like I was church.

"I used to dream about this," he murmured, lips brushing the inside of my thigh. "Used to lie awake thinking about how you used to taste. Wondering if I made it all up."

His mouth met me—hot, unrelenting.

I cried out, one hand fisted behind his neck, the other pressed against the wall to keep myself upright. He devoured me with a hunger that bordered on worship. Took his time. Read my body like it was a love letter he'd lost and just found under his pillow.

My knees buckled for real when I came.

He caught me.

Carried me.

Laid me gently across his bed like something precious, then hovered over me, watching my chest rise and fall.

"You good?" he asked, voice hoarse.

I laughed, breathless. "I don't even know what planet I'm on."

He smiled. Crawled over me. "Then let me bring you all the way home."

And when he entered me bare—slow, deep, full—I damn near cried. Thank God for hysterectomies and blind trust in a man who seemed destined to be my person.

My body welcomed him like he'd never left. Like time had folded in on itself and erased every pain except the one that knew how to ache for him. His hands gripped my thighs, pushed them open wider as he moved with a rhythm that knew my name.

I wrapped my legs around his waist, anchored my heels at the small of his back. He cursed, then kissed me again, this time with fire. He whispered things—low, guttural confessions—things like *I missed you, I still dream about you, I never stopped wanting this.*

I arched into him.

Matched him.

Tore at his back when he hit that spot, that place inside me no one else had ever known how to reach.

"Don't stop," I begged.

"I'm not," he growled. "Not ever."

When I came again, it wasn't quiet.

It was a release—years of waiting, of wondering, of hurting—all unraveling in a wave that drowned us both.

He followed soon after, body shaking, head buried in the crook of my neck like he was trying to fuse our souls back together.

When it was over, he didn't move.

Just stayed inside me, breathing with me. Letting the silence speak.

I closed my eyes. Let myself float in it. Thanking God for the hysterectomy, I'd had years before, because the dick he'd just given me, would have me pregnant tonight.

I was safe. Full. Found.

The first thing I felt and saw upon waking was the warmth of his body still pressed against mine and the faint rays of sun peaking in through the sliding glass doors of his bedroom.

The sheets were tangled around my legs. The aftershock of our love making, *fucking,* pulsed dull and low in my belly. He was naked as the day he was born, sprawled beside me with one arm slung heavy over my hip and his face half-shadowed by early morning sun.

Corian. He looked so peaceful. So damned handsome.

His sharp jawline sliced straight through my second thoughts about last night. He was sleep-softened but still rugged, his beard brushing against the pillow. His hand on me was possessive even while he slept.

My thighs ached. My mouth was dry. My heart?

Confused as hell.

Do I stay?

Do I sneak out like a ghost with my dignity wrapped in this sheet—before reality can catch up to me?

Because the truth is... last night healed me and wrecked me all over again. Not just my body—my mind, my heart, my carefully rebuilt armor. Corian held me like he'd never let me go. Touched me like he still knew every part of me. And damn it, I let him.

So now what?

Snuggling into his chest feels like surrender. Like forgiveness I haven't fully given. Like hope I haven't dared to speak out loud.

But slipping out the door would mean I'm still scared—that I don't trust him. Or worse, that I don't trust *me*.

And maybe... maybe I'm just not ready for the answer either way. And funny how Kima could so easily enter my thoughts in my time of need. I could clearly hear her guidance, 'Or how about just savor the dicking down you go last night and shut them silly thoughts off. Didn't you just say you were thirsty.'

Thirst won over all the overthinking.

I wrapped the sheet around me, tiptoed across the hardwood out of his bedroom and into the kitchen.

The glass was cold against my fingers. The water? Heaven. I was halfway through it when I heard the back door creak open behind me.

"Daddy, I'm making breakfast, you want—"

I turned.

She froze.

Ja'Kari.

Shit.

The look on her face wasn't shock so much as something worse—recognition.

Her eyes flicked once to the sheet barely hanging on my body, then to the glass in my hand, then to the cornbread crumbs still on the counter from last night.

Her brows lifted slightly... then her lips slowly curved into a smile full of delicious, wickedness.

"Well *damn*," she said drawing out the *a.m.n.* in damn, blinking like she was adjusting to the sight of me in all my 600-thread count, Egyptian Cotton, wrapped glory. "Dinner must have been *real* good last night."

My mouth worked around the glass. "I – uh –Ja'Kari. Hey. I didn't know—"

"Yeah–uh– me either," she grinned, sauntering to the fridge. "Didn't realize dinner would extend into breakfast too." Her face wrinkled into an apologetic grin. "I stayed at my fiancé's last night to give my dad the house so he could have a little... privacy."

My face got hotter. I adjusted the knot of the sheet at my chest.

"We usually eat Sunday breakfast together," she said as she pulled out eggs and cheese from the refrigerator. She cracked an egg one-handed into the bowl she'd reached around me to grab out of the cabinet, cool as a cucumber.

"I'm honestly glad you're still here. Kinda was rooting for it. You will stay and join us for breakfast won't you?"

I blinked. "Excuse me?"

Ja'Kari turned, leaned a hip against the counter, arms crossed, eyes dancing with mischief but I detected no shade in her words. "Girl, the look on your face right now is priceless. Please don't be embarrassed on my account."

How the hell I wouldn't be is beyond me.

She continued, "Look. Whatever transpired between the two of you last night that has you standing in his kitchen dressed like a sexy bed sheet goddess, I am here for it. Happy for y'all."

I blinked again.

She grinned wider.

"I... I should probably—" I stammered.

"Good morning."

I whipped around just in time to see Corian stroll in like a *damn billboard* for post-coital satisfaction. Bare-chested, sweatpants slung low, beard still deliciously scruffy. He looked like he hadn't slept—because well he hadn't much—and didn't appear the least bit sorry about it.

He looked at me. Then at Ja'Kari. Then back at me.

"Sorry," he said, eyes landing on me then swung back to Ja'Kari, voice scratchy and full of heat. "Morning kinda' crept up on us."

Ja'Kari rolled her eyes. "Relax, the both of you. I should have called and made sure the coast was clear. But since we're all here now, may as well enjoy some breakfast."

I gave him a narrow-eyed glare that could've boiled *his* damn eggs.

"Mmm," he grunted, raising a questioned eye at me. "Stay for breakfast?"

"Sure," I glared at him again, "Let me at least make myself presentable first."

"You look good to me just like that," he muttered. Then added, under his breath, "Or in nothing."

"Boundaries!" Ja'Kari snapped, pointing a spatula like a gavel. "Y'all grown. *Hell...* I'm grown but I'm still your child."

Corian backed off with a slow chuckle, then reached for a coffee cup.

I gave Ja'Kari a quick look full of embarrassment. "I think I'll go put my dress back on now."

She smiled. "Take your time. I'll keep the grits warm."

I nodded, ducked out of the kitchen like it might erase the heat radiating from every inch of me. Slipped back into Corian's room. Closed the door and sat for a second, just long enough to exhale.

What the hell is happening?

Thirty minutes later, I emerged in my dress from last night, hair in a quick topknot, face bare, soul… still spinning. I'd also had the thought to grab Corian's button down and tossed it into his chest as I passed by him at the island in the kitchen.

The table had been set.

Somehow, Ja'Kari had made a whole spread—cheese grits, scrambled eggs with chives, turkey sausage, and fresh-cut fruit that had no business being that juicy looking.

She handed me a mug of coffee without ceremony and motioned for me to sit.

Corian took his seat. Shirt now on, eyes full of something dangerously close to affection. I avoided his gaze and focused on the food.

The three of us ate.

At first, it was quiet. Awkward. The kind of quiet that pressed against your skin and reminded you that yes, you absolutely just got caught in a sheet by a grown man's daughter.

But then Corian said, "Guess who else is a huge Beyonce fan?" His words were directed at Ja'Kari.

She looked at me and lit up. "I knew I liked you!" Then she proceeded to tell a story about dragging Corian to a Beyoncé concert last year and how he fell asleep during the *ballads* and only woke up during "Partition."

"He tried to act like he was just resting his eyes," she said, rolling hers. "But he was snoring. *Snoring.*"

"Only because I'd worked a 14-hour day," Corian grumbled into his coffee.

"Don't let him lie," Ja'Kari said, grinning at me. "He was up bright-eyed when the beat dropped. Then tried to say, 'This one got a lil bounce.'"

I laughed—*really* laughed—at her perfect mimic of Corian's deep voice. Corian just shook his head.

And just like that, the awkwardness started to fade.

I found myself watching them, the way their rhythms synced without trying. How she teased him but respected him. How he softened around her in a way that was quiet but undeniable.

And slowly... they folded me into the conversation. Ja'Kari asked what I thought about the community center project. Asked about my brother. She even said she liked the paint colors I'd picked for the inside of the event space. Which caused me to raise my eyes to Corian's and smile. The fact he'd been sharing some of my decisions to his daughter oddly made my chest tighten in a good way.

Being around the two of them was nice. It was subtle. Easy.

And I realized something I hadn't expected to feel in this house, at this table.

Welcomed.

We lingered over coffee longer than I meant to. Laughing. Watching Ja'Kari move around her father's kitchen like she'd been running it since birth.

And despite the very awkward way this morning started, she was... kind.

Disarmingly kind and funny.

And maybe even a little conspiratorial in the way she kept stealing glances at me and her dad who had just finished clowning me about how I used to love to pick out outfits from magazines and fantasize about what my wardrobe would be when I was rich.

"Well, that hasn't changed. Shopping is my religion and luxury brands are my flock." I chuckled.

"I've been needing to get up to Atlanta," Ja'Kari said, reaching for her phone like it doubled as a social calendar. "Need to go and look for my wedding dress finally. You should come, Ms. Cara."

"Interestingly enough, Kima and I were just talking about hitting Ponce City Market and that new pop-up vintage spot in the West End next weekend."

"Girl, yesssssss." She smirked. "Sounds like we're going shopping," Ja'Kari cheered.

I shook my head, a little perplexed. Shouldn't looking for wedding dresses be something you did with your mother? I thought but was still grinning when I stood to rinse my mug. I hadn't expected any of this—not the awkwardness, not the welcome, not the warmth. Certainly not an ally in Corian's daughter.

I looked over at Corian and mouthed that I needed to go. His face wrinkled in brief disappointment but soon followed behind me after I thanked Ja'Kari for breakfast then went to gather my things and he met me at the door to walk me out.

The sun stretched wide across the yard, gold and blinding. My heels clicked against the porch as we stepped out.

Neither of us spoke right away.

He held my car door for me.

I hesitated.

"You okay?" he asked, voice low.

I nodded once, then gave a shrug that felt too honest. "I don't know."

He gave me a look. Don't quite know what it meant, but I felt like he'd conveyed with his eyes that he'd wait however long it took to figure it out with me. That he wasn't going to push. That he knew better now.

"One thing at a time, right?" He said, reading my mind.

I looked down at my car keys, then back up at him. "Let's just get through the build."

He stepped in just close enough for his voice to hit different.

"No pressure, Cara. Just... don't disappear this time."

I swallowed. "I won't."

He leaned in, kissed my forehead.

A few moments later, I slid into my car, started the engine, and pulled away.

Part 3 – Reunion and Conflict

(Bridge)
Now years have gone by, never
forgot your smile
Remember arms, 'round your
waist, gripped tight for dear life
Steel hearts done softened, got
miles to go
On leather roads, chasing dreams
that lead to home

Chapter 27 — Corian

The smell of fresh drywall dust and joint compound filled the air. We were standing in what would soon be the multipurpose room of the new community center, the walls newly sheet rocked in the portion of the old gin that we chose to keep. Construction work still continued in the new build areas, but in the last 4 weeks, even that would be done and ready for Cara's interior design plans to start being implemented within the next couple of weeks.

The echo in the empty room made everyone's voices sound a little louder than they actually were, which was probably why Marcus was over there talking like he was addressing the U.N.

"...and if we push the staging closer to the far wall, that'll give us more space for the line dancing. We'll need extra room if Kima plans to bring all her wild girlfriends down from Macon."

"Excuse you," Kima said from where she was beside Cara, hips in mid-swing, biting into a peach she'd brought from her car, as she continued showing Cara the moves to one of the popular line dance songs called Danger or something like that. She tossed over her shoulder after dropping low and winding her body back up. "We don't get wild. We get downright nasty with it."

"Same thing," Darren muttered, turning away from them, but not before I heard him said under his breath, "big, fine ass."

Cara did her own little shimmy before crouching back down on the floor beside the makeshift layout of the ride route we'd sketched in tape. She looked good. Too good. Her hair was pulled up in that messy knot she liked when she wasn't trying too hard, and her jeans fit her like they were sewn around her hips and ass.

She pivoted in her low position searching for me. Our eyes locked, and she said, "I'm thinking the trail ride loop should circle around the old hayfield and come in from the east side," she said, tapping the outline. "That way, riders return through the main gate with the community center behind them."

I was supposed to be paying attention to her map skills. But I wasn't.

I was watching the way her back curved as she leaned in, how her shoulders flexed when she pointed. Watching the way her voice dipped just a little when she was focused.

"You always look that serious when you're squatting like that?" I asked, sidling up beside her.

She giggled softly but didn't look up. "Only when I know you're watching."

Darren snorted. "Aww hell. Here they go again."

"Ignore him," I said, grinning. "He's just mad Kima don't flirt with him like that."

Kima rolled her eyes. "Please. Darren couldn't handle none of this."

Darren looked up. "Try me."

"Ohhh?" Ja'Kari chimed in, walking in with a box of water and a big 'I see you' grin in her uncle Darren's direction.

Cara looked up at me again, eyes dancing. "Your *people* are ridiculous."

"Hell they are just as much your crazy ass people as they are mine," I said, looking around at our ragtag trail ride planning committee. I replied, offering her a hand to help her stand. Then whispered for only her to hear, "As a matter of fact, they just recognize how fuckable you are to me and maybe their rooting for a little happy ending for us?" I wiggled my eyebrows at her hoped she'd bite and follow me to the completed restrooms off the entrance of the community center.

"You better get your hand away from my sister's backside before I slap the fool out of you," Marcus called.

"My bad, big dawg," I said, busted. Throwing my hands up in mock surrender, but I was grinning hard.

Ja'Kari popped her water cap and leaned against the drywall taking a sip. "So what's the final verdict on the event name?"

"There isn't one," Cara answered, looking around the space. "Not yet anyway. So far we've only agreed it should honor Mr. Ecklands' vision here."

Kima nodded. "Yeah. A celebration of legacy, healing, and the future."

"Exactly," I added. "Full of love and heart."

That sobered the mood a little. In the right way.

Cara stood beside me, brushing drywall dust from her jeans. "We'll keep it simple. A community ride in memory of Mr. Ecklands, followed by an afternoon fair and then later a southern soul inspired party. Line dancing, good food, live music. Maybe even a libation ceremony. Let the elders pour blessings into the space."

"And sparklers," Ja'Kari added. "Kids love 'em."

"Don't forget the food trucks," Marcus said. "I'm working on securing three—fish, BBQ, and one that does peach cobbler funnel cakes."

My stomach growled just hearing it. "Add a bar. Once the sun goes down, all children need to be put to bed cause it will be a grown folks party. I know a few folks who can set up cocktail stations, but we'll need a permit."

Darren raised a hand. "I'm already working on that. Got the forms on my desk."

Cara looked around the room then, her eyes softening at the sight of us all.

"You realize we've almost completed everything, right?" she asked, her voice a little quieter.

"Yep. In just over two months we've almost completed the list," I said quietly, turning to her. "I think there probably were some unlisted items we've fulfilled too..."

I looked at her then, really looked at her. Her eyes shone. Not tears exactly, but the weight of it all.

"Accurate," she said. "Mr. Ecklands brought us back together."

"This makes the second time." I grabbed her hand and pulled her into my side, pressing my lips openly on her forehead.

"Please don't tell me this nigga bout' to start crying over there." Darren said to Kima loud enough for everyone to hear him. "He starts crying, we're all gonna be forced to hug." He said this raising a brow at her suggestively. Kima rolled her eyes.

"Oh hush, Unc." Ja'Kari said. "They are cute together. You act like crying is weak."

"I ain't crying," I grumbled. "That's sweat."

"Mm-hmm," Cara teased. "Sweaty-eyed."

Everyone laughed.

The mood lifted again.

We spent another hour finalizing the details—decor, sponsorships, getting local businesses and the local radio station involved, a list of elders to invite, and who was on goat-wrangling duty for the petting zoo. That one somehow landed on Marcus.

By the time the sun had started to fall, painting the sheet rock gold through the open windows, we were all sitting on whatever we could find—milk crates, toolboxes, a random folding chair Ja'Kari pulled from her trunk.

It felt like old times and something new all at once.

And just as Darren assigned a DJ shortlist, a loud honk came from outside.

Everyone turned toward the front window.

And there he was.

"Is that lil—?" Cara started.

"Yep," I said, already smiling. "That fool is finally home."

Jaxon stepped out of his matte-black Lucid wearing shades, boots, and a hoodie that probably cost more than the ranch's monthly feed bill.

He stood beside the car like he was waiting for someone to announce him.

And because I'm petty, I did.

"Jaxon Demetrie, everybody!" I called out, voice booming. "Back from L.A. to grace us common folk with his presence!"

Jax flipped me off but was grinning by the time he reached the door.

"Y'all missed me?" He asked, stepping inside like he never left. "Don't lie."

"Missed your ass like a root canal," Darren muttered.

"Evening, ladies," Jax added, eyeing Kima and Cara. "Y'all look like Black excellence and poor choices wrapped in one." He said before swinging his eyes around the room at Darren and me.

"You're late," Cara said, hands on hips. "We just finished planning the whole damn celebration and as you can see, the building is almost done too."

He looked her over. "I'm late, but still on time with all the code you need to run the VR and tech center," he said with all the cocky swag he'd carried since birth.

I groaned. "Lord, help us."

But even as I teased, even as I shook my head at my baby brother acting a fool—I felt it.

That hum.

That rhythm.

Like something good was finally coming together.

Cara caught my eye again, her smile a quiet thing just for me.

And for the first time in a long time, I believed we just might make this work.

The planning wrapped with enough jokes and crosstalk to fill a reunion cookout. We all lingered in the space a little longer than necessary, laughing, plotting, and pretending we weren't half-exhausted from the Georgia heat and drywall fumes. But eventually, people started filing out—Darren headed back to check on the horses, Ja'Kari and Kima were talking about coordinating T-shirts, Marcus muttered something about catching the Braves game.

Jaxon was last to leave, flashing his phone at me. "Y'all got one more day to finish all the old-school prep. After that, I'm putting this thing on the metaverse, *aight*?"

"Boy, get gone," I said, clapping his back. "You headed to go see mom and dad?" I asked as he made his way out too.

And then it was just me and her.

Cara.

She'd walked out ahead of me, and when I stepped outside, she was standing at the edge of the porch, her arms crossed as the evening breeze caught her hair, lifting strands like a halo. The sky was fading into a peach-and-indigo swirl, cicadas singing a lazy praise song into the dusk.

Her car sat parked just beyond the gravel, glinting in the last light of day.

"You trying to sneak off without saying goodbye?" I asked, pulling the screen door shut behind me.

She didn't look back right away.

"Not on your life," she said softly. "I just don't want the day to end."

My heart did that thing again. That shift.

I walked over, stood behind her—not touching, just there.

"We're not done," I said. "Not by a long shot."

She glanced over her shoulder, the corner of her mouth turning up. "You always so sure of yourself?"

"When it comes to you?" I leaned down, close enough to let my breath tease her ear. "Never been more certain."

She didn't pull away. Didn't lean in either.

Just let the moment hold.

"This thing between us..." she started, still staring out over the fields, "it feels like... déjà vu."

"Maybe it is," I said. "But maybe it's also our opportunity to write another chapter of our story." I chose the word "write" rather than "end" because I didn't want this to end ever and didn't want to put that energy out into the universe.

She turned then, slow, like she was deciding how much of herself to give. Her eyes met mine. Dark, searching, open. "You keep talking like I'm staying."

I stepped closer. Close enough for her knees to brush mine. "Just hopeful."

Her fingers grazed my forearm, barely there. "Hope can be dangerous, Corian."

"I'm dangerous," I murmured. "You already knew that."

She smirked. "Not like this."

And then I kissed her.

Slow. Deep. No rush. No heat we hadn't already tasted.

But with everything behind it—every damn thing we hadn't said back then and were brave enough to say now.

Her lips parted for me, soft and willing, and I slid my tongue against hers like I was reacquainting myself with her for the umpteenth time.

She sighed into my mouth, her hands curling into my shirt, tugging me closer.

When we broke apart, it wasn't because I wanted to.

It was because if we didn't, I was going to lift her ass right on up and take her on the entry way railing; passersby be damned.

She licked her lips, breath ragged. "You always kiss like that?"

"Only you."

She exhaled, stepped back. Just a bit. Just enough to look composed again, even as her chest rose and fell a little faster than before. "I should go."

"So should I."

She turned and walked toward her car. I followed, slow, watching the sway of her hips. She had the confidence of a woman who knew she had me strung out and still wasn't quite done playing with me.

She opened the car door, paused.

"Corian?"

"Yeah?"

She looked over her shoulder, eyes dark with promise.

"I'll be over later, and I know Ja'Kari will be home so please go easy on me and don't make me regret it."

Reaching her car, I brushed a hand over her waist, then dipped my lips to her neck for one last slow taste. She shivered.

"You won't," I whispered against her skin. "But I can't promise I'll let you go before sunrise."

She laughed, pushed me back gently with a palm to my chest.

Then she slid into her car and started the engine, the loud roar cutting through the stillness.

I stood there, arms folded, watching her taillights disappear down the dirt road, the dusk folding in behind

And I knew—no matter what—this time, I wasn't letting her go.

Chapter 28 — Cara

I'd made it to the stop sign off of Old Hwy 27 before I was able to breathe again. I wasn't ready to leave Corian's side. Not really. But I needed a moment to collect myself. To stop the tremble in my thighs from how that man had looked at me while describing saddle logistics and parking options.

All I planned to do was go back to Marcus's and pack a quick overnight bag, but that's all I needed to calm my hot ass down. I groaned when I thought about how close I was to taking him up on his offer of a quickie in the not quite finished bathroom of the center while all our friends, who'd volunteered to help by the way, worked while he was breaking my back just down the hall. *Get your hot ass together, Cara...*

He talked about horses like he was daring me to ride him next.

My skin prickled just thinking about it. I took off and the rumbling of the car seat from the powerful engine of the Porsche did not help. My mouth was dry. My thoughts? Completely unhinged.

Over these last few weeks, Corian was well beyond just flirting. He was pressing on every memory we ever made. Revising old wounds into mere faded battle scars. Whispering things like *stay* with nothing but his eyes and that devastating little grin of his.

And I let him take me there too.

Worse—I was craving it. Craving for him to ask me to stay this time.

I was still about ten minutes from Marcus's, but I had to get the AC humming because just the thought of Corian had me misting in sweat. I expertly handled the sports car while digging through my purse for lip balm, then my phone.

Two missed texts from Kima that were only a string of links to funny ass TikTok videos.

And another unread message.

From Michel.

I stared at the screen like it was a grenade.

Michel: *Ma belle. Just checking in. I know we never talked much about your trip back home and how long you'd actually be there, but there are some rumblings with the investors. Have you checked in with your team? I stopped by the other day and overheard Jean-Pierre say things weren't the same without your energy. How long do you think you'll be gone?*

My stomach flipped. Not because it was unexpected. Michel had always been attentive. That European brand of "I may not own you, but I want to"—kind of possessive. Even though I'd put him, *us*, on pause. It still was a bit jarring to get this message from him out of the blue. Then it kind of pissed me off. Was he slick using the Rue d'Orleans project as a way to check in on me? True, he was one of the major investors in the project, but damn...

He'd called a couple of times since I'd been back here, but I hadn't answered or returned them. As far as I was concerned, I'd told him we were through. But this was the first time he'd texted me and brought my work or team up. Then I also remembered I hadn't really checked in with them in a while either.

Jean-Pierre had sent me some revisions to the renderings for the lobby of Rue d'Orleans. And I'd only given them a cursory look.

I hadn't touched the damn pitch deck I promised to finalize for the design investors.

The ding of another message pulled me back.

Michel: *I miss you.*

Here he go with the bullshit. Three words.

But they didn't land like they used to.

Not like Corian's hand on the small of my back. Not like his slow, sinful kisses in front of the stables two nights ago. Not like the feeling of being *wanted* by someone who didn't need to prove a damn thing.

I locked my phone and tossed it in the passenger seat like it was toxic.

Then reached for it again to hit Kima up as a distraction.

I texted Kima and told her the Atlanta shopping trip was a go. Ja'Kari was in too. Lord help me. distracting myself with finalizing shopping plans with Kima cleared my mind of all thoughts of Michel. Or my team for that matter. I pulled up to Marcus's. Ran inside giving him a peck on the cheek then quickly went to the guest room to pack my *spin the night bag.*

Chapter 29 — Corian

I was brushing down Steel Jr. when I heard her pull up.

When she finally called and told me she was on the way, I told her I'd likely be in the stables and to drive around to the front.

I didn't move at first. Just ran the soft-bristled brush along Steel's flank, steadying both of us. The boy flicked his ear, like he could smell her too.

I hoped she packed an overnight bag. I wanted her to stay because I had a surprise for her.

And now she was here.

I set the brush down and stepped around the stall just in time to see her silhouette pause outside the barn. The overhead light caught her just right—bare legs under that long sweatshirt. She looked almost as fresh and free as that first day she'd come to the stable when we were younger. Except then she had on an oversized sweatshirt with oversized jeans and flip flops. Tonight she had on an oversized sweatshirt with the tiniest of black cutoff shorts peaking out from beneath it and a pair of sharp pointed toed cowboy boots. The leather looked like butter and money. Her silvery curls were piled high, and even in the dim light, she looked like a dream wrapped in temptation.

I leaned against the stable door, arms crossed.

"You get lost on the way?" I asked, voice lower than it needed to be.

Cara looked up, a slow smile spreading. "No. You are so impatient."

"Naw. You just like making me wait."

She walked in, her steps deliberate. Her eyes never left mine. "That's because you do this thing with your mouth when you're impatient."

"What thing?" I tilted my head.

"That thing where you press your tongue to your cheek, like you're trying not to cuss me out and kiss me at the same time."

I grinned, heat rolling low and steady in my gut. "Maybe I am."

She stopped in front of me, just close enough for her breath to ghost my neck. "Maybe I like that."

God.

This woman.

I cupped the back of her neck, slow, letting my fingers slip into that thick, wild hair. Her eyes fluttered once. Her lips parted.

I kissed her.

Not rushed. Not claiming. Just the kind of kiss that says, *I see you. I've been waiting.*

Her hands slid around my waist, fingers pressing into the small of my back.

"You smell like leather and cedarwood," she whispered when our mouths finally parted.

"I live in a stable," I teased.

"Yeah, but you wear it like cologne."

She looked past me, toward the far stall where I'd left the door open to the back lot.

"What's back there?" she asked.

"Come see."

I led her out the rear exit of the stable, the warm night folding around us. Cicadas low and humming, sky inked with summer haze. Off to the side of the fence, under a floodlight I'd rigged to an old motion sensor, the Chevelle sat gleaming—matte black and chrome, hood propped open like she was still in mid-recovery. I'd moved it back there as soon as I'd gotten home, knowing I would be showing it to Cara tonight.

She froze.

"Is that a…" Her voice caught.

I nodded. "'69 Chevelle. Found it in a junk lot about ten years back. Rusted all to hell. Engine barely coughed."

She walked up to it like she was approaching something sacred. Her hand reached to trail over the front panel as she slowly walked around the car, taking in every detail. "This… this is just like my daddy's."

"I know."

She turned. "You remembered?"

"I told you. I never forgot anything about you," I said quietly. "I saw it, and all I could think about was how you used to talk about that car. Said it was the last place you remembered feeling safe when you were little."

She blinked fast, and for a second, I thought she might look away. But she didn't. She stepped closer, pressed a palm to my chest.

"You did this… for me?"

"I guess I always hoped…" I shrugged. "That one day, if you ever came back—if I ever earned the right—you'd ride with me in it."

She didn't say anything at first.

After a few moments went by, she tilted her head to the side then looked up at me. "Do you remember that night... out on Slosheye Trail?"

I paused, brows pulling. "When I rode you out on the bike?"

She nodded slowly. "To the old cemetery."

"Hell yeah, I remember." My voice dipped, curious at what made her ask that now, but memories stirring all the same. "We dared each other to write down our dreams. Said we'd read 'em out loud on the oldest grave we could find."

She smiled, soft and crooked. "Because some old ghost story said if the spirits didn't terrify us, they'd help make our dreams come true."

"The spirits of Slosheye," I muttered, chuckled under my breath. "Whole damn trail was supposed to be haunted. You remember that crooked sign? The one someone spray-painted 'WALK IF YOU WANT TO DIE' on?"

She laughed, the sound rich in the dimming light of the sky. "And yet we went anyway."

"We were stupid teenagers," I said, eyes narrowing as the vision of it came back. "Didn't even make it to the graveyard, not really. We chickened out when the wind started howling and those cows in the next field started bellowing like crazy as if they'd seen a haint."

"But we *did* make it to the pond," she whispered, eyes flickering with something brighter now.

I swallowed, nodding. "I vaguely recall laying in a bed of wildflowers like it was the damn Garden of Eden."

"It was our first time," she said, voice quiet.

I blinked. Gave a single nod but stayed quiet. It was also the moment I realized I was in love with Cara Mackey. She pressed her palm to my chest, right over the spot where my heart kicked hard against bone. She looked toward the car, toward the path leading back behind the stables.

"I want to ride with you in this car tonight. Down Slosheye Trail."

A beat passed before I said, "You sure?"

She nodded. "I want to retrace our steps and go back to that pond. I want to remember how we started."

I lowered the hood of the car and walked her around to the passenger door, firmly closing it after she slipped in. I made my way around to the driver's seat, thanking both God and Mr. Ecklands for the foresight of clearing the pathways and trails from the old Cotton Gin to the pond. Because that was the only way this beast of a car would make it back there.

The Chevelle rumbled down that dirt path—headlights brushing against pine branches. It was dark. The southern dark of the country, untouched by streetlights. There was something cozy about it now.

The pond opened up before us lit by a silver sliver of moon that cut through the majestic trees that surrounded the water.

I parked under what might have been the same old cedar we used to lie beneath and killed the engine.

She opened the door before I could get to her side.

I walked to the front of the car.

Then turned.

She reached behind her neck, pulled the sweatshirt over her head in one slow motion, and tossed it onto the hood of the car. The small black cutoffs were next.

Underneath, she wore nothing but a pair of black lace panties and confidence.

My breath left me.

"Out here? You sure?" I asked, voice thick.

"Back to our beginning? Only thing I've been sure of since you've come back into my orbit."

I walked to her like I was moving through molasses. Touched her like a man starving for softness. Kissed her again—deeper this time, with a hunger that came from years of silence and every unsaid word between us.

She climbed backwards onto the hood without breaking our kiss. Pulled me between her thighs like she was done pretending we had time to waste.

Her back arched. Her moan caught against my tongue.

And God...

The way she opened for me.

The way she welcomed me.

It wasn't just sex. It wasn't just nostalgia. It was fire and forgiveness. It was sweat and primal desire.

We made love on the hood of that Chevelle like the universe had been waiting for us to come back to this moment. Slow at first—hands and mouths all knowing, learning and relearning curves and contours, tracing old scars and new stories. Then fast—bodies colliding like thunder and flame. Only the good old steel of an American muscle car could have sustained the battering of our unchecked love making, *fucking*, and love making again.

She gripped my shoulders, nails digging in as her hips rolled up to meet mine. She gasped my name into the warm night air like a song. Like a curse. Like a promise.

"Corian," she whispered. "God... don't stop. Don't you dare stop."

"Never," I growled against her skin. "You're mine, baby. You hear me?"

Her body trembled around me, her release washing over us both like a tide pulling every ounce of grief and regret out with it.

And I gave her everything I had.

Every thrust.

Every whispered confession.

Every broken piece of the man I used to be, turned whole again under her.

When it was over, I held her in my arms, our bodies cooling in the night air. Her leg was draped over mine, her cheek against my chest. The stars blinked overhead like they were giving us their blessing.

Neither of us spoke for a long time.

Until finally, she lifted her head.

"That was..."

"Yeah," I murmured, brushing a kiss to her temple. "It was."

She sighed, content, and I felt her melt into me like we were made for this exact moment.

She smiled. Kissed me again—this time soft, almost shy.

"You're trouble."

I pulled her closer. "I've been called worse."

We stayed there for a while longer—bodies tangled, hearts open, the pond quiet behind us.

And then...

"I love you," I said.

No hesitation.

No fear.

Just the truth.

Cara didn't move.

Didn't flinch.

She just laid her head back down on my chest and whispered, "I know."

And right then?

That was enough.

Chapter 30 – Cara

The weekend in Atlanta was supposed to be an escape. No community center, which was literally less than two weeks from being complete. No trail ride planning; it was all planned, and the invites were already out. No slow-burn tension in the shape of a certain cowboy who looked like sex in boots. Just a girls' trip with Ja'Kari and Kima—shopping, Bellinis, and *gut busting* laughs.

We were already deep in the mix. It was Saturday morning, and we'd left Lily on the two-hour road trip to Atlanta at 8 AM this morning.

"I'm just saying," Kima said, adjusting her oversized sunnies as we strutted through Ponce City Market, "if these vintage Levi's don't fit my ass like freedom, I'm fighting the entire state of Georgia for my *hunnid* and fitty back."

Ja'Kari cackled, one hand on a fringed leather crossbody bag. "Sis, that's what tailoring is for."

"Tailoring?" Kima stopped dead in her tracks. "I *am* the fit and these motherfuckers better fit like they were made just for me."

I laughed so hard I snorted. "You know you could have just tried them on before buying them, right?"

"Yes, I could have. But the way these unsanctioned hot flashes be doing me, I might air this bitch out from the irritation of it all," she said, waving a hand, fanning her brow.

"Kima, girl, stop playing. You are not in perimenopause yet," I swatted her arm.

"No, I'm not. But, *bitch*, let my big ass blame it on something other than me sweating from trying to shimmy *it* and these wide ass hips in these skin-tight jeans. You know vintage means no stretch."

"That part," Ja'Kari tossed over her shoulder.

We were gliding through the market like it was a runway. Bellinis in hand—courtesy of Kima's contraband thermos—and a playlist in Ja'Kari's tote bag speaker that ping-ponged from Megan to Ma Rainey with no apology.

I was dressed in a wrap dress I hadn't worn since Paris, feeling just enough sexy, just enough Southern. Kima had on a cute pair of high-waisted mom jeans cropped just above the ankle with a pair of fresh white chucks and her signature graphic tee. Ja'Kari had on a simple black tank, with a flared tennis skirt that damn near had her ass cheeks hanging out the bottom. The age gap of it all. Yet, we were having a good old time..

That is... until my phone buzzed. Again.

Back-to-back.

As usual, Kima clocked it instantly.

"That's the third time in twenty minutes. Who's blowing up your line like that? Please don't tell me it's fake as Cowboy Carter requesting you come bounce on his saddle."

I smirked, checking the screen. "Nope. I wish. Worse," I said glancing to make sure Ja'Kari was out of earshot.

"Worse damage than that man's hands on your hips, trying to blow your back out? I find that hard to believe."

I flipped the phone so Kima could see who the avoided call was from: *Michel.*

Ja'Kari, was already halfway down the aisle in an oversized denim jacket that was longer than her skirt. Actually, the combination had no business looking that good. I winked at her and gave her a thumbs up when she stopped midway raising a brow and striking a model pose. I was glad she'd busied herself with trying on clothes, because I didn't want her to see that my lover from the not-too-distant past was blowing up my phone.

I shoved the phone into my purse. "It's nothing."

Kima looked at me sideways. "Nothing don't call you three times back-to-back like that."

We breezed into the next shop, past a rack of sequined cowgirl hats and overpriced candles shaped like Greek busts. The sexy guy behind the counter gave us an appreciative once over. Oblivious to my mess, Ja'Kari grinned at him, then made a beeline to a rack with a dress that had caught her attention.

"Y'all, help me decide," she sauntered over holding the interesting bright, peach-colored piece up, pressing it against her body "I know we have an appointment at the bridal shop, but I was thinking maybe a non-traditional wedding dress. Something like this." She looked back and forth between Kima and I, expectant.

"Let's go!" Kima said, snatching the dress from her hands. "It's giving 'Say Yes to the Dress: Country Edition'."

I just lowered my head, holding my laugh in at the dejected look on Ja'Kari's face.

"It's not that bad." she pouted.

"But it is," I looked at her apologetically to soften the blow. Then wrapped my arm around both hers and Kima's shoulders and led us towards the exit. It was time we headed over to the Bridal shop down on Auburn Avenue.

The moment we stepped into Adele's Atelier, the world outside dulled in comparison.

It was like walking into a dream painted in soft gold and ivory—the kind of place that didn't just sell dresses but conjured *moments*. Velvet curtains draped high above arched doorways, their folds puddled like spilled silk onto polished marble floors. Delicate crystal chandeliers hung overhead, catching the light and scattering it across the walls in shimmering fragments.

Rows of gowns floated along brass racks—silks, tulles, lace so fine it looked like it had been spun by moonlight. Some were dramatic—cascading ruffles and plunging necklines that begged for a cathedral. Others were minimalist, all clean lines and whispered elegance, waiting to be brought to life by the right woman. I'd never been inside a bridal boutique before. I was as awestruck as the look on Ja'Kari's face.

The scent inside the boutique was a mix of white peonies and sweet champagne, subtle but luxurious. In the back, a grand mirrored platform waited for its next transformation, flanked by plush cream settees and small gold tables that held crystal flutes already half-filled with bubbly.

The sales associate who greeted us wore a soft gray jumpsuit with fashion-forward heels and a kind practiced smile.

"Welcome to Adele's," she said, voice smooth as a string quartet. "You must be Ja'Kari," she reached out to grasp Ja'Kari's hand. "Are we ready to find the one?"

Ja'Kari let out a breathless little laugh. "Let's get it."

Kima clapped her hands. "We're about to shut this whole boutique down."

And as we followed her deeper into the beautiful space—her heels clicking like confidence led us across the marble to the settees.

Ja'Kari disappeared into the velvet-curtained fitting room. Kima and I sat gingerly on the silk-covered settees and clinked our two champagne flutes together.

Then the front door opened causing both Kima and I to look in that direction.

I recognized her instantly. Same short petit frame and pixie cut. Yes, she'd aged over the years. But how could I ever forget her or the sound of her voice? All was confirmed when Ja'Kari walked out with her first wedding dress on.

"Mom?" she said, as if she was just as surprised to see her mother, Monica, as Kima and I were. Ja'Kari moved towards her with tiny almost hopping steps due to the white lace mermaid gown that hugged her like a glove.

Yep. *Monica.* The ghost of wives past. Although I'd never officially met her, everything about her was etched in my memory. I mean, why wouldn't I remember. The small second I encountered her all those years ago, caused a ripple effect through my entire world. And now she was here in the bridal boutique her daughter had invited me to. Eyeing me like I was dog hair on a Chanel suit. Obviously, she knew who I was too. Note to self, I should have followed my first mind that day sitting in Corian's kitchen when Ja'Kari invited me on this outing and politely said no to this.

"I thought you and Brian were going to be out of town?" Ja'Kari said when she pulled away from her mother's embrace.

"Now you know I was not going to miss my only baby's wedding dress try on, now," Monica said smiled up at her beautiful daughter before narrowing her eyes and cutting them over at me. "And look, I get the added bonus of finally meeting the woman that thought it would be ok to play mama and help my daughter on such an occasion that only her actual mother should lead," she said, smiled so hard and fake, that shit had to hurt. "Hello, *Clara*. Can't say it's a pleasure to finally meet you... here."

I blinked rapidly, taken totally aback by what was just said. I looked to Ja'Kari first just to be sure this wasn't some sort of setup. But the shocked and apologetic look on her face made it clear that it was not. Then I looked back at her mother. Opting to not show my ass on what was already pointed out as a *special mother daughter occasion*. "It's Cara and no, we haven't met have we. The pleasure is all mine," I said standing and reaching out to shake her hand.

Monica just looked at my hand in disdain. But the fake smile didn't budge from her face. "Mm. Not officially. But trust me, you're presence was definitely known throughout my marriage." With that she moved passed me, taking a glass of champagne from the tray and plopping down on the settee. "Well let's get this show on the road. Go stand on the pedestal, honey so I can see this dress." I was all but dismissed.

Ja'Kari shot me a quick glance—guilt and frustration battling behind her lashes. "Mama, I invited Cara. And Kima too. They're helping me today."

Kima stepped closer to me, her stance casual but her tone not. "We're just here to hype your daughter. No disrespect meant unless you want this smo—"

I cleared my throat effectively cutting Kima off before she threatened to whoop Monica's ass.

"Of course," Monica said, eyes never leaving mine. "I just thought... something as special as this would be a... family affair."

My spine stiffened. But I didn't take the bait.

I said smoothly. "As Kima was saying, we're just here to celebrate your beautiful daughter. No disrespect was meant."

She nodded once, then turned to Ja'Kari with a less severe smile. "That one's nice. But let's try an A-line dress like the one I sent you. It'll flatter your hips better."

"Whew," Kima whispered, "the devil does indeed wear Prada."

Ja'Kari mouthed *I'm sorry*.

I just shook my head and mouthed back, "*It's your day,*" and winked at her.

I backed away, holding a hand up to stay Kima as I stepped out the front door to breathe and pulled out my phone.

5 missed calls7 texts.

From Michel. Jean-Pierre. And now Delia.

Shit.

I hit Michel's name.

He picked up on the first ring.

"Cara."

"Michel, I was going to call you tonight, but I see all these missed—"

"Initially when you left, you said a couple of weeks. It's been almost ten," He said, cutting me smooth the fuck off.

"Ok, and?" I responded heatedly. "Last I checked, I worked for Cara Mackey. Not you, Michel."

"Well if you did work for me, you'd be fired for this. The Rue d'Or-leans project permits have been pulled, because of your design decisions and you are not even here. Leaving your team to deal with the fall out."

His words stopped my breath. "What?"

"We're facing a full shutdown," Michel continued. "One of the his-torical societies filed a complaint. Something about improper restoration methods. The mayor's office is involved. And now investors are pissed and threatening to walk."

"What the hell? My team would have told me about this," I wanted to yell, but how would I know, but my confidence wavered. I hadn't really been making myself available to my team lately. Caught up in the community center... in Corian. Changing my tone, I asked, more to myself than Michel. "Why hasn't anyone from my team called me?"

He paused. "Because I'm on the money side of this, *Ma Belle*. I hear these things first. But trust me, they're probably scrambling now."

I pulled the phone away and scanned my messages. They'd all sent messages. Jean-Pierre. Delia. Even Bonet, the intern on the project. All panicked. All urgent.

Michel's voice softened. "You are the face of this. The passion. And now you're... what? Playing cowgirl while your project is falling apart?"

The guilt hit like a slap.

"You must come back as soon as possible and fix this."

Kima appeared beside me, face serious now. "Everything okay?"

I shook my head but held up a finger and asked her for a second for me to finish the call with Michel. "I'll be on the next plane." I ended the call.

I looked at Kima, defeated. "No. Not even close to being okay."

The joy from earlier? Gone.

Replaced by a sick churn in my stomach and a weight on my chest that I couldn't shake.

I had stayed in Lily too long.

And now everything I'd built in Paris was falling apart.

I forced a breath, looked through the glass doors toward the fitting room where Ja'Kari was standing with her mom.

Their closeness sent a longing through me. Mother and daughter, a bond that I'd lost at such an early age. A bond that I'd never had the opportunity to experience with a child of my own.

I didn't know who I was in this moment. I was torn between wanting to be the woman building a future in a town that once broke her and the version of me who had built an empire that was now crumbling.

And for the first time since coming home... I didn't know which way to run.

Chapter 31 — Corian

I entered through the front screen door of our parents' home and even if I were trying to sneak up on them, I couldn't coming in this way. The screen door creaked, *loudly*, like it always did. It was a sound as familiar as my mother's voice calling one of our full government names from the porch just beyond it. I stepped inside just in time to hear Jax curse under his breath.

"Don't slam that damn cabinet, boy," Mama called from the back.

I grinned and caught the door behind me before it added to the drama. The house smelled like fried chicken, fresh biscuits and gravy. Darren was posted up at the table, still in his riding boots, laptop open, and AirPods in. Jax stood at the stove like he owned it, one eyebrow arched while he stirred something that smelled too good for a man who just flew in a week ago. Mama had to have given him lessons in cooking over the last few days because I swear when this boy left for college, he would have sat in his room and starved to death if someone didn't basically hand deliver him a plate to the table.

"Look who finally made it," Jax said without turning.

"Y'all start without me?" I asked, tossing my hat on the sideboard.

"We've been here all day," Darren said, tugging one bud from his ear. "Some of us actually know how to be on time."

Mama poked her head in from the laundry room. "Don't let them boys guilt-trip you, baby. You got that center to finish."

She always had a way of balancing the scale when my brothers got to *chirpin'*. I leaned down and kissed her cheek.

"Smells like your boy's been throwing down," I said.

Mama rolled her eyes. "You know I had to come in here and rescue him and my kitchen earlier. Damn near started a grease fire."

"I was *experimenting*," Jax huffed. "Y'all act like ya' *mans* can't innovate in the kitchen."

Waynan Demetrie cleared his throat from the recliner in the front room. "Ain't nobody asked for you to turn collard greens into liquid morse code, Jaxon."

The three of us burst out laughing.

Darren shut his laptop with a satisfying snap. "Hence the reason we don't have any vegetables with this meal." He snickered.

Ma opened the deep freezer off the back porch, bringing something in to pop into the microwave for thawing and heating. "Now you know, I ain't letting no family dinner at *my* table go down without at least one side of collard greens. Got some macaroni and cheese out here too if y'all boys want some."

I made a bee-line right for the deep freezer and grabbed the frozen container of that too.

"Alright, while that's heating, let's handle some business first," Darren continued in the mist of the commotion going on around him in the kitchen. "I leave in three weeks for Turkey."

"Three weeks?" I frowned. "I thought it was five."

He nodded. "We moved it up. The Turkish breeder wants to close before Democracy and National Unity Day, one of their major holidays. Not trying to let anything get in the way of this deal."

Waynan grunted. "Deals don't mean shit if y'all forget where you came from."

"We haven't," I said, locking eyes with him. "That's why we're sitting in your house, eating your food, building a future on Demetrie soil."

Mama came over and pinched my cheek. "That's why you're my favorite."

"Boy, don't let her lie to you," Jax said. "I'm the cute one."

"You're the expensive one," Darren muttered.

Jax flipped him off.

"Anyway," Darren continued, "we need to finalize the AR installation with Jax's team before I go. If we get the immersive exhibit up and running by soft launch, it'll be a game changer and Jax, while I'm there I'd like to get you online to demo some of the more ranch specific tech to the buyers."

Jax crossed his arms. "Can do. I already got two developers on-site here Monday for the live test at the community center. They walked me through some of the features last night and it gave me chills. It's going to blow those buyers away."

I looked around the room at my brothers and felt a weight in my chest. Not the heavy kind. The good kind. The kind that comes from knowing you're walking in your calling with your woman and whole family with you to boot.

"Now that that's settled, the trail ride is two weeks away and we still need to schedule the dress rehearsal for it too," I added.

"And you?" Jax smirked. "What are you handling, big bro?"

"I'm making sure the horses are ready. And the legacy stands tall."

Darren raised an eyebrow. "That legacy includes that fine woman riding shotgun in your life again?"

Jax whooped.

"Oh, we going there today?" I puffed up my chest but couldn't stop the corners of my mouth from edging up at the brotherly love going around the room.

Mama clucked her tongue and waved a dishrag. "Don't y'all start mess in my kitchen. But for real Corian, why haven't you brought that pretty lady around. Ja'Kari called and told me you couldn't keep your hands off the girl. She was a beauty when y'all were young. Bet she's even more gorgeous with age."

Waynan didn't say a word, but the look he gave me could cut steel. That old school, never-forget-what-you-left-behind kind of look.

"You got something to say, Daddy?" I asked, voice even.

He leaned forward, in his chair in the living room, peering into the kitchen with his elbows on his knees and jaw set. "You sure you're ready to have that woman back in your life full-time?"

I blinked. "Why wouldn't I be?"

"Hell, didn't she run off and leave your ass once? You think she won't do it again?"

Mama sucked her teeth. "Now why you gotta stir the pot?"

"I'm just saying," Pops said. "You been pining for that girl since before Ja'Kari was born. Now she back for a New York minute and you losing focus."

"I haven't lost focus. If anything, Cara has helped me regain some purpose," I snapped. "I'm still here. Still building. Still grinding. And I'm not gonna apologize for loving the same woman I loved since I was eighteen."

Silence fell over the room sharp and sudden..

Then Darren exhaled. "Well damn."

Mama walked over and rubbed my shoulder. "Ain't nothing wrong with a man knowing his heart."

Jax, of course, had to be Jax. "As long as she don't break it again."

Just then, my phone buzzed.

A name I hadn't expected to see on my phone screen.

Monica.

I stepped away and answered. "Hello?"

Her voice was sharp. "You really let *her* take our daughter wedding dress shopping?"

I blinked. "What?"

"Cara. Mackey." Monica punctuated Cara's first and last name adding base in her voice before each pause. "Whatever her name is. Ja'Kari mentioned one of your little friends would be there helping her pick out gowns. So I pulled up and low and behold, *your* high school sweetheart is there at our child's big day of picking out her gown, laughing like she belonged. You let the same woman who blew up our life *play mama* to our daughter?"

I rubbed my temple. "She wasn't playing anything. Ja'Kari invited her."

"And you didn't say no?"

"Ja'Kari's a grown woman. I'm not gonna tell her who she can and can't invite anywhere. Plus, Ja'Kari said you couldn't make it."

Monica's voice dropped. "You always did let that woman lurk up and through our marriage like a goddamn ghost, ever waiting to just go *peek-a-boo I'm back!* I guess you finally got what you wanted all these years."

"Monica, I'm not exactly sure what the hell is going on right now, but Cara was invited by our daughter. So if you have an issue with that, get over it. Ja'Kari is grown and makes her own choices. Perhaps you should ask her why she invited Cara Instead of calling me trying to start shit. Ain't no fish biting here."

"Well, enjoy your fairytale," she said coldly. "But don't let her rewrite the story. You and I both know how it really went down."

She hung up before I could respond.

I stood there, staring at my phone like it might give me answers.

It didn't.

Just like it didn't tell me how to protect the peace I had just started to build with Cara.

I just barely made it through dinner after that call from Monica. What she'd said to me cut deep. God only knows what she may have said to Cara. *Why fucking now?* Just when I was getting comfortable in this thing with Cara, my past came around to bite it in the ass.

The panic I felt all those years ago when Cara walked away came back now. Especially since I hadn't heard from her since this morning and all my calls were going to voicemail.

After dinner I'd come out on the porch. Needed a moment alone to think.

I tried her number once more. Straight to voicemail.

That made five calls in total. No reply.

I leaned on the porch rail, arms braced, the weight of everything pressing down on my spine.

The screen door creaked open behind me.

I didn't turn.

Mama's steps were slow, familiar. A rhythm I knew in my bones.

"You gone stew all night out here," she asked, "or you want company?"

I gave a tired smile. "Just thinking."

"Mm-hmm. That 'thinking' look always comes with a jaw that could break steel."

She eased beside me on the bench, her house dress soft and faded, slippers whispered across the boards. A glass of iced tea in one hand, a floral fan in the other, working overtime in the humid night.

We sat in the quiet for a beat. The cicadas kept singing like they didn't care my whole chest felt hollow.

"You want to talk about it?" she asked.

I surprised even myself when I just spit it out. "Monica called."

She nodded, waiting for me to say more.

"Apparently she popped in on Ja'Kari's and Cara's shopping trip today and accused me of letting Cara play house with our daughter."

I turned my head toward her. "She said I let the woman I pined after our entire marriage waltz back in like she's got a claim to what she built."

Mama hummed, fan still moving steady. "Monica always did have a gift for twisting the truth to fit the wound she refuses to heal."

"She ain't wrong, though," I said quietly. "Well she's wrong about Cara trying to play house with our grown daughter, but I did pine. Even when I tried not to. Even while being faithful to Monica our entire marriage, I did pine for Cara."

"She knows that," Mama said. "And that's the part that stings her most."

I shifted, rubbed the back of my neck. "What if I'm wrong about Cara, now? She has a whole life in Paris, but I feel it in my bones that we are meant to be."

She paused, her fan stilling.

"What if I'm just filling in the blanks with who I wish she still was? She's not even answering my calls right now. What if she's already gone again, Mama, and I'm just standing here like a damn fool waiting on a call that ain't coming?"

She turned to me then. No judgment. Just that calm she'd always had.

"You want the truth?"

I nodded.

"She left all those years ago to better herself," Mama said. "And she told you the plan. She never left you. You let her go. Then you broke what you had when you got Monica pregnant."

I flinched. Didn't expect her to say it like that.

"Monica didn't trap you. But she sure didn't make it easy to look back. And you thought doing the 'right thing' meant burying the *real* thing."

I swallowed hard. "I thought being a man meant standing in my mess."

"And maybe it did," she said, softer now. "You raised a daughter with love. You held this family together when your daddy lost his leg. You built a life out of bricks and regret."

She touched my knee then. "But now you've got a second chance. Not with just any woman. With *her*. And baby, real love don't show up twice unless it's meant to stay."

"But what if I mess it up again?"

"Then you own it. Like a man. But don't you dare walk away outta fear." She looked at me fully now. "That ain't the Demetrie way."

A lump caught in my throat. "I been calling her all day, Mama. She ain't picking up."

"Maybe she's not ready to talk. Maybe she's scared too. Who knows what Monica may have said to Cara."

I shook my head. "Yeah well that and she's built a life over there. In Paris. She's got a team, a reputation, a whole world that don't include me."

Mama's eyes gleamed. "But her heart still does, baby. Or else she wouldn't have stuck around this long. Wouldn't be opening herself to all this mess and memories."

Mama leaned back, fan swaying again. "You want to know what kind of man you are now?"

I glanced at her.

"You're the kind who can love better than he did the first time. The kind who earned the right to try again."

And with that, she stood, kissed my temple like I was still her boy with scraped knees and a bruised spirit, and walked back inside.

Leaving me alone with the quiet hum of the porch swing and the weight of love I wasn't ready to lose.

Chapter 32 — Cara

The lights of I-75 blurred past the window, but I barely saw them. My phone sat in my lap, dark now. Silent. As if even it had run out of things to say.

Kima drove, one hand on the wheel, one on a fast-food cup sweating peach tea into the console. She hadn't said much since we pulled out of Atlanta. Just... gave me space. The kind only a real friend could give without making it feel like distance.

I stared out at the dark ribbon of road ahead, my thoughts a tangle of broken promises and blinking notifications.

The call with Michel kept replaying. His voice. That sharp, clipped tone that used to unravel me. Now? It just left a bruise.

Because he was right.

I'd told myself Paris would understand. That a few extra weeks back home was fine. But the truth? I hadn't checked in with anyone but Delia in over a month. Hadn't opened the project files in nearly as long.

And now? The whole damn hotel was at risk. My name. My vision. My career.

Kima glanced over at me, her voice soft. "You good?"

"No," I said, blunt. "But I will be."

She nodded like that was enough—for now. And it was.

Ja'Kari had stayed behind in Atlanta with her mom, smoothing things over after Monica's little pop-up performance at the bridal boutique. I didn't ask what happened after I left. I wasn't sure I could stomach it.

I texted Corian.

Just one line: "Made it back safe. Need a little space. Will explain soon."

He hadn't responded.

And I didn't blame him.

Because this time? It wasn't about the past. It was about the present unraveling at my feet.

And I had no idea how to hold it all together.

Kima had dropped me at Marcus's house before heading home, her hug tight and her parting words soft: *"Whatever you decide, you're not alone."*

But right now, alone was exactly how I felt.

I was still sitting at Marcus's breakfast bar in one of his oversized tees, hair a mess, laptop open and untouched, when he walked in with two takeout bags from Bird Dog BBQ.

"I figured you hadn't eaten," he said, setting the food down like a peace offering. "And before you say no, I got the peach cobbler too."

I blinked at him, lips twitching. "You trying to guilt me into a meal?"

"I'm your little brother. Guilt is my love language." He sat across from me, started unpacking ribs and mac and cheese like he knew damn well I wouldn't say no.

I watched him a moment—his broad shoulders still cut like he never missed a gym day, even though the NFL was behind him now. He was settled, grounded. Still funny as hell. And despite everything we went through as kids... he'd turned out pretty damn solid.

"You ever miss it?" I asked quietly. "The field?"

He shrugged. "Some days. Not the pain, though. Not the pressure. I like my life quiet now. Predictable."

I scoffed. "Must be nice."

He narrowed his eyes at me. "That bad?"

I hesitated.

Then I let it out.

"The project in Paris is falling apart. Investors are threatening to pull out. The city's on my ass about a historical restoration violation and I'm just... here. Stuck. Torn."

Marcus leaned back, chewing slow. "And you think you need to fix it all?"

"I *do* need to fix it all. It's my name on the contracts. My vision they bought into."

He nodded. "Yeah. And who was there helping you bring that vision to life?"

"My team."

"So maybe let them help you now."

I didn't say anything.

He pushed the container of cobbler toward me. "You always think you gotta hold the whole world on your back, Sis. But look where that's gotten you. You're burnt out. You're doubting yourself. And you're trying love a man who's waited thirty damn years for you while also managing a whole international build with a pissed-off French ex breathing down your neck."

I blinked. "You knew about Michel?"

He smirked. "Girl, I *know* everything. Kima called me after y'all got back. Said your eyes looked like somebody had poured regret into 'em and set you on fire."

I laughed despite myself, covering my face. "I swear, I'm gonna block her."

"No you ain't." He leaned in, serious now. "Whatever you decide to do—go back to Paris or stay—I got your back. Always. But make sure it's your decision. Not one made out of guilt. Not one made outta fear. Yours."

I nodded, throat tight.

Marcus reached for his fork. "Now eat this damn food before it gets cold. We'll solve the rest tomorrow."

The food helped. A little. The cobbler helped more.

But it was the silence after Marcus went to bed that finally pushed me to open my laptop.

I sat cross-legged on the guest bed, wrapped in a throw blanket, my phone and laptop side by side, both buzzing with long-ignored messages. My inbox was a wreck—Jean-Pierre had sent three follow-ups, Delia had escalated her subject line to *URGENT - Call ASAP*, and Bonet, sweet baby intern Bonet, had forwarded a photo of a municipal citation stamped in red at the front entrance of the hotel with the caption: *This real? Please advise.*

I swallowed hard.

The warm glow of the lamp suddenly felt accusatory. Like the walls of Marcus's peaceful, quiet home were bearing witness to my unraveling.

I clicked into the email chain between Michel and the investors. The threads went deep. Legal consultants. PR concerns. Historic council letters. And tucked in the middle of one of the longer replies from Michel, a sentence I hadn't expected:

"I know Cara. She'll fix this. She's just... lost right now."

I stared at the screen.

He wasn't wrong.

But he also wasn't the one to guide me back.

With shaking fingers, I finally clicked "Join" on the Teams meeting link I'd asked Jean-Pierre to set up before we left Atlanta. It was 1:30am in Lily and 7:30am, Paris time. The whole team would be on.

The screen opened on Jean-Pierre's tired face. He looked like he hadn't slept in two days.

"Cara," he said softly, relief flooding his features. "Finally."

Delia appeared in the second box, brows pinched. "You're alive."

"I'm sorry," I said, the words falling heavy. "I should've called. Sooner. I should've—"

"We were scared," Jean-Pierre interrupted. "That something had happened. Or that you'd abandoned it all."

Delia didn't speak. She just stared at me. Waiting.

I took a deep breath. "I didn't abandon anything. I needed time. But I should've stayed more connected. I left too much hanging without clarity, without support. That's on me."

Delia's jaw flexed, the tension written all over her face..

"It's not just about being disconnected, Cara. You are the center of this. The vision. The name. When the face of a project disappears, people assume it's collapsing, and I think that's what's happening."

I winced. "I know."

"I defended your design with the historical society," she said. "But we're at the tipping point. We need you here."

I nodded slowly, guilt thickening in my chest.

"I'll fly back," I said. "Give me forty-eight hours. I'll be in Paris by the end of the week."

Jean-Pierre blinked. "Really?"

"I owe it to all of you. And to myself."

Delia's face softened a fraction. "Good. We'll prepare."

The call ended. But the weight in my chest didn't lift.

I sat still for a long moment, just staring at the darkened laptop screen. My reflection stared back—tired, bare-faced, eyes rimmed with too many thoughts.

I had come back to Lily to honor a legacy. To heal. To reconnect.

And I had.

But I couldn't pretend the rest of my life wasn't calling.

The work I loved. The people who believed in me. The version of myself that fought to build something from nothing.

I pressed a palm to my chest, steadying the ache.

How do you love two lives at once?

How do you tell the man who makes your whole body remember what it means to belong that you have to leave him again?

How do you make it feel different... when the choice still feels like a betrayal?

I didn't have an answer.

Not yet.

But I knew what I had to do.

And it would start with telling Corian.

Chapter 33 – Corian

The old cotton gin was humming with energy. And this time, it wasn't the ghosts of the past. It was the promise of the future.

The tin roof rattled with the wind, but the inside smelled like sawdust, fresh wiring, and new beginnings. We'd framed out two of the tech-enabled stables already—the ones that would become the core of our equine therapy program—and I was overseeing the final electrical checks on the east wing when I heard Jax cursing in the back.

"Yo, Corian! These mounts for the VR rig need bracing. What did your contractor use, hot glue?!"

I wiped sweat off my brow, already headed his way.

Jax was crouched near the loading dock with a wiry guy in a black tee and tool belt, gesturing wildly at a wall mount for the AR interactive platform.

"They install this wrong, and it'll fall the first time somebody gets excited in a simulation."

"Handled," I said, nodding at the guy to reinforce it. "And no more yelling. You scare off one more volunteer and I'm docking your pay."

"I don't get paid," Jax muttered.

"Exactly."

Darren leaned against a temporary workbench, clipboard in hand, tapping something into his phone. He was calmer today. Focused. Probably double-checking his notes before his trip to Turkey.

Three weeks. He'd be gone in three weeks for three weeks to negotiate the horse breeding deal that could change the future of our ranch and the whole damn community center.

And we were almost ready.

Almost.

"You see this?" Jax said, thumbing toward the east wall. "This shit's starting to look like a real facility."

"Because it is," Darren added, glancing up. "On time. Under budget. Cara's renderings came together like magic."

The mention of her name did something to my chest.

I hadn't heard from her in damn near two days. A couple dry-ass texts. No call. No voice. No *her*.

Not the way I needed. Not the way that tells a man he ain't just a little moment, a short detour in her big life.

But she'd said she needed space. Said something was going on with her project back in Paris and she needed to be on the same time zone as her team. I gave her space. Even though every second of it made my chest feel like it was lined with barbed wire.

I adjusted the framing chalk line, double-checked the angle, and was about to move on when I heard it, the steady crunch of the Porsche's tires on gravel, low and certain.

My spine straightened before my brain could catch up.

That sound lived somewhere deep inside me now.

Cara.

She stepped out of the car slowly, sunglasses on, hoodie zipped, bag slung over one shoulder.

Not her usual confident strut. Not the slow tease of a woman who knew she'd have my attention the second she arrived.

She looked... I couldn't put my finger on it, but I didn't like it.

She walked toward me, careful, deliberate. Like she didn't want to kick up dust she wouldn't be around to clean up.

"Hey," I said, wiping my hands on my jeans. I couldn't stop the small grin forming. "You bring me lunch or something?"

She shook her head slowly. Then pushed the glasses up onto her curls.

"I'm flying back to Paris."

I didn't respond.

Couldn't.

The wind kept blowing. Tools kept buzzing in the background. But everything else stopped.

"You're what?" I asked.

She swallowed hard. "I didn't want to say anything until I had more details. I knew you'd have questions. I didn't want to... make it real yet. But the calls keep coming, the team needs decisions, and the investors are threatening to pull out."

Her eyes flicked to mine, guilt and urgency tangled up behind them. "I have to go.." I stepped back before I even realized it. Like her words had physically burned me. Like I needed room to brace myself.

"Before we finish," I paused, staring at her, knowing my words weren't just about the community center or Mr. Ecklands' legacy, "here?"

"I can't let them pull the project. It's spiraling, and I'm the face. I'm the lead."

I looked down at my hands. Callused. Dirty. Stained with the very place she helped imagine. Finally, I asked point blank. "You coming back?"

Her shoulders sank before she looked away, but not before I saw the shimmer of tears in her eyes. "I don't know."

"You told me this—this place, we—meant something."

"It does," she said quickly. Too quickly.

"But you're still leaving."

"I have to," he r words landed with finality.

Jax's voice shouted something from across the room, but I couldn't make sense of what he was saying. I only saw her. Hair pulled up. Face closed off. Wearing goodbye like it was stitched into the hem of her hoodie.

"Running again?" I asked, voice like gravel.

She blinked. Hurt. "This isn't about running. It's about the life I built before I came back."

She paused—then stepped closer, like she couldn't stand the space between us but didn't know how to close it.

"That life didn't stop existing just because I came home. I have responsibilities. People depending on me. And I... I've been trying to figure out how to be both things."

Her voice wavered. "But I never said I was staying gone. I said I had to go."

I looked at her—really looked. And damn if it didn't make me feel like the dirt under her feet had more certainty than I did.

I took a breath, deep and slow. Because anything faster might break something inside me.

"Well," I said finally. "Thanks for letting me know."

"Corian—"

But I was already walking away. I couldn't take it, the feeling that we were no longer, again. Not right there. Not in the building that had her fingerprints on every damn beam.

I heard her turn back toward the car. The door shut gently.

And just like that, the air left the gin.

The boys kept working. The tools kept buzzing. But it felt like the whole damn project had split straight down the middle.

I didn't say a word.

Didn't call out to her. Didn't ask her to stay. Didn't demand a damn thing.

I just watched Cara climb into her car, wrap her fingers around the steering wheel like it was the only solid thing left, and drive away.

Dust curled in the air behind her, a soft and slow goodbye.

The sound of the construction crew hammering something back into place echoed from inside the building, but it all felt like background noise. Like I wasn't standing in the middle of my life watching the best part of it slip away

I turned on my heel, jaw locked and stomped toward my truck. Jax called after me, saying something about the VR rig, but I didn't answer.

I slammed the door, cranked the ignition, and peeled off so fast the tires spit gravel toward the edge of the job site. I didn't even look back. Didn't need to.

I knew if I did, I'd see the community center rising behind me—steel bones and fresh paint—and I'd wonder why the hell it all suddenly felt so empty.

The road blurred in front of me as I sped through Lily, barely tapping the brakes at stop signs. Ten minutes later, I was turning down the long gravel path toward the Demetrie ranch, the house rising slow over the hill like it had been waiting for me to come home broken again.

But I didn't stop at the house.

I veered off toward the stables.

Steel was already watching me when I pulled up, pacing along the gate like he'd sensed it—my storm.

I jumped out the truck, grabbed the saddle and bridle from the tack room without even closing the door behind me.

"C'mon, boy," I murmured, my voice rough.

He didn't argue. Didn't flinch. Just stood steady while I threw the saddle on, cinched it with shaking hands, and climbed up like muscle memory had taken the wheel.

I didn't need a destination.

Just needed motion.

We tore out across the pasture like fire and fury, hoofbeats pounding the ground like war drums, like protest, like grief.

I didn't look at the house. I didn't think about Paris.

I just rode.

Tight circles through the trees. Sharp turns along the back fence. Breath ragged. Mind spiraling.

Because dammit—I was doing the work. I was showing up. I was building the damn dream.

But I couldn't make her come back no matter how bad I hoped she would.

I rode until my thighs burned and Steel's flanks gleamed with sweat under the afternoon sun. Until the ache in my chest drowned out the buzz of my phone ringing in my pocket for the third time.

Her name lit up the screen.

Cara.

But I didn't answer.

Because I needed to breathe. To feel something steady underneath me.

To remember who the hell I was before she walked back in and lit a match under all the places I'd tried to bury.

And yeah—maybe I'd still love her tomorrow.

But today?

Today I needed to ride it out.

By the time I rode Steel back into the barn, the light was fading low across the Demetrie land. That deep, amber haze that only hits right before dusk. Everything quieted down. Even the pain.

I unsaddled him slow, brushing him down in silence. My hands moved out of habit, but my mind... my mind was pacing like it didn't know where the hell to settle.

She left.

Flew back to Paris.

I leaned my forehead against Steel's withers, inhaling the clean scent of sweat and earth. He huffed softly, like he understood. Like he'd been watching the whole damn saga unfold and was just waiting for me to get my heart back in line.

I pulled away, tossed the brush back into the bin, and wiped my face on my forearm.

No tears.

Just sweat.

Just frustration.

Just a man standing in the aftermath of almost.

The worst kind of heartbreak is the one that doesn't explode. It drifts. Slow. Subtle. Again. A solemn ending. A suitcase packed with folded guilt and soft goodbyes.

I stepped outside the barn and let the screen door slam behind me.

The sun was almost gone now, just a sliver of gold hanging over the tree line.

I stood there, hands on my hips, chest still rising hard from the ride. And I told myself the truth.

I couldn't stop her.

Wouldn't beg her to stay.

That ain't love. That's control. And I already tried that once—back when I was too young to know better and too proud to say I was scared.

I was scared now too. Still. But I wasn't eighteen anymore. And I wasn't walking away from the kind of love that comes once in a lifetime and knocks the wind out your chest every time you see her smile.

Cara had dreams. Big ones. Bigger than me, maybe. Bigger than Lily.

And she'd always chased them with a fire I'd been too damn stupid to match back then.

But now?

Now I was building something too. Legacy. Community. A future.

And I wanted her in it.

If she couldn't choose it now, I'd let her go.

But once this trail ride was done... once the center opened, and the dust settled, I'd get on a plane, find her and tell her flat out: I still love you. I've always loved you. And this time, I'm not backing down.

Not again. Not from us.

Chapter 34 — Cara

I hadn't even made it out of Charles de Gaulle before the walls started closing in.

It wasn't the terminal itself—sleek glass, white light, the hum of international travelers moving like a current.. It was me. My skin. My breath. My bones. They felt too slow. Too heavy. Too Southern. Like Georgia had clung to me in layers that were unfamiliar to Paris.

The air was dry. Sterile. No honeysuckle, no pine. No trace of barbecue smoke or red clay.

And the driver holding the sign with *"Mlle. Cara Mackey,"* barely looked up from his tablet when I waved.

"Bonjour," I said, voice stiff from the 9-hour flight and no sleep.

He glanced over, nodded once, and opened the door to the back seat without a word.

Okay then.

I slid into the car and tucked my trench around me, trying not to think about the fact that I'd left Georgia without saying goodbye to the one person who mattered most.

Corian had called. Twice. I hadn't answered yet. Not because I didn't want to hear his voice—but I'd been so busy putting out fires I didn't have time to think since being back in Paris.

The first missed call was because I'd been doing everything shy of flat out bribing the preservation office to reinstate our permits and couldn't break away. The second missed call... I didn't call him back out of sheer guilt. Because the last thing I told him before leaving was that I wasn't sure if I'd be coming back—I couldn't stand the incriminating look in his eyes as if he believed that statement meant I was unsure of us.

It wasn't that I didn't want to hear his voice—I knew if I heard him ask *why* I was running again, I'd fold. I'd fall apart.

And I couldn't do that. Not right now.

Not after Michel made it sound like my entire career was on the brink of collapse if I didn't return and fix the mess of my project. Not after the frantic voicemails from Jean-Pierre and the panic in Delia's texts. Not after I promised I'd fix what I'd abandon here.

So I kept my phone on Do Not Disturb and watched the Parisian streets flash past the window.

Everything was familiar.

And everything felt wrong.

The Seine was still winding, the gray rooftops still charming, the boulangeries still pushing out perfect croissants. But it didn't touch me. Not the way it used to.

The streets were too narrow.

The people too fast.

The silence inside me too loud.

By the time we pulled up to the job site, my chest felt like it was wrapped in wire.

From the outside, the hotel looked worse than I'd imagined. The front entrance was blocked with fencing and scaffolding, and the side alley—the one we'd planned to convert into a chic courtyard garden—was filled with dumpsters. No signage. No press banners. Nothing. Just bones. And not the elegant kind.

I stepped out of the car and was immediately greeted by Jean-Pierre—his tie askew, hair frazzled, iPad in hand.

"Cara," he breathed like I was a mirage. "*Merci Dieu*. Thank you for getting back to Paris, so quickly. Shit is bad."

My jaw clenched. "What the hell happened?"

He glanced toward the building, face tightening. "Everything."

Jean-Pierre led me inside the site through the temporary construction entrance, rattling off updates like he was trying to get ahead of an avalanche. "The subcontractors walked off last week. They claim delayed payments from funders. It's been snowballing."

"Delayed payments?" My stomach twisted. That didn't make sense. Michel had assured funding was secure.

Jean-Pierre splayed his hands, unsure of how to respond, just continued rattling off the issues causing the stop work on the Rue d'Orleans project. "And now the preservation office flagged us for unauthorized adjustments. Camille said it's like someone intentionally ignored protocols." Camille was the Director of the Preservation Society of Paris.

I blinked at him as we moved through the gutted lobby. "Jesus, Jean-Pierre. I've been gone eight weeks. Not eight years."

"Exactly," he said, breathless. "Eight weeks is a lifetime in Paris construction."

We turned the corner into what used to be the grand salon. I stopped short.

The floor tiles we'd sourced from Morocco were still crated. The lighting installations? Unopened in the corner. Worse—half the walls had been stripped of their original trim. My heart sank.

"Who approved this demo?"

Jean-Pierre flinched. "Michel did."

Of course he did. Michel had given unsanctioned guidance to my team, creating chaos, but interestingly enough when I talked to him before jumping on a plane to come back, he'd left this part out. Last I checked, a stop work order did not mean undo work that was already done.

The bastard had enough clout as an investor to override certain delays... but not enough vision to know what would set the historical society on fire.

"Where's Delia?" I asked, scanning the room like she might pop out of the dust.

Jean-Pierre pulled out his phone and texted furiously. "On her way. She's been back and forth between here and city hall trying to handle the fines. But I think she's... overwhelmed."

Overwhelmed. Great. So was I.

I walked through the space slowly, letting the failures speak to me. It wasn't just the budget, or the red tape, or the shoddy comms. It was the *tone*. The absence of *me*. My eye. My presence. This building didn't carry *my* signature anymore—it looked like someone tried to whitewash my soul out of it.

And all signs pointed to Michel.

Jean-Pierre glanced over, hesitant. "Okay... so, Camille just texted back."

"Good. She was sending me straight to voicemail when I was trying to call on the car ride over."

"She wants to meet with you. Personally. She said no more emails. No more calls. She wants face-to-face accountability."

I shut my eyes. Counted to three. "Fine. Set it up."

Just then, the back door opened, and Delia stepped in—strikingly beautiful as usual but visibly shaken under her leather trench and dark curls.

She looked me up and down.

"About damn time you made it back," She said, before quickly rushing over to give me a hug.

I embraced her back and over her shoulder, murmured, "Nice to see you too."

She dropped her bag and slipped out of her coat, placing both on the makeshift table in the center of the space, ready to roll up her sleeves to pitch in where she could. but not before adding, "No one could have planned for this ticking time bomb with the historical renovation police. Up front, you need to know that Michel's been throwing around his money weight and micromanaging everyone, ever since the stop work order went public. The press is also sniffing around for a story. They smell blood in the water, Cara."

"I left to handle some family shit, and literally come back to a dumpster fire."

"Yeah well, we in it now," she said, softer now.

"Fuck. I didn't mean to be gone this long," I admitted. "I just... I got caught up."

Delia sighed. "Uh-un. Cut that shit out. You're back now. How do we get ahead of this?"

I opened my mouth.

But before I could answer, my phone buzzed.

Michel.

Of course.

I declined the call.

Then I looked at my team—Jean-Pierre, still nervously scrolling through his calendar, Bonet ready to carry out anything administrative, and Delia, though not my employee, stood there arms crossed, looking like she was ready to go to war for the cause.

"Alright. First things first, this week is all about doing *whatever*," I emphasized, "needs to be done to get Camille to lift this stop work order. Jean-Pierre is already working on setting a meeting with up. Bonet, start power dialing all the contractors for the installs and see what incentives they need to drop everything and prioritize the Rue d'Orleans as soon as we give them the greenlight."

I rattled whatever I could think of off the top of my head. Then looked to Delia, "Give me a run down on where we are with construction. Before I left, 60-percent of the building was ready for flooring installation with a fast follow of wall treatments."

She reached in her bag and pulled out the construction schedule. My girl was ready. "Before the stop work order, all the wet areas were finished. All remaining construction is in the parking areas. And I'm confident in saying that unless you're planning to *feng shui* that area out, you and you're team can begin full-scale design implementation, in some cases *again*," she paused to twist her lips and shrug her eyebrows at mention of the work that had been undone by Michel's order, "on the hotel's interior, while the landscape artists build out the garden's and exterior spaces and courtyards."

I nodded. "Good. Good. In the meantime, I need to figure out why this shit blew up in the first place. In fifteen years of owning my firm and completing hundreds of renovation projects around Paris and Europe, I've never had a stop work order put in. If it's anything we do good and are the experts at, is historical preservation and the laws that govern it."

I exhaled and walked to the edge of the space where the floor met the stained wall.

Ten days. I wanted this project to be back up and running in ten days. Less if I had anything to do with it!

I had to fix this mess. To reclaim mine and my firm's reputation.

And to remind everyone—including myself—that I was capable of doing just that. Even if I couldn't stop thinking about the man I'd left behind.

I left my team with a laundry list of tasks before, closing the door behind me in the project site office and braced myself. First order of business, fix the mess I'd made with him. I stared at my phone, thumb hovering over Corian's missed calls. My breath quickened as I hit the call button.

"Cara?" His voice was rough, cautious. It unraveled me instantly.

"Hey." My voice cracked on that one syllable. "I'm sorry I haven't answered. It's... bad here."

Silence stretched for a beat. "You okay?"

"I'm... barely holding it together. Michel—" I paused, he wouldn't know who Michel is. I shifted my tone. "I think this might be a sabotage job on my project. I have to fix this. People are counting on me."

Another silence, heavier. "Cara, you could've told me that's why you were rushing off. I would've understood."

"I know." I closed my eyes. "But I was scared that if I didn't just pick up and leave, I would have allowed," my words trailed. My heart knew what my mouth couldn't say. If I'd given him a single inch of influence on my decision, Corian would have won out and everything I'd built here was going up in smoke. "Um, I just had to drop everything and get back here."

"Including me." he stated softly.

My heart clenched. "Corian, no." My words sounded hollow even to my own ears. I'd gotten wrapped up in the community center and him and let my team and the Rue d'Orleans investors down here. And now I was letting him down being back here and leaving us and my returning open ended.

He exhaled slowly. "It's late here. Go ahead and take care of business."

My eyes burned. "I'm trying to. I swear, Corian. Let me put this fire out here and we can talk about where you and I go from here."

"I won't press you, Cara," he said firmly. "But don't shut me out. I'm here. Waiting."

"Okay," I whispered.

"Okay." His voice softened a bit. "Take care."

The call ended, leaving my heart pounding and clear for the first time since I stepped off the plane.

I stood straighter, fortified by the calm certainty of Corian's voice still echoing in my ear. I picked up the phone again. Now it was time to handle Michel's ass.

He boldly picked up on the first ring.

"Cara."

"I'm here," I said, voice flat. "Say what you need to say." My anger at what I suspected happened to my project was stoked by the sound of my name on his tongue.

He blustered at the heat in my tone. "Ok. I'm glad you're back to take care of this catastrophe. You've been gone over two months. What did you think would happen?" *Did this motherfucker just get indignant with me?* He kept going. "Not just physically—you checked out *mentally*.

Spiritually. You left your entire team twisting, had no regard for the money I and the other investors have tied up in this project while you played small-town savior."

"I told you I needed time to handle some things back at home. And according to *my team,* things were going fine until work was suddenly halted. No explanations given."

"You didn't take *time,* Cara. You *abandoned* the most ambitious restoration project of your career to what relive a childhood that ended in the last century."

My breath stilled, rage flickering just beneath the surface.

"I stepped away because I needed to. The reason for doing so does not concern you. And now that I think about it, a stop work order without justification sounds like a money play. It would have taken big bank, like the type of big bank that you have to pull off."

Oh it was crystal clear to me now. And yes, I'd pretty much accused him of sabotaging my project.

His silence was instant.

I pressed. "You bypassed my team. You signed off on the vendor switch without Delia or Camille's approval. You *knew* the historical board had concerns with that company and you ignored protocol. You caused this."

"I made a decision," he said, calm but cutting. "One I wouldn't have had to make if you'd been where you belonged."

"No," I fired back. "You didn't *make* a decision—you made a *move.* A play. You wanted me back in Paris, and you used the project to manipulate the whole situation," I hissed at him over the phone. And the motherfucker didn't even deny my accusation. My next words came out of my mouth in near real time with the realization. "You couldn't stand seeing me choose something other than you. So you made sure I had no choice but to come running back."

"I invested millions in this project."

"And I invested my *name,* Michel. My reputation. You want to talk about stakes? You won't be the one fielding questions when the press asks how this went sideways. I will."

"You nor your firm would have won the Rue d'Orleans project if it weren't for me," he said, "let alone gained the prestige, had the articles written about you.

I stopped cold. "Say that again?"

His voice softened. Patronizing. Like I was the intern, not the woman who designed the vision that had every lifestyle magazine in Europe calling. "Cara, *ma belle*, you're brilliant—but the world didn't start noticing until I put my credibility behind you."

My teeth unclenched. "You mean the credibility you're now using as a shield to cover your ass?"

"No. I mean the weight I carry as an investor who saw your potential and still does."

"You saw an opportunity," I corrected. "And when I stopped making you the center of my universe, you couldn't handle it."

He said nothing, and I continued.

"You've always needed me to orbit you. But Michel, I'm not a moon. I'm a goddamn sun."

A pause.

"I take it things with him are serious?"

"What?" I said in shock at this next tactic he tried to use. I chuckled. "Yeah. It is serious, but this isn't about him." Yeah, that shit *backfired*. Michel was grasping for straws. There was no way he could have known about Corian, let alone any '*him*'. I knew the fact that there was a 'him' and he wasn't it, would cut Michel deep and I let him bleed.

"But it is," he said in a weak ass come back. "Because before him, you were *here*. You were the version of yourself who wanted the world. Now you want... porch swings and sunset trail rides?" He asked in an incredulous rendition of a southern drawl.

I laughed, bitter. "You think love and ambition can't live in the same woman?"

"I think you're forgetting how fragile ambition with no talent is. One misstep, and you lose it all," he said patronizingly.

"No," I chuckled calmly. "I know exactly how fragile it is. Which is why I'm back. To clean up the mess *you* made. Thank God I have talent in droves to do so."

He took a beat, then changed his tactics to more forthcoming. "You could have told me when you were leaving Paris you'd be gone this long," he said. "Eight weeks."

"I told you I needed space."

"You said two weeks," he countered.

"And it turned into more," I said bitingly.

His exhale was sharp. "It's been a mess here, Cara."

"I'm aware, Michel. But at whose hand?"

"You didn't check in."

"To who? You? I don't give a damn how much money you have or how much influence it brings you. I don't answer to you and I certainly don't belong to you. Furthermore," I said, "I'm tired of having to prove my worth to people like you who only remember my value when I use my talents to make them look better."

Silence.

I kept my voice even. "You knew what you were doing, Michel. You had your hands on the purse strings, but don't ever forget this place bears my fingerprints. This is my vision."

Another pause. His tone softened. Another shift in his tactics. "I didn't want to lose you, Cara."

"You never had me." Then I ended the call.

Chapter 35 – Cara

A week later, Bonet sat at her desk, tapping furiously at her laptop. Jean-Pierre had already scheduled follow-ups with the preservation committee. And Delia, bless her, had somehow rallied the contractors up.

I stood in the center of it all, arms crossed, watching the motion I'd once orchestrated like a symphony—and now barely felt part of.

It should've felt like victory. Like homecoming.

But all I could think about was how quiet Corian had gone.

It had been a mad dash of activity around here and my team and I had been working around the clock, recasting schedules, reordering finishes and furniture. I hadn't reached out to him like I wanted to.

Because I didn't know how to hear that voice and not come undone. He'd left the ball in my court, so he wasn't reaching out either.

He'd told me he loved me. Not with flowers or speeches—but with his hands, his eyes, his body, and his damned patience. And now?

I was 4,300 miles away, pretending this life—this dream I'd built brick by brick—was enough.

Delia passed by with a tablet and paused. "Meeting in thirty with the investors. You good to lead?"

I nodded, even as my throat tightened. "Yeah. Let's show them what the hell we're made of."

I stood in my office a little longer than I should have, reflecting. Paris had always felt like momentum to me—everything fast, curated, exquisite.

But this morning? It felt still.

I passed the concierge with a tight smile and adjusted the drape of my trench preparing to enter the board room. Jean-Pierre had already texted four times. Bonet twice. Delia was looping in the preservation office. The meeting with the full team and key investors was starting.

The monitor in our boardroom showed that everyone was logged in and ready to get started. The vibe was tense.

The investors sat like they'd come to a reckoning. Three men I recognized, two new faces Michel had wrangled I'm sure. At the head of the table, Michel leaned forward, hands clasped like a priest offering penance. Camille Laurent sat to his right.

"Gentlemen," I said. "Madame Laurent. Thank you for meeting on such short notice."

Michel sat back, his mouth tight. "We were just discussing the permit reinstatement process—"

"That's almost handled. Camille," I said nodding to the Director, "agreed on the course of action that needed to be taken, and my team and I have completed all requests and are ready for the scheduled inspection in two days. Our plans are airtight." One of the newer investors raised a brow. "That's quite a turnaround."

"I'm quite a woman," I said smoothly, flipping to the next slide of my deck. "The updated timelines are in the packets that were delivered to the preservation society this morning. Financial projections have been adjusted to reflect the delays and reconveyance of work strategy But there's still the matter of the overdue return of payments from Michel's recommended contractors." I cut my eyes in his direction before continuing. "We need resolution there quickly so those funds can be paid to the contractor I previously approved and hired."

Michel gave me a side glance. I stared unflinching at him across the Zoom screen.

"I'll be reviewing every contract, line item, and change order by Monday. No more surprises. If something needs to be rerouted, it goes through me first. That includes vendor approvals, contractor payments—and Michel's involvement in those decisions."

A beat of silence.

Then the oldest investor—gray beard, tortoise-shell glasses—cleared his throat. "We were told you were... unavailable. That you had stepped away."

"I stepped out," I said. "I didn't disappear."

"And now?"

"I'm here now." I let the weight of those words land as I looked around the room at Jean-Pierre, Delia, Bonet and the host of staff designers. "My team is aligned and is fully capable of maintaining even in my absence as long as no intentional...derailments happen." I cut my eyes in Michel's direction again, without lingering on him too long.   Michel shifted in his seat. I continued, this time directly to the only one at the table who could lift the stop work order. "Camille, this project is still ours—" my eyes swept proudly over my team, "and we've made the requested adjustments. I am asking that you lift the order."

"You've had... distractions," one of the other investors offered, cautiously, before Camille could issue a ruling.

I met his eyes. "And yet, here we are."

Madame Laurent lifted her glass of water, swirling it idly. "Your team seems to think you've returned for good."

"I've returned to finish what I started," I said. "Everything else is noise."

Michel didn't flinch, but I felt the weight of his silence.

"I know the last few weeks raised concerns," I continued. "But my commitment to this project has not wavered. I built the design, recruited the core team, and earned every inch of support you've given. I intend to deliver. Period."

The room held its breath for a beat longer.

Then the gray-bearded investor nodded once. "You deliver on those forecasts, and we'll stay the course."

The others murmured their agreement.

I closed the binder, calm as still water.

Michel was the last to speak. "You came back strong."

"No other way," I said.

He looked at me, eyes scanning for weakness. He didn't find it.

"The motion to lift the stop work order is granted," Camille said, "pending the upcoming inspection."

My team exploded in joy. We could start work again in two days.

Why didn't I feel ecstatic? Later that night, I sat in the windowsill of my flat overlooking the Seine and the *Champs Elysées*. I usually sat here to think and clear my mind. Sometimes strumming a chord on my daddy's guitar. I caught glimpses of it in my periphery a few times. I drew my eyes away from it in search of my phone that had just buzzed.

I padded barefoot to the kitchen, poured a glass of wine I didn't really want, and leaned on the counter to read the screen.

Kima.

CALL ME. I'M NOT GONNA TEXT THIS.

I blew out my breath and hit the video call button.

She answered on the second ring, lips already pursed, head wrapped in a gold scarf like she'd been ready to lay down some truth.

"Damn," she said, eyes scanning my face. "You look... sad"

"Sad is a word," I said, a twisted smile on my lips that didn't do much to change her perception.

"You okay?"

I shrugged.

She sipped from a ceramic mug, eyes narrowing. "That bad?"

"Worse," I admitted. "The project here is back on track." I said, catching her up on the last week and a half. "Michel was the one who stirred this shit up. Thank God I made it back just in time for me and my team to set things straight. We pulled a Hail Mary."

Kima's face softened. "Then why aren't you out celebrating, Girl?"

I opened my mouth. Closed it.

"I'm floating," I said finally. "Unanchored. I got back just in time to save it, but..."

"You don't want to be there." Kima's words hit harder than I expected. I blinked back the sting of tears.

Kima leaned forward on her elbows. "You left Georgia like your feet were on fire. But don't act like I didn't see your face every time someone said Corian's name when you were here. Or the way you breathed in Lily like it was oxygen once you got over the bad memories and could remember the good."

"I had to come back. They needed me here."

"You needed you," she said gently. "You're a boss. You build things. But you've been building for everybody else for a long damn time. When are you gonna build for yourself?"

I bit my lip.

She didn't let up. "You in love with him?"

I looked away.

Kima whistled low. "Damn. You really are. And let me guess—haven't even told him?"

I looked back at her. "I panicked."

"You? Miss Blueprint? You don't panic."

"*This...* he wasn't in the blueprint."

We both sat with that.

Then she smiled. "Wanna know something wild?"

I raised a brow.

"The whole damn town's still rooting for you two. Even Ja'Kari. Darren. Hell, even Waynan."

My mouth dropped. "Waynan?"

"Girl, he told Corian last week, 'Don't mess up this chance. Black love don't come around twice in one lifetime.' Heard it with my own ears when he and mama Demetrie came over to check out the community center. That reminds me," she snapped her finger. "It is beautiful Cara," she switched to the back camera and panned the space. She was at the center. "While you were there fixing a mess, the plan you created here was implemented beautifully."

I pressed a hand to my chest, breath catching. I'd only seen a glimpse of the entry way and the areas that led to the horticulture wing, but what I saw was more beautiful than any high-end boutique hotel I'd ever designed.

Kima flipped the camera back, mug in hand. "We miss you, Mackey. The porch don't hit the same. The trail ride's the day after tomorrow and your name's on everybody's lips. Don't make us come drag you back."

My heart twisted.

"I just need to finish up here, then I'll try to come back."

"You said that before. Then you didn't come back for thirty years."

I flinched.

She didn't mean it to cut—but it did. Because it was true.

There was no clever comeback. No laugh to ease the ache. Just silence between us, thick and awkward.

"I should go," I said quietly. "It's late."

Kima nodded, lips pressed tight. "Alright. Just... don't wait too long, Mackey. Second times don't always come back around."

She winked before ending the call.

The wine sat untouched on the counter. My phone, face down. My suitcase—half unpacked—mocked me from the hallway.

And I realized, standing there barefoot in the kitchen of the perfectly curated life I'd built... I had never felt more alone—because the only place I truly wanted to be was back in Georgia. With Corian.

Part 4 — Homecoming

(Outro)

So here we are now, back where
we belong

Picking up the pieces, rewriting
our song

Steel horses, leather roads,

This time, together— never leave
you alone

They say Iron sharpens iron, so
can leather for steel

Back at the crossroads of love

I grip your reins, you grip my
wheel

(Chorus – Final)

Ridin' on Steel horse, down a
leather road,

We carved our own way

Had to keep living, never stopped
loving,

Two hearts have found their
place

No more letters, left unread

The ghosts of our past, finally
put to bed

Ridin' on a Steel horse, down a
leather road,

Real love done found its way

...Home

Chapter 36 — Corian

The morning air smelled like horses, smoked hickory, and fresh-cut grass. Not some poetic metaphor—just Lily on a day bigger than the town itself.

I stood in the main hallway of the new community center—clean walls gleaming, light pouring through the tall windows we fought zoning for. Every damn detail screamed her name.

The drawer pulls in the youth kitchen? She sketched them by hand and had them custom cast. The reclaimed wood benches in the gallery hall? She sourced them from a mill an hour outside town—insisted on the raw grain showing. The palette on the mural wall? Cara's colors. Cara's eye. Cara's heartbeat built into every inch of the damn place.

She should've been here.

We should've cut the ribbon together.

But she wasn't. And I hadn't heard her voice since the morning she'd arrived back in Paris.

I swallowed hard and turned toward the sound of bootsteps.

Darren strolled in, his shirt half-tucked, phone in one hand and a clip-board in the other. "Turkish consulate confirmed the horse inspection. I leave in a week."

I clapped him on the shoulder. "Proud of you."

He smirked. "I'll make sure they know Demetrie horses don't just run—they glide."

Jax was already outside, setting up the VR equipment for the middle and high schoolers we'd bused in from over at Dooly. The headsets and horse simulation program was blowing their young minds. The kids were losing it—in the best way.

And Ja'Kari? She and Marcus were tag-teaming logistics. Checking coolers, directing vendors, organizing parking. My daughter was smil-ing—until her eyes found mine.

She was mid-laugh with one of the volunteers, clipboard in hand, looking like the kind of woman any father would be proud of. But the moment our gazes met, her smile faltered just enough to let me know she saw it.

The ache. The absence.

She didn't say anything. Just held my eyes a second longer than neces-sary, like she was trying to will some kind of comfort into me from across the lawn.

Because she knew.

This moment should've been shared. Cara helped bring it all to life. And now, all this beauty was missing the one person who helped me believe it was even possible.

Cara deserved to be here.

And Ja'Kari knew that, too.

By 9 a.m., the sun had climbed just high enough to cast a soft, golden light across the front of the newly completed community center. Rows of folding chairs stretched beneath a white canopy strung with lights. Neighbors, elders, reporters, a handful of elected officials—all gathered, their murmurs quieting as I stepped up to the mic.

I took a breath. Let my eyes travel the crowd, land on the carved wood sign above the doors: *The Ecklands Community Center for Black Heritage & Innovation.*

"This morning," I began, voice steady but thick with meaning, "we stand on sacred ground. Not just because of the dirt beneath our boots—but because of the legacy sown into it. A legacy John Ecklands and his wife, Mrs. Bonita Ecklands, spent their lives nurturing."

I paused, letting the moment breathe.

"When Mr. Ecklands asked me and Cara Mackey to take this on, I thought we were here to restore a building. But what he really entrusted us with was a dream. A continuation. A promise that the youth of Lily, Georgia, would have more than just history to inherit—they'd have tools. Opportunity. A place to belong."

I cleared my throat, heart tightening as I looked around the grounds.

"My family—the Demetries—have bred and trained horses here for three generations. But today, we're not just raising animals. We're training minds. Building futures. Creating space for Black youth to learn STEM, agriculture, art, and damn sure how to ride with pride."

That got a few loud claps. I let them roll, then continued.

"This center is a blueprint for what happens when we believe in our kids, our roots, and our power. It's a living, breathing example of what happens when a town doesn't just preserve its past—but invests in its future."

I glanced toward the back—and saw Marcus step away, answering a call just as I was about to give praise to his sister.

I looked up at the center again—at the reclaimed wood benches, the bronze plaques Cara designed, the colors she picked that somehow made the place feel both new and already lived in. It all threw me off, but I kept going.

"There's someone who helped design every inch of this place. Who looked at an old cotton gin and at first saw ruin—she turned it into redemption. A sanctuary. A place for our people to breathe, to dream, to build."

My throat tightened, but I didn't stop.

"She's not here today... but if you look around—at the colors on the walls, the curve of the benches, the way sunlight hits that atrium—it's all her. Every part of this center carries her signature. Y'all know her name."

I paused, voice dipping lower.

"Cara Mackey. Give her some love."

The crowd erupted in claps and cheers. But I heard the space between it—the ache, the question. The wondering of why she wasn't standing next to me.

"She should be here," I said, quieter now. "This was her vision too."

Silence stretched, long and reverent. A breeze moved through the trees like it was agreeing with me. Or maybe just reminding me to breathe.

I scanned the crowd—saw Ja'Kari's proud smile soften at the corners, saw Kima brush a tear. Saw Marcus step off to the side, phone pressed to his ear with a tight expression I didn't have time to clock.

And my heart... split a little.

Because for all this joy, all this pride...

She was still gone.

I cleared my throat.

"To the family of John and Bonita Ecklands... thank you. Ms. Bonita, thank you for being here. For the legacy you and Mr. Ecklands built. For trusting us with it. For believing something this beautiful could rise from what was left behind."

I nodded once and stepped back.

The applause was thunderous. Echoed off the brick.

I had to pause. Swallow hard. Because if I said one more word with her name thick on my tongue, I might not finish.

I stepped back, handed the mic off to the mayor, and let the sound of the people carry the rest.

10a.m. The Ride Begins.

By mid-afternoon, the land was alive.

Friesians gleamed like black glass under the sun. Tennessee Walkers strutted with their heads high, and tails arched. Every corner smelled like grilled ribs, fried fish, and wood smoke. Food trucks lined the gravel curve. Music poured from the speakers—OutKast, Cowboy Carter, and some throwback Johnny Cash just for good measure.

Over sixty riders had registered. Black cowboys and cowgirls from three counties. It was beautiful. There were riders of every age and shade ready to ride slow and deep through the pine groves.

I swung onto Steel Jr.'s back. He tossed his head, eager. I rubbed his neck.

"You ready, boy?"

He snorted.

Ja'Kari rode beside me, radiant in a bolo tie and boots she'd threatened to bedazzle. Darren was mounted behind us, already teasing Kima who was trying not to smile too big under her wide-brim hat. Jax walked alongside the VR demo tent, letting kids try the headset between funnel cake runs.

Everyone was here.

Everyone except her.

We started slow, music following us down the trail, the land golden and wide beneath the weight of so much legacy.

Every turn in the trail brought a memory—of her laugh, her scent, the way she leaned into me when we rode together as teens. And when the path curved just past the old pine grove, revealing the new stretch we'd cleared to reach the pond, my breath caught. Because now, even the land remembered her.

Or maybe it was just the flashback of the way she'd looked that night at the pond—barefoot, bold, moaning my name like it was sacred. The way she'd opened up, body and soul. The way I'd told her I loved her and meant it with everything I had.

I thought that night changed us.

I thought she'd stay.

But maybe loving somebody doesn't always mean they can stay. Maybe it just means you don't close the door if they ever come back.

I adjusted my reins. Looked toward the horizon.

And decided.

If she won't come home...

My resolve grew even stronger that I was going to her.

Chapter 37 — Cara

I stood at the edge of the rooftop terrace, fingers resting on the cool iron rail as Paris moved in soft blurs beneath me. The skyline shimmered with late summer light, the spires of *Saint-Eustache* catching the sun like they had no idea my heart was cracking in quiet, even beats.

We'd saved the project. The final permits had been approved, and the stop work order fully lifted. The investors were staying. The grand opening was back on track.

I was here in body. Yet my mind ... was on dirt red roads.

A slow breath escaped me. My reflection hovered faintly in the glass doors behind me. Same curls. Same caramel skin. Same woman who'd flown back across the Atlantic to prove she was still in control.

But I wasn't. Not really.

Behind me, the door opened with a soft click. Delia's voice, low and certain, clipped through the air. "You really just gonna stand up here pretending you'd rather not be back there?"

I didn't answer.

She walked up beside me, heels clicking against the concrete rooftop, letting her question linger.

Then—softly—she said, "You know the only reason I came to Paris?"

I glanced at her, surprised. She didn't wait for permission to continue.

"Okiyo Bamdi," she said with a half-smile. "Yeah, the ex-MI6, six-pack-having pain in my ass? Him."

That got a ghost of a smile out of me.

"I met him when I wasn't looking," Delia said wistfully. "When I wasn't ready. I didn't even believe I could love somebody after everything I'd been through." Her voice softened further. "But he... he saw me. Not just the work. Not just the title. Not just the carefully managed moods and rhythms and brilliance. He saw the bruises. The flinches. The doubt."

I looked down, throat thick.

Delia took a breath. "He didn't save me. But he held me like I could save myself. Every day. He taught me how to forgive myself. How to stop punishing myself for surviving."

I felt that. Deep. Right where my breath had stalled since I left Lily.

"I almost let him go. Almost chose safety over soul," she whispered. "But I didn't. And now? I've never known love that felt so... earned." She turned to me fully then. "So if there's a man in Lily, Georgia who makes you feel like that... even a fraction of that? Run, not walk. Fly. Catch the damn flight and go get your joy."

She was quiet a beat, then added, "Your career will wait. But that kind of love? It don't knock twice. And maybe... Just maybe if you leave now, you might make some of that trail ride you told me about."

My hands trembled on the railing. I didn't cry, just shook all over. I reached for my bag and pulled out the red leather journal.

And flipped to the page with the last lines of the song.

They say iron sharpens iron...So can leather for steel.

I stared at the words. I'd written them, but now the meaning of them rang true. That one damn line had carried me for years.

It was about him. It had *always* been about him.

About the way we loved each other hard. The way we survived, even when the world pulled us in opposite directions. The way we never let go—even when we pretended we had.

I ran my thumb over the ink, lips parting on a shaky breath.

Delia didn't say a word.

She didn't have to.

"Thank you, Sis," I whispered, leaning in to hug her tight. "I got a trail ride in south Georgia to be at."

"Go get him," She gave me one last squeeze and released me.

I took off and hailed the first cab I could to take me to my flat. I wouldn't actually make the trail ride. But it was scheduled to start at 10am on the East Coast and if I could get on the next flight, I could be back in Lily by 10pm while the party and concert of local performers was in full swing.

Back at my apartment, I grabbed a small leather satchel and threw some essentials in it; my phone charger off the counter, necessary toiletries and my make up bag. Before heading to my closet, I stopped in the hallway, pulled out my phone, and dialed Marcus.

It was about 9:30am in Lily, but he answered on the second ring. "'Bout time I hear from you," he admonished.

"I need to know—did they start yet? The ceremony?" I asked.

There was a pause, then background noise. Cheers. A mic squeal.

"Corian just stepped up to the podium. The dedication speech is about to start. You good?"

I pressed a hand to my chest. My heart was racing.

"I'm coming home."

"Wait—what?"

But I was already hanging up.

Not out of rudeness, but because hesitation had no place in this kind of love. The kind that knocks once, *in our case twice*, hard and loud, and dares you to open the door.

In my closet, I stripped off my slacks and silk blouse before reaching into the recesses of the closet to find the denim dress and boots that had lived in the back there for years, never thought I'd wear them. I ran to the bathroom and pulled my hair into a soft, wild bun, hands shaking, heart thundering. Just before leaving the apartment, I doubled back to grab the one thing I needed most.

The guitar case sat by the bookshelf like it had been waiting on me to remember who I was.

Daddy's old Gibson.

I'd only learned one chord real well. G major. The good one. The one that felt like a porch and a breeze and a first kiss under a southern sky.

I picked it up now. Fingers trembling.

Then I turned off the lights, locked the door, and took a cab straight to the airport.

Nine hours later, I landed in Atlanta.

Customs felt like it took a year. My guitar case hit the carousel with a thud. I didn't stop for coffee or air or anything but keys.

Two hours from Hartsfield to Lily.

I didn't care.

I drove like the road was pulling me home, every mile another heartbeat.

By the time I hit the county line, my chest was burning from holding back everything I needed to say to him. Everything I'd left unsaid. Everything I'd almost let slip through my fingers—again.

Because Corian Demetrie wasn't just the man I loved.

He was the man I *chose*.

And this time?

I was coming back on purpose.

Chapter 38 – Corian

The kids had started loading up—parents packing them into SUVs with sticky fingers, smiling faces, and VR headsets still spinning in their heads. We'd sent them home with prize bags and full bellies, and now?

Now it was grown folks' time.

The lawn had changed.

Coolers clinked open. The cash bar was doing numbers. Libations were being poured heavy and wide, and folks who'd been quiet during the dedication were now dancing like their knees forgot their age.

I stood at the mic again, sweat trickling down my back, but my heart was lighter than it had been all day. I grinned at the crowd, mic in one hand, other hand wiping my brow with a towel someone handed me.

"All right, y'all," I said, my voice carrying across the buzzing crowd. "The sun's still up for now, but y'all know what time it is. Kids are headed home. That means it's time for us to act like we ain't gotta be up in the morning."

The crowd roared.

I turned toward the edge of the stage and waved up one of the old heads—Uncle Sly, who was already a few drinks in and ready to cut up. He stumbled up with a wide grin and slapped me on the back.

"Don't mind me if I cuss a lil' bit, this whiskey talkin'," he said into the mic to wild laughter. "Now I want all y'all with good knees to hit the dance floor—and the rest of us gon' two-step from our chairs."

The DJ didn't even wait.

The beat dropped, and the grass became a dance floor.

Line dance crews formed instantly. Kima, Ja'Kari, and what looked like half the women in Dooly County hit it hard—boots stomping, curls bouncing, fans snapping. The choreography was tight, synchronized like they'd been rehearsing for weeks.

The crowd whooped as they hit the drop on "Mississippi Slide" then slid right into a remix of "Dangerous" featuring Twista and Morgan Wallen that had the uncles looking confused and aroused at the same time.

Even Jax was out there, trying to learn the steps and failing gloriously—until some woman in daisy dukes and a rhinestone bra top pulled him into a slow grind that had him grinning like he'd just won the lottery.

I stood back, watching it all with my arms crossed, smiling despite the ache.

The trail ride had been everything. The center was standing tall. My brothers were thriving. My daughter was laughing.

And still...

The DJ had just finished spinning another track—something with a little bounce to it—when Marcus climbed the steps to the stage and leaned into Uncle Sly's ear. Whatever he whispered made the man go still for half a second. Then he grinned.

"Hold up now," Uncle Sly said, cutting the music. The crowd groaned. "Y'all sit tight. We got a surprise. And I don't mean the kind that come in shot glasses."

People laughed, shifted, looked toward the stage.

Lights dimmed.

A hush rolled over the crowd like thunder before a summer storm.

Then someone—quick and quiet—brought a single stool and placed it center stage. Left just as fast.

The weight in my chest shifted. The breath in my throat stalled.

Spotlight hit the stage.

And there she was.

Cara Mackey.

Denim dress. Boots. Hair in a soft, wild bun.

She didn't speak. Didn't smile. Just started picking—slow and deliberate. Her fingers moved across the strings like she'd been doing it her whole damn life.

A hush swept through the crowd.

Then she looked up, Eyes scanning Until they found mine and locked.

I stopped breathing.

That's when I noticed... *I mean really noticed* the guitar. An old Gibson. Beat-up but beautiful.

And then—God. She opened her mouth. *And sang.* I stood there, stunned. Because I didn't know she could sing. Didn't know she could play. Didn't know I could feel like this—like I was witnessing something sacred, something private being laid bare under a single light.

Her voice? It wasn't just pretty. It was full. Woman-grown. Ragged at the edges, rich with heartbreak and hope. And it cracked me wide open before the first verse even ended.

Started out with dreams, hearts
full of fire
We were just kids, living wild and
wired
But life came fast, tore us apart
Left me with a broken soul and a
faded heart
They say iron sharpens iron, but
you're leather I'm steel
On this crossroad of love... you grip
your reins, I gripped my wheel

My knees damn near buckled at the beauty. People around me went still. Some gasped. But me? I moved.

Slowly. Steadily. Toward the stage.

Because I recognized those words.

She wasn't just singing some ballad. Wasn't covering Beyoncé or Faith or one of them country girls with soul.

She was singing words I'd read before. Thirty years ago I'd only glimpsed them. Thought it was a poem. It was this song.

The one from her journal. The one she never allowed me to read.

Now she sang it like her soul was on fire.

The crowd started to sway. And when the chorus hit again, voices joined her like they'd always known the words.

Ridin' on a steel horse, down a
leather road,
Tipped your hat and was on your
way

Had to keep living, but never
stopped loving,
Place too small I couldn't stay
Jaded on love, letters unread
Vanished like a ghost, story un-
said
Ridin' on a steel horse, down a
leather road...
Glass hearts were meant to break

I was at the edge of the stage now.

Tears blurred my vision. I didn't care.

Because I wasn't the only one crying. Her voice cracked on the next verse. Just barely. But she didn't stop.

She played harder. Sang louder. Gave it all to the crowd—but her eyes never left mine.

Necessity called, I had to roam
You took your path, I took my
own
Family drama, it weighed me
down
Two dreams too big for this
one-light town
They say iron sharpens iron, you're
leather I'm steel
On the crossroads of love...
You grip your reins, I gripped my
wheel

She stood for the last verse.

No longer just a woman with a guitar.

She was fire. She was home. She was the truth I'd spent half my life aching for. She hit the bridge in the song, and I knew she'd spent the same aching for us.

> *Now years have gone by, never*
> *forgot your smile*
> *Remember arms, 'round your*
> *waist, gripped tight for dear life*
> *Steel hearts done softened, got*
> *miles to go*
> *On leather roads, chasing dreams*
> *that lead to home*
>
> *So here we are now, back where we*
> *belong*
> *Picking up the pieces, rewriting*
> *our song*
> *Steel horses, leather roads,*
> *This time, together—never leave*
> *you alone*
> *They say iron sharpens iron, so can*
> *leather for steel*
> *Back at the crossroads of love...*
> *I grip your reins... you grip my*
> *wheel.*

The last chord rang out like a prayer.

Silence.

Then the crowd exploded.

But not louder than the pounding in my chest and the way her voice wrapped around every note.

She was walking towards me.

And I was reaching for her.

She finished the last line like she was exhaling history.

The crowd stood.

Didn't matter if they understood every lyric or every line—I did. I felt the words in my soul. Felt her. Felt us.

My chest burned. My throat locked up. But my feet kept moving. Up the stairs. Onto the stage and towards the only woman who ever truly had me.

She lowered the guitar slowly, her fingers still trembling against the strings. Her eyes met mine—wet, wide, terrified and free all at once.

I closed the space between us.

Didn't say a word.

Just reached for her—like my heart had been waiting thirty years to beat again.

My hand found her waist. Her breath caught. Her mouth opened just slightly. But I beat her to the punch.

"You ready to stop *runnin'*, Mackey?" I asked, low and hoarse, the words vibrating between us.

She blinked. Swallowed. And whispered the only thing I needed.

"Only place I'm running is to you," she whispered.

And that was it.

I pulled her into me and kissed her, not giving a damn that we were on a stage in front of the whole town. Not careful. Not polite.

But deep. Full. Messy with memory and magic.

She kissed me back equally as fervent.

The crowd screamed, chairs clattered as folks tried to get a better look, and fans popped.

Somebody yelled "Finally!"

But all I cared about right now was her.

and when her arms wrapped around my neck, and I lifted her clean off the floor, kissed her through every ounce of regret, of time lost, of silence and distance and damn near giving up.

And right there—on that stage, under a starry Georgia sky in the middle of July, with the whole damn town watching—I knew one thing for sure. She was mine.

Again.

Still.

Always.

To Be Continued...

To Be Continued...

About the Author

Cher Terais is the ultimate Renaissance woman! With a passion for travel and an eye for gorgeous interior design and architecture, she's crafted beautiful stories centered around black love and its complexities.

Take a journey with her from busy street markets to distant escapes in her books that will take you around the world.

Originally from Warner Robins, Georgia, Cher spent time in the Army before moving to the Middle East as a Program Manager. Her travels allowed her to dive into diverse cultures as well as serve as a springboard for more trips around Asia, the Caribbean and Europe. Proud mother of two daughters and one grandson, Cher encourages them to pursue their dreams of no limits!

Follow her on social media (@cher_terais (all major platforms) @cher_terais_author on IG) to learn more about this amazing author who calls the suburbs of Atlanta home!

A Wanderlust Romance Series

Bali Blue

Mess on the Mara

Tempest in Tulum

The Leather and Steel Series

Steel Horses Leather Roads

Stay even more connected by scanning the QR Code below to get bonus content for Cher Terais' books.

https://linktr.ee/Cher_Terais

Love the journey? Don't let it end here.

Step into **The Chapter Lounge** — my private book club community made just for readers like you. Join the conversations, get sneak peeks, exclusive content, and connect with fellow romance lovers who crave the same escape you do.

Join here: https://tcl.chersbookedclub.com/lit-lovers

(Scan the QR code below)

Want to travel like the characters in this book?

Join me for **The Luxe Nomad Webinar**, where I share my blueprint for traveling the world without breaking your bank account — just like the heroines in my stories.

Learn how to live well, travel smart, and do it all in style.

Save your seat: https://webinar.chersbookedclub.com/home-page-warm

(Scan the QR code below)

Ready to turn the page... in paradise?

Join me on one of my **curated group trips** inspired by the stories you love — from the beaches of Bali to the savannahs of Kenya. These aren't just vacations — they're unforgettable experiences filled with sisterhood, luxury, and soul-deep restoration.

Explore upcoming retreats and reserve your spot at:

https://trips.chersbookedclub.com/opt-in

(Scan the QR code below)

The trip doesn't stop here! The Booked Club and The Chapter Lounge communities have launched!

Sign up for my mailing list for more details!

www.ingramcontent.com/pod-product-compliance
Lightning Source LLC
Chambersburg PA
CBHW020122120726
47903CB00007B/2069